REVEALATIONS

REVEALATIONS

RUTH DRABKIN

Beneath the Silence, Beyond the Clock

For the early risers, the quiet keepers of morning—brewing coffee, stocking shelves, bringing light to a sleeping world.

For those who live between the lines—who work the late hours, mop the floors, chase down the truth, and still find the strength to smile.

This is for the underdogs, the secret holders, the dreamers with tired hands and feet, and the doers with open hearts.

And to the ones we've lost—your light still lingers in every story I tell.

PROLOGUE

The smell of burnt espresso and stale grocery store air clung to Penny's uniform as she wiped down the counter, her muscles aching from another shift behind the bar. To any passerby, she was just another overworked barista in a coffee shop tucked inside *Rock n' Roll Alfie's*, a Hollywood grocery store that catered to the eccentric and the elite. But Penny wasn't here for the coffee.

She was here for the truth.

When she first took the undercover assignment, she thought it would be simple—play the part, blend in, and gather intel on a suspected human trafficking ring. But Alfie's was its own beast, a place where everyone had secrets, and nothing was ever as it seemed. Employees schemed, customers whispered, and somewhere in the chaos, criminals lurked behind friendly smiles.

Now, months later, Penny had seen more than she ever expected. Murders passed off as accidents. Drugs moved between the aisles. People who vanished without a trace. And through it all, she had to keep pouring lattes, smiling at the very people she suspected, and pretending she wasn't watching their every move.

But no cover lasts forever.

Sooner or later, the truth would come spilling out. And when it did, Penny knew one thing—*not everyone would make it out alive.*

CHAPTER ONE

WELCOME TO ALFIE'S

No one becomes a cop to serve lattes. At least, that's what I told myself as I stared at my reflection in the passenger-side mirror, adjusting the stiff new ball cap that said Sunset Star Coffee in a font that tried way too hard to be chill. It was the kind of aesthetic that screamed "influencer," even though the only thing I seemed to influence lately was the growing suspicion that someone at headquarters hated me.

My real name? Raven McCool. Yeah, I know—sounds fake. No, I didn't pick it. And yes, I've heard every joke. But for now, I go by Penny Padlock—a name HQ assigned to match the persona: quirky, reliable, just mysterious enough. Think locked diary... with latte art.

I am divorced, in my late twenties, and nowhere near what you'd picture when someone said 'cop.' I have

long, reddish-brown hair that I usually wear in a ponytail while working the kiosk—sleek, functional, but still
kind of flirty. I'm slim and undeniably cute, with sharp
brown eyes that take everything in. People tend to do a
double take. Maybe it's the attitude, equal parts sweet
and sassy, or the rebellious streak I never really bother to
hide. I don't exactly blend in, but the higher-ups were
confident I could get the job done.

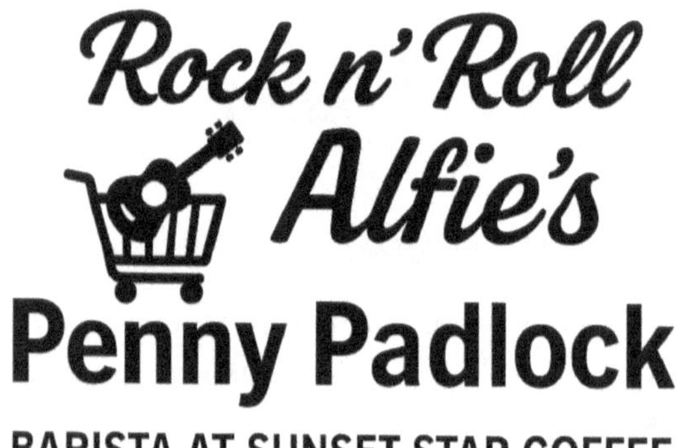

I am a cop. Undercover. And my first solo assignment? Barista at a grocery store on Sunset Boulevard in
the heart of Hollywood. Specifically, Alfie's. Or, as the
locals liked to call it, Rock n' Roll Alfie's, because apparently nothing screams "edgy rebellion" like discount-
ed rotisserie chicken and a dubious selection of house
wines.

Sunset Boulevard or Sunset Strip is known world-
wide for its famous restaurants, strip clubs, fast sports

cars, and nightclubs that partied like it was always Saturday. If something shady was going to happen in plain sight, this was the place.

Los Angeles, for all its glamor and grit, is also one of the biggest grocery store capitals in the world—with over 6,700 of them dotting the county. Grocery stores are like cathedrals here. They sprawl, they shine, they swallow entire city blocks. And they all have their own rhythm. Alfie's had a beat that never stopped, and Sunset Star Coffee was right in the middle of it.

I will be stationed inside the Sunset Star Coffee kiosk—an open-air caffeine trap lodged between the florist and the sushi counter. My job? Blend in. Observe. Report. And if necessary, unravel whatever criminal undercurrent was pulsing beneath the surface of this high-turnover, fluorescent-lit madhouse.

And something was definitely off.

My first red flag? The guy I was replacing got mysteriously transferred after a "milk frothing accident." That, and the number of incidents reported here in the last month: an armed robbery in the parking lot, a Manager with sealed priors, and a delivery guy who disappeared mid-shift and reappeared three days later in Bakersfield wearing someone else's name tag. I wasn't just here to serve coffee. I was here to find out what the hell was going on.

Inside my bag were two uniforms, a burner phone, a pen disguised as a voice recorder, and the tightest schedule known to man. My handler, Detective Gus Dabrowski, thought this op would be "good for optics."

"It's undercover work, McCool. Not everything's gonna be high-speed chases and international heists. Blend in, make connections, figure out who's got blood on their hands and who's just bad at stocking shelves."

Easy for him to say. He wasn't the one about to clock in next to a break room microwave with radioactive spaghetti sauce splattered inside.

Orientation was held in a conference room that smelled like expired coffee and stale ambition. A peppy HR trainer with pastel nails and a headset microphone told us about Alfie's "values," which apparently included community, consistency, and always smiling through trauma. I sat between a 17-year-old who kept snapping her gum and a former DJ named Dennis who looked like he hadn't slept since Coachella '07.

We were a ragtag group—cashiers, baggers, produce clerks, sushi chefs, service deli workers, and overnight restockers. A mix of teens working their first jobs, jaded veterans of the grocery grind, and a few middle-aged folks who clearly didn't want to be there. A couple of them had the same last names, and that's when I started noticing it.

Nepotism. It was everywhere.

One girl in produce kept glancing over at a meat department guy like she wanted to vanish through the floor. "He's my cousin," she whispered to the girl next to her. "He tells my mom everything."

The HR trainer's daughter was in our group too—she proudly declared she'd be working in the bakery. Of course. Summer job for the princess while the rest of us figured out how to clean a cheese slicer without losing a finger.

Every department had someone who was related to someone else. A mom and son in restock. A niece and uncle in the deli. And the kicker? One of the security guards was married to someone in accounting. The whole store felt like a family tree with price tags.

"We pride ourselves on exceptional customer service," the trainer beamed, pointing to a PowerPoint slide that featured stock photos of people hugging pineapples. "We are not just a store. We are a lifestyle."

Behind her, someone sneezed so violently it rattled the projector.

We watched a series of outdated training videos that looked like they'd been shot on DVDS. One featured a reenactment of a customer trying to return a watermelon with a bite taken out of it. The Manager in the video kept nodding and saying, "We understand your frustration." I was tempted to write "Be less understanding" in my notes.

Then came the dreaded icebreakers. We had to stand, say our name, department, and our "fun fact." Mine was: "I once ate 20 marshmallows in under a minute." Totally false, but I wasn't about to share anything real. Dennis said he once DJed for a house party that got broken up by Snoop Dogg. No one questioned him.

For the next three hours, we were lectured on safety protocols, food handling standards, and proper break-room etiquette. Apparently, expired yogurt was an HR issue. Who knew? I jotted mental notes while also practicing my fake laugh. You never know when you'll need to seem thrilled about mandatory apron inspections.

Then came the quizzes. Open-book, sure, but the questions were bizarre. One asked what you should do if a customer attempts to climb into the refrigerated seafood display. (Answer: Alert management. Resist the urge to film.)

Eventually, our trainer passed out goodie bags with pens, magnets, and coupons for $1 off any Alfie's-brand frozen peas. I felt incredibly special.

Once the paperwork was done, we were herded like cattle through the backroom and into the heart of the store. Jorge, the front-end Manager, led the "grand tour" like he was hosting a reality TV episode titled Grocery Store Gladiators.

"To your left, we have the cheese wall—yes, it's a thing. Please don't sample anything unless you want to meet our loss prevention team."

We zigzagged through the bakery, where the air smelled like sugar and despair, then past produce, where a team member was using a Sharpie to touch up some bruised avocados. Jorge proudly showed us the meat department, the florist station, and the sushi counter that, judging by smell alone, had seen better days.

In the dairy section, someone had spelled "help" in spilled yogurt. I pointed it out. Jorge laughed. "Yeah, that's just Tony. He gets bored on overnight shift."

The break room was a horror story in itself: beige walls, flickering fluorescent light, a microwave with mysterious stains, and a couch that may or may not have been sentient. There were lockers with half-peeled name tags and a printed sign above the fridge that read, "If it's not yours, don't eat it. If you don't know what it is, throw it out."

As we ended the tour, Jorge handed each of us a laminated store map, a name tag with magnetic backing, and a "welcome treat." I got to pick one item off the shelf—anything under five bucks. I chose a cold bottle of green tea. Dennis the DJ chose an entire rotisserie chicken.

"Respect," I told him.

He nodded solemnly. "Protein builds focus."

On the way out, I passed by the front where Betsy, the Manager of Sunset Star, was talking to a vendor with way too much charm in his smile. She barely glanced at us new hires but gave me a once-over like she was trying to calculate my weaknesses. My instincts itched. Something about her felt... off.

The next day, I arrived early for my first shift at Sunset Star Coffee. I wore the full kit—black Alfie's polo tucked into khakis, the Sunset Star apron tied tightly around my waist, and a polite-but-dead-inside smile. The kiosk was already bustling. Steam hissed. The register beeped. A woman argued with a Barista over whether almond milk "frothed with feeling."

I stepped behind the counter and was immediately greeted by Trina, who looked me up and down like I was a stray cat in a Gucci boutique.

"You must be Penny," she said, headset tilted just so. "We don't stir drinks here. We swirl."

It was early. The kind of early where customers came in bleary-eyed, clutching their phones and mumbling their orders with morning breath that could singe your eyebrows. Penny had joked to herself that the kiosk should offer a side mint with every order—except it wasn't really a joke.

And the cash. Oh, the cash. Folded bills tossed on the counter like she was a wishing well. Damp, crumpled, sometimes stuck together with... something. Unfolding them felt like a violation of personal space. It was petty to care. But it also happened every. single. day.

And it was only her first week.

Sunset Star had its own language, its own tempo, its own rules. And Penny Padlock—Raven McCool—was fluent in it by the end of the week.

But as the espresso steamed and customers lined up with bad breath and broken stories, Penny couldn't shake the feeling that something dark was brewing— something no amount of syrup could cover up.

CHAPTER
TWO

SUSPICIOUS GROUNDS

Trina didn't like me. That much was clear by the way she tossed a rag in my direction and said, "Might as well wipe the counters if you're just gonna stand there like a mannequin from the clearance bin."

I smiled back. "Of course. Just let me know if I'm blocking the espresso aura."

She snorted and turned her attention to the customer, a screenwriter who insisted on pitching his pilot while ordering a flat white. I grabbed the rag and started wiping down the already-clean counter, watching out of the corner of my eye.

Day two on the job, and the cracks in the store's foundation were already showing. Not literal cracks—though those were there too, in the linoleum by the juice aisle—but the kind that came from people hiding secrets in plain sight.

I was starting to form my mental suspect board. And the first pin went to Trina.

Trina had been with Alfie's for eight years, which in grocery time was basically elder status. She acted like she'd built the kiosk herself from reclaimed barn wood and resentment. But more than that, she was too aware—of where everyone was, what they were doing, when shipments were late. She wasn't just a Barista. She was watching everything.

And that made her dangerous.

Barista training continued that morning—and if yesterday had been awkward, today was flat-out humiliating. Dante showed up early again, flashing that model-smile and already halfway through prepping the espresso station. Tristan, the regional trainer, hovered behind him with a cup of cold brew like he was watching a prized student defend a thesis.

Meanwhile, I was still figuring out how to keep my milk pitcher from screeching like a banshee every time I steamed oat milk. We were expected to learn everything—how to steam milk to exactly 150 degrees for lattes, 130 for kids' drinks, and always using a thermometer unless we had Jedi Barista instincts. The pressure to create silky microfoam with zero bubbles made me question my life choices.

Then came syrup pumps—one for small, two for medium, three for large, and four for extra-large. Each size had its matching cup, both for hot and iced drinks. If you messed up the ratio, the drink was either sugar sludge or disappointment in a cup.

We were drilled on writing everything clearly on the cups—milk type, number of shots, flavors, and customer name. After making the drink, we had to call out the full order and the customer's name like it was a Broadway audition. Mess up the announcement, and you risked the wrath of a caffeine-deprived actor or influencer.

Then came the dirty work. We had to wash dishes in the backroom sink—scrubbing steaming pitchers, blender lids, and pastry tongs. Pastries and sandwiches had to be date-dotted correctly, color-coded depending on whether they expired in two or three days. Miss a dot or put the wrong date? That was a reportable offense.

We had to restock cups by size, refill the ice bin, heat sandwiches for the display, and make sure each item was rotated correctly. There were strict rules on how long items could stay under the heat lamp before being pulled. Not to mention constant cleaning—wiping counters, deep-cleaning the espresso machine, sanitizing all surfaces, and sweeping under the counter hourly.

The irony? None of it actually seemed to be done by anyone except the new hires. I noticed old spills under the sink, moldy date stickers left on trays, and dried caramel stuck to the counter's edge.

Tristan's main focus? Dante's latte art. "This guy was born to steam milk," he said, beaming as Dante poured a perfect rosetta pattern.

Then came the POS training. Dante and I were stationed side by side, learning the register system—a glitchy touch-screen with too many buttons and a personality of its own. We were taught how to ring up every item, from cold brews with four pumps of mocha to breakfast sandwiches with custom mods. It got more complicated when employees came by.

Coworkers from other departments expected discounts—some subtle, others not so much. "Hook me up, Penny," a produce guy winked as he ordered a triple espresso. "We're all family, right?"

According to policy, they were supposed to get 10% off drinks during their breaks. But no one ever entered it the same way twice, and half the time, people asked for extras "off the record." Dante happily comped almond milk or extra shots. I tried to stick to the rules and got eye-rolls in return.

I turned back to my own attempt, which looked like a seahorse having a nervous breakdown. There was a pop quiz at the end of each module. Dante aced them. I scraped by while wondering why the regional trainer acted like we were in a latte Olympics.

After one session, Tristan clapped Dante on the back and said, "If we had ten of you, we'd take over the west coast."

I bit my tongue. Hard.

The longer this training went on, the more I felt like I was being pulled in a thousand directions. I wasn't here to become the Barista of the year—I was here to investigate a crime, to gather intel, to uncover something real. Instead, I was elbow-deep in milk foam and paperwork.

Every task, every overly precise rule about syrup pumps and date-dot stickers, every lecture from Tristan or side-eye from Trina chipped away at my focus. I was overwhelmed, tired, and starting to lose track of why I was even here.

At night, I collapsed into bed with espresso still clinging to my hair and caramel syrup stuck to my forearm. My sketchpad lay on the floor half-finished. Instead of connecting dots, I was mentally restocking the ice bin and reviewing heating times for cheddar breakfast melts.

Rock n' Roll Alfie's wasn't just exhausting—it was starting to feel like a distraction. A deliberately exhausting, overly micromanaged distraction.

Every shift felt like a test I hadn't studied for. I had to memorize everything: food menus, drink recipes, POS shortcuts, heating instructions for breakfast sandwiches, and exact steps for taking out the trash. I had to refresh the coffee bar with clean carafes and full bean hoppers every hour, restock cup towers and ice bins, wipe the syrup bottles, and label everything to Sunset Star standards.

Meanwhile, customers flowed in and out all day long—many of them regulars who came in up to three times a day and expected boutique-level service from a kiosk inside a grocery store. And while I was expected to juggle all that, I was also trying to do the real job: investigating a possible financial irregularity, strange behavior among employees, and general corruption.

I was starting to crack under the weight of all the layers. Somewhere beneath the espresso foam and empty sandwich wrappers, I could feel my case slipping away from me.

I started to wonder: was that the point?

At lunch, I took my overpriced turkey sandwich to the break room, trying to blend in. It wasn't hard—everyone was either half-asleep or glued to their phones. I sat next to a cashier named Lynn, who was watching true crime TikToks at full volume.

"You new?" she asked without looking up.

"Yeah. Coffee kiosk. Penny."

She finally glanced over and gave me a once-over. "You'll last a month. Maybe."

"Optimistic."

She shrugged. "This place eats people."

We ate in silence for a beat, then she added, "Watch your back with Trina. She's real cozy with management. Betsy's her godmother or something."

My ears perked. That wasn't in the HR welcome packet.

"She makes it hell for anyone she doesn't like," Lynn continued, taking the lettuce off her sandwich. "Ask Karina. Oh wait, you can't. She quit after two weeks."

"Thanks for the tip."

She leaned in, voice low. "You didn't hear it from me."

Later that day, we had a team huddle in the loading dock. Betsy stood on a milk crate like she was about to announce a merger.

"Everyone, Friday is the start of our summer 'Happy Shopper' initiative," she said, voice bright enough to cause cavities. "That means double points for customers and double effort from us!"

A few groans rippled through the group. Jorge was pretending to take notes on a clipboard. Trina stood next to Betsy like a shadow with mascara.

"We need enthusiasm," Betsy continued. "Energy. Positivity!"

"Pay raises?" someone called from the back.

She ignored it. "And team building. Don't forget, Friday's mixer is mandatory. There will be activities. Name tags. Games."

Dennis muttered, "Great. I've always wanted to relive high school gym."

When it ended, people scattered like dry leaves. I lingered, pretending to rearrange the napkin display while listening in as Trina and Betsy talked near the breakroom door.

"She's not bad," Trina said.

"She's watching too closely," Betsy replied. "Keep her busy. Distract her if you have to."

My heart skipped.

They were talking about me.

Back behind the bar, Trina handed me a clipboard with drink recipes. "You need to memorize these. No substitutions unless authorized."

I scanned the list. Half of them were ridiculous. Who needed a maple lavender foam on a double ristretto at 9 a.m.?

"I'll study up," I said.

She narrowed her eyes. "I hope so. We run this place tight."

I held her gaze. "I can be tight."

"Good. Don't embarrass me."

After closing, I went home, kicked off my shoes, and pulled out my sketchpad again. The board was growing:

Trina: Knows too much. Close to Betsy. Threatened by new hires.

Betsy: Manager. Manipulative. Possibly running something behind the scenes.

Lynn: Gossip source. Possibly an ally.

Dante: Overconfident. Favored by trainer. Why?

Karina: Former Barista. Left suddenly. Track her down?

Mystery Clue: "She's watching too closely." Why? What did they think I'd find?

I scribbled one more question:

Who's protecting who—and from what?

The next morning, before clock-in, I spotted Lynn by the self-checkout lanes.

"You hear about the espresso machine?" she asked, tossing her apron over one shoulder.

"No. What about it?"

"It shorted out last week. Almost took out Jorge."

I blinked. "How does that even happen?"

"Ask Trina. She fixed it herself. Said it was 'just a fuse.'"

More notes for the board.

Mid-shift, I caught Betsy speaking with a customer I hadn't seen before—a man in his fifties, all beige clothing and expensive shoes. He handed her an envelope, which she slid into her apron without breaking eye contact.

No receipt. No smile. No "have a nice day."

When she walked past me, I smiled. "Everything alright?"

She didn't smile back. "Peachy."

She disappeared into the back office.

That night, I added a new heading to the board: Envelope Man.

Underneath it, I drew a dollar sign and circled it.

Friday was coming fast, and I could already feel the tension rising like steam from the espresso machine.

I wasn't sure what kind of game was being played at Alfie's yet—but I was definitely in it now.

CHAPTER THREE

FOAM AND FRICTION

The customer in front of me wore rhinestone sunglasses, a sequined trucker hat, and an expression like I'd just insulted her Yorkie.

"I said extra-hot, skinny, sugar-free hazelnut latte with almond milk, not oat milk," she snapped, thrusting the cup back at me like it had personally wronged her.

"Of course," I said, taking the cup and internally rolling my eyes. This was the third drink I'd remade for her, and it was only 8:42 a.m.

"Hollywood royalty," Trina whispered from the other end of the bar. "Comes in three times a day. Hasn't tipped since 2019."

I steamed new milk and tried to focus, but my body was running on fumes. Between the impossible training expectations, customer service theater, and all my real work going undone, I was hanging on by a shot of espresso and spite.

Dante breezed by, handing off a cappuccino like it was a love letter. "You're doing great, Penny," he chirped.

I forced a smile. "Thanks, Dante."

He was the golden child, the rising star of the Sunset Star universe. Trina doted on him now too, laughing at his dumb jokes and praising his "natural warmth." I watched her show him how to refill the whipped cream canisters with a sweetness she'd never once directed at me.

I hated how good he was at this.

Later, I was assigned to trash duty. It involved hauling out three dripping black bags and sanitizing the bins in a cramped alley that smelled like day-old sushi and bad decisions. It was also where the delivery trucks backed in, and where I found Jorge leaning against the wall, smoking a cigarette he pretended wasn't lit.

"Rough shift?" he asked.

"I'm living the dream," I said.

He chuckled. "You'll get used to it. Or you'll quit. That's the usual path."

"Is it just me, or is this place... intense?"

Jorge exhaled smoke sideways. "It's Hollywood, baby. Everyone's pretending to be something else. Even in grocery stores."

I wanted to ask more, but Betsy popped her head out the back door.

"Penny, back on bar. Now."

"Yes, ma'am."

Back inside, I wiped sweat from my forehead and restocked the cup tower, double-checking the inventory log as I went. The numbers weren't adding up. We were short four sleeves of large iced cups and two bags of dark roast.

I made a mental note to follow up later. Maybe someone was just forgetful. Or maybe something else was going on.

The line of customers had tripled in the twenty minutes I was gone, and there was no backup in sight. Trina had vanished again—she had a gift for slipping away mid-rush and reappearing only when the hardest part was over. I'd seen her disappear behind the break room, come back forty minutes later drenched in sweat and radiating the pungent smell of musty body odor. Even the customers noticed. One woman leaned in and whispered, "Is something dead in here?"

The source? Trina's bra—likely soaking wet and overworked like the rest of us.

I stepped in just in time to help a customer with a complicated order involving three blended drinks and a hot tea with lemon. Trina reemerged only long enough to criticize my pouring technique and log a half-hearted order.

"Where were you?" she hissed, as if she hadn't just pulled a disappearing act herself.

"Trash," I replied, biting back everything else I wanted to say.

I was being left alone more and more, with barely any training and no support. Every drink I made required a full wash of my hands afterward—Sunset Star policy. No gloves allowed, just soap and scrubbing, dozens of times a shift. Between that, calling out each customer's name, writing every detail on each cup, restocking lids and sleeves, and refreshing the bar setup, it felt like I was trying to run the entire kiosk solo during a caffeine apocalypse. Every shift I was thrown into chaos, juggling demanding customers with only half the tools I needed. It wasn't just exhausting—it was infuriating.

And always looming above it all were Trina and Betsy, whispering by the pastry case, talking like co-conspirators. I was beginning to see their real power: they didn't just run the kiosk—they ruled it. They protected each other, targeted others, and manipulated every flow of power inside Alfie's like it was their personal chessboard.

They weren't just my coworkers. They were my conflict.

We worked in tense silence until the rush slowed. As I stepped away to start wiping down the espresso machine, I overheard something strange.

"Just make sure the drawer balances this time," Betsy whispered to Trina by the pastry case.

"I triple-checked it. If she sees it again, she's going to ask questions."

I turned my back and pretended to stir syrup into a carafe.

See what again? Who was asking questions?

By the end of the day, my feet were numb and my brain was fried. I scribbled into my sketchpad with what little energy I had left:

Inventory errors. Cup sleeves missing. Coffee bags undercounted.

Cash drawer? Skimming?

Customer complaints rising. Training still not complete.

Trina and Betsy = possible coordination.

I stared at the page. What had started as a simple "observe and report" job was now spiraling. I didn't know what I was in the middle of, but I could feel the tension rising, minute by minute.

And I wasn't the only one feeling it.

Before that, I started noticing more about the people around me—the web of personalities that made up Alfie's. There were cliques: produce stuck to produce, the deli gossiped with the sushi crew, and everyone silently agreed that restockers were on a different planet altogether.

I met Biola in the bakery department—a regal woman with salt-and-pepper hair twisted into a tight bun and the kind of judgmental side-eye that could pierce drywall. She offered me a smile when no one was looking and handed me a slightly burnt chocolate chip cookie like it was a test.

"You're new," she said, not a question.

"Penny. Coffee kiosk."

"Biola. Bakery." She glanced behind her, then leaned closer. "I'm Betsy's mother."

I froze.

"She doesn't like when I tell people that," she added with a wink.

The next moment, she was back to slicing banana bread with military precision. I filed her under: Knows More Than She Lets On.

Everywhere I turned, there were odd dynamics. Two cashiers never made eye contact. A deli worker and a Manager seemed to be communicating via passive-aggressive post-its. People smiled when necessary, but no one seemed to really trust each other.

And then there were the customers.

Some were regulars—too regular. One guy came in five times a day, always ordered the same thing, paid in cash, and never made eye contact. Another woman would ask for obscure seasonal drinks that weren't even on the menu anymore, then linger near the florist section while muttering into her phone.

I tried not to be paranoid, but every interaction now felt like it could be something more. Drug runners? Informants? Or just very strange Angelenos?

I started jotting quick notes after each suspicious encounter.

Customer: tall man, faded Dodgers cap, orders decaf but adds five espresso shots—suspicious energy.

Customer: pink tracksuit, heavy perfume, stares at fire exit every time—possible casing?

The deeper I looked, the more I saw. This grocery store wasn't just quirky—it was coded. Layers and patterns that didn't fully make sense yet.

Dennis, the DJ-turned-deli-worker, approached me while I was grabbing a water from the break room fridge.

"You ever feel like this place has too many cameras?" he asked, cracking open a can of sparkling tea.

I paused. "You mean security?"

He nodded. "There's more in the stockroom than on the sales floor. That's weird, right?"

It was.

I added it to my list.

Back on bar, I closed out the register for the night. As I counted out the till, I noticed a receipt tucked underneath the drawer. It wasn't for a transaction—just a list of drink codes scribbled on the back and a name: T. Harmon.

Another name for the board. Another thread to pull.

I looked up at the empty kiosk, the shiny surfaces hiding a mountain of secrets.

Something was brewing at Sunset Star—and for once, it wasn't coffee.

CHAPTER
FOUR

THE DIRTY CHAI

The next morning, before the sun could finish rising over Sunset Boulevard, I was back at Sunset Star Coffee, scrubbing caramel off the counter with a rag that should've been retired during the Obama administration. My back ached. My hands were cracked from all the washing. And my patience? Hanging by a thread thinner than Trina's excuse for a timecard. Trina, who was overweight, always sweating, and smelled like she hadn't discovered detergent. Her clothes clung to her body in a way that made you want to hold your breath when she walked past. Married, miserable, and mad at the world, she wasn't a team player. She was nosy, invasive, and always in someone else's business. The worst part? She got away with everything. Everyone knew she was having a fling with Ted, the Assistant Store

Manager. That's why no one called her out. That's why she disappeared mid-shift without consequence. That's why Betsy—her best friend and co-conspirator—always covered for her.

"You opening alone?" Dante asked, strolling in with a croissant in hand and not a care in the world.

"Apparently." I wiped my brow with my sleeve. "Trina's out sick—again."

"She looked fine last night," he said, chewing.

"Must've been a sudden case of strategic vanishing."

We opened late. No one noticed because customers were too busy trying to jump the line or order their drinks before the bar was even set up. I was halfway through restocking the ice bin when a man stepped up to the counter and ordered a "dirty chai."

"Excuse me?" I asked.

"Dirty chai. You know—chai syrup, two espresso shots, steamed milk. Make it iced."

I nodded, scribbled on the cup, and got to work.

As I poured the syrup, the name settled into my head like a song lyric I didn't want. A dirty chai. That felt... too on the nose. A chai, corrupted. A drink that looked sweet but came with a jolt.

Like Betsy and Trina.

I served the drink and watched him sip it with a twitch. He glanced around like he was waiting for someone. He wasn't the first customer like that. And probably not the last.

I noticed something shift when he came in. Trina stopped mid-sip of her Red Bull and stared. Betsy's hand clenched so tight around the pastry tongs, I thought she might bend them. Neither said a word, but their body language screamed discomfort. They kept glancing toward him like he'd walked in wearing a badge—which, as far as I could tell, he hadn't.

Still, the tension was real. I wasn't sure who this man was, but he made them nervous. And that alone made him interesting.

He returned the next day. Ordered the same thing. Sat near the floral department with a tablet and earbuds, but didn't touch his drink for nearly thirty minutes. Just watched. Not in a creepy way—more like someone calculating. Studying.

I made a mental note to keep an eye on him, too.

Around eleven, Betsy decided to make a drink herself—a rare sight. She tied her apron on like she was auditioning for a cooking show and waltzed behind the bar just as I was finishing a caramel macchiato.

"I'll take the next one," she said with a toothy smile, nudging me out of the way.

The customer ordered a simple iced vanilla latte. Easy. But Betsy steamed milk instead of pouring cold, added two pumps too many, forgot the espresso entirely, and handed it off like it was a masterpiece.

Not two minutes later, the customer came back, holding the cup with a pinched look. "This isn't right. It's hot. And weirdly sweet."

"Oh, you must've said hot," Betsy replied, deflecting without blinking.

"I said iced. And I didn't ask for extra vanilla."

Betsy turned to me. "Can you fix this?"

I took the drink and remade it, silently fuming.

After he left, one of the other Baristas—Minnie from closing shifts—leaned over and muttered, "That's why she never makes drinks. Customers complain every time."

"She prefers ringing people up," said Nate from re-stock, who'd somehow appeared with a broom and a smirk. "Less chance of exposure."

It all made sense. Betsy was never behind the bar unless it was for show. She'd once been Alfie's book-keeper—back before she got promoted to Manager by Joe, the Store Director. Rumor had it she wore short skirts and flirted her way into the role. There was always something a little ghetto about her demeanor, like she was trying too hard to look in control while constantly dodging accountability. She didn't want a co-Manager unless it was Trina, and she made sure no one else ever got close to her turf. She didn't have a ring on her finger, but she was now pregnant with her fifth child. That part mattered to her—the ring, not the baby. She wanted the image, even if everything else was a mess underneath... She didn't know what she was doing—and didn't care to learn.

Just after lunch, chaos erupted.

A loud crack—like a firework—snapped through the front of the store, followed by another. Screams echoed from the sliding entrance doors. I instinctively ducked, coffee still in hand, heart pounding.

Gunshots. Outside. Parking lot.

The armed security guard posted at the front rushed toward the doors, hand on his weapon. Customers panicked, abandoning carts, some running toward the elevators, others ducking behind produce displays.

I grabbed the kiosk's landline but hesitated. Calling 911 would mean identifying myself—too much risk. So I used my burner phone.

"911, what's your emergency?"

"Active shooter outside Alfie's. Two shots fired. Parking lot level. People are panicking."

I gave only what they needed, then hung up and turned to the Baristas.

"Secure the kiosk. Shut down the brewers. Stay down."

Betsy appeared from the break room, eyes wide but already calculating. "We need to lock the side stairwells and elevators. Now."

There were four elevators connecting the main floor to the upstairs parking garage. Wide, slow, and impossible to monitor all at once. I bolted toward the closest set, heart hammering, and hit the lock override key we'd been trained on—well, barcly trained on. The elevators stuttered to a halt.

One down.

I rounded the back hallway, passing a frozen bakery worker pressed against the wall. "Get to the break room," I barked. "Lock the door behind you."

The guard came through on the store PA. "Situation under control. Suspect fled on foot. No known injuries."

The store breathed again—but barely.

Customers slowly reemerged. Someone started crying in the produce aisle. Others just grabbed their bags and left. But the damage was done. Fear hung in the air like burnt espresso.

And through all of it, Betsy and Trina looked rattled—but not for the reasons you'd expect. They weren't scared of the shooter.

They were scared of what might come next.

Midway through the shift, I caught Betsy in the back office—door open, phone in hand, speaking fast and low.

"I don't care what Harmon said," she snapped. "Just move the numbers. She won't catch it."

Harmon. Again.

I ducked away before she saw me and added another note to my mental board. Or rather, the actual board I kept taped inside a sketchpad at home. I was going to need new pages soon.

The customers were a blur. Half of them came in for the same drink every day, like clockwork. Others ordered oddly specific drinks—two shots of espresso, oat milk, one pump hazelnut, half-pump caramel, cinnamon dusted—but never drank them. They'd just hover. Watching.

I started to suspect they weren't all here for caffeine.

By mid-afternoon, I was alone on bar again. The rush hit like a freight train, and Dante had vanished to "check the milk temp in the back fridge," which I was pretty sure was code for texting in the loading dock. The line stretched all the way to the floral department.

I smiled, nodded, filled cups, scribbled names, steamed milk, washed my hands. Every single time.

And not a single coworker offered help.

As I finished another dirty chai for a woman in designer joggers and oversized sunglasses, she leaned in and said, "You don't belong here."

I froze. "Excuse me?"

She smiled, took the cup, and left without another word.

A chill ran through me.

I marked her down: dirty chai lady, mirrored sunglasses, cryptic.

After close, I stayed late to finish the logs—temp checks, cleaning charts, milk disposal forms. Someone had signed for morning cleaning but nothing had been done. The mop water was still clear. The trash bin hadn't been changed.

I filled everything out myself, like I always did.

Before I left, I flipped through the back pages of the logbook. A few were missing.

Not blank. Missing.

Ripped clean out.

I snapped a photo with my burner phone and slid the book back into the drawer.

Something was definitely off.

And the more I looked, the more I saw it.

Later that night, I sat on the floor of my studio apartment, flipping through my sketchpad. Names, drink codes, inventory shifts, strange behavior. Every thread pointed in the same direction:

Trina and Betsy.

They weren't just sketchy. They were running something.

And I wasn't going to let them keep the lid on it for much longer.

CHAPTER
FIVE

THE WRONG CUP

The next day, Alfie's was buzzing like nothing had happened. No signs left behind of yesterday's chaos. No extra security. No press. Just the lingering scent of citrus cleaner and paranoia. But the vibe was different. Tighter. Employees whispered instead of joked. Betsy smiled a little too much. Trina laughed a little too loud. It was all for show.

And the man with the tablet? He was back.

He ordered his usual dirty chai. I handed it to him with a calm smile, even though every part of me buzzed with alert. Betsy watched him from the register. Trina peeked around the pastry case, pretending to adjust muffins.

I was scheduled to cover a half-shift that morning and left just before noon. Charles was on bar—a tall, long-haired guy from Wisconsin who rode a skateboard to work and was always late. He had that easygoing vibe, the kind that made you wonder if anything ever got to him. Cool, detached, and barely holding it together. He handed off drinks like he was floating through a dream.

Donny—the cheese Manager turned reluctant co-Manager—stopped by the kiosk just before his inventory meeting with Joe.

"I'll take whatever has the most caffeine," he joked. "I need to learn all the drinks if I'm going to co-manage Sunset Star, right?"

He usually stuck to iced green teas with eight pumps of simple syrup, but today he reached for something new—something he hadn't ordered.

"That one's mine," Mike said from the counter.

But Donny had already grabbed the dirty chai and walked off with a shrug.

Charles barely looked up. "Oh—uh, sorry, man. Want me to make you another one?"

Mike didn't answer. He just watched Donny walk away, then nodded slowly.

I didn't see it happen.

But I heard about it in gut-wrenching detail.

Donny had been walking down the hallway behind the dairy cooler, sipping the drink, laughing to himself about how it wasn't half bad. He collapsed near the supply closet, his head hitting the wall hard enough to leave a dent in the drywall. A produce clerk found him moments later, convulsing, foam at the corner of his mouth.

The paramedics said seizure. Possible allergic reaction. But there was something more frantic in their tones than that. By the time I got the call, Alfie's had been swarmed by EMTs, the breakroom sealed off, and HR already rewriting the incident.

I got the call on my burner an hour later. Donny had collapsed in the service hallway behind the dairy case. Paramedics had been called. Initial reports said it looked like a seizure, maybe a reaction.

But the whispers said poison.

And deep down, I believed them.

It wasn't just the drink—it was the timing, the randomness of Donny being the one to grab it. Too coincidental. Too perfect. And the worst part? No one seemed to care that it might've been intentional. Management was already talking damage control instead of investigation.

I rushed back in on my day off, claiming I left something in my locker. Betsy was already in crisis mode, walking fast, talking faster. Trina hovered like a bat on alert.

"We think it was food poisoning," Betsy said to a concerned customer, flashing her PR smile. "We've got food safety on it. Just a fluke."

But it wasn't a fluke. Donny had taken a drink meant for someone else.

Someone like Mike—the so-called auditor, tablet always in hand, eyes always scanning like he was writing a report in his head. The dirty chai had been his. But Donny got it instead.

In the break room, the tension was razor sharp. Nate from restock looked pale. Lynn avoided eye contact. Minnie whispered to me near the vending machine.

"Donny never gets drinks," she said. "That wasn't even his order. He just picked it up."

My stomach turned. If the drink was intended for the man who made Betsy and Trina nervous, that meant someone had planned this. Someone wanted him gone.

And someone else got caught in the middle.

Donny didn't deserve it. He was a goofball, sure, but he was trying. The guy just wanted to learn his drinks, manage a team, maybe stop sweating cheese for once in his life. Now he was in the hospital under observation, and Alfie's was treating it like a shift error.

I clocked in for my next shift with one goal: watch everything. I stuck close to the kiosk, triple-checking every cup, every label. I intercepted orders, watched Betsy's every move, and shadowed Trina from the coffee bar to the break room and back.

No one else had gotten sick. Not yet. But paranoia was creeping in like mold under a drain mat.

And Mike—the so-called auditor—was still coming in, still ordering the same thing, still watching from his perch by the floral section. But I could tell he'd noticed the shift. He was sharper now. His eyes stayed on Charles a beat too long. He never left his drink unattended.

If Donny was the wrong target, that meant Mike was the right one.

And Mike wasn't stupid. He'd started watching more carefully. Asking more questions. I caught him lingering by the customer service counter, talking to Ted in a low voice. Ted looked uncomfortable. Which told me everything.

Even Charles seemed spooked. He started triple-checking every label, actually wiping the steamer wand between drinks. I'd never seen him move faster than a casual stroll before.

And someone wanted him gone... Still sipping. Still unbothered.

I didn't know who Mike really was. But it was clear now: he wasn't just here for the chai.

And if someone was willing to take a man down for just sipping the wrong drink, then Alfie's was a far more dangerous place than I'd realized.

How was I supposed to explain this to Gus, my supervisor? I'd signed up to investigate shady behavior, maybe a theft ring, not a near-homicide involving poisoned beverages. Would another team come in? Would forensics sweep the kiosk, pull security footage, run cup prints? Or would they pull me out, bury this whole thing under corporate silence?

Everything started to spiral. Fast.

Word spread like wildfire. Customers were nervous. Regulars asked questions. A local blogger posted something cryptic about an "incident at the cheese case," and it got shared fifty times within the hour. HR responded by sending out a memo titled "Employee Wellness & Safety Reminder."

Meanwhile, the staff was mourning.

Donny was gone. His presence lingered like a ghost in the walls. People spoke about him in hushed tones, like mentioning his name might stir the air in the breakroom. He'd been well-liked earnest, maybe a little awkward, but the kind of guy who meant every word he said. Always talking about his kids, beaming like a proud dad with a full wallet of crayon drawings. He was genuinely excited to learn the ins and outs of the kiosk. That morning, he'd shown up early with a box of mini blueberry muffins for the team—still warm, like he'd planned it that way.

Betsy and Trina—despite their well-known dislike for Donny—taped a picture of him on the kiosk bulletin board with a sticky note that read, "We'll miss you, Donny." The gesture felt hollow, performative. But people noticed.

Customers noticed. Minnie cried while wiping down the counter. Nate from restock muttered something about switching departments. Even Ted kept pacing around the office like he didn't know what to do with his hands.

And me? I wrote everything down. Every look. Every whisper. Every tremble in a coworker's voice.

Because Alfie's wasn't just complicated anymore.

It was officially dangerous.

That night, I sat in my apartment staring at my sketchpad, the one I'd been filling with names and notes and suspicions. And now? A new page. I titled it: "Case Escalation."

I kept thinking back to my last undercover gig—a chop-shop sting in El Monte. It was dirty, yes, but predictable. Small-time thieves, greedy guys with missing teeth and big mouths. No poison. No collapsing coworkers. No fake smiles posted next to real grief.

This? This was different.

I'd expected shoplifting. Maybe embezzlement. Definitely not attempted murder in the middle of a grocery store.

And when I finally worked up the nerve to message Gus, I couldn't bring myself to type it all. I just sent: Need to talk. It's bigger than we thought.

The next morning, I hovered by the service desk, watching Ted talk to Mike again. I tried to ease into the conversation.

"Hey, Ted. You doing okay? It's been a rough week."

Ted gave me a tight-lipped nod. "Fine. Just busy."

"You've worked with Donny a long time, right?"

Ted's face hardened. "Yeah. And I don't need you playing Detective around here. You've got customers to help."

I blinked. "I wasn't—"

"Go clock in, Penny. This isn't your department."

He walked away before I could say anything else.

So Ted wasn't ready to talk. Maybe he had something to hide. Or maybe he just didn't like me poking around where Trina might be involved.

Either way, he'd confirmed one thing: I was onto something.

Before I clocked in, I stopped by the security office under the pretense of needing footage for a "missing wallet." I asked to review camera feeds from the day before—specifically the kiosk. The guard, a guy named Raul with a perpetual energy drink in hand, barely looked up from his screen.

"Be quick. I'm not supposed to let anyone watch these unless it's a real emergency."

"It is," I said, voice even.

I scrolled through the footage—sped-up hours of Baristas swirling, steaming, and scribbling names on cups. Then I saw it. Charles placing the dirty chai down. Mike looking at it. Donny grabbing it before Mike could speak up. I watched it twice. Three times.

I paused at the exact moment Donny took that first sip. He smiled. He didn't know.

I closed the file and thanked Raul, making a note to follow up later. The footage might disappear. Or worse, be "accidentally deleted."

I ran into Minnie by the time clock.

She was standing there holding her badge but hadn't scanned it yet. Her eyes were rimmed red. The usual bright pink in her cheeks was pale.

"He trained me," she said softly. "Donny. My first day here, he stayed late to help me label all the cheese wheels. He didn't have to do that. He even bought me a coffee the next morning just to check in."

She paused and added, "This place gets under your skin, you know? You work here long enough, and people become your second family. Not always the family you'd choose, but still... when one of them gets hurt—"

Her voice cracked. She pressed her lips together and stared at the timeclock.

"I can't believe he's just... gone. I mean, I know he's not dead. But it feels like we all lost something."

She wiped her eyes quickly, like she was embarrassed. "I keep thinking I'm going to hear him singing in the dairy case or doing that dumb turkey impression by the rotisserie chicken."

I nodded slowly. "Yeah. It's hard."

"You know what sucks?" she said. "I don't even know what happened. No one tells us anything. It's like we're supposed to pretend he just left early."

I didn't have an answer for her.

She finally scanned her badge. "See you on bar."

Later, I got a text from Gus. It was short: Careful. Corporate's watching now.

Whatever I was in the middle of—it had just gone national.

Before I left for the night, I lingered in the kiosk a little longer, wiping down surfaces that were already clean. I could feel eyes on me. Lynn was watching from behind the service counter. Nate, still pale, lingered too long near the cooler. Even Trina passed by, slower than necessary, arms folded like she was daring me to speak.

Everyone had questions, but no one wanted to ask out loud. It wasn't just grief in the air anymore—it was fear. Paranoia had set in, quiet and slow, creeping into every shift and every sideways glance.

I started wondering if someone was watching me. If maybe I was getting too close, asking too many questions. And what if the poisoned drink had been a warning to more than just Mike?

That night, I double-locked my apartment door and closed the curtains. Then I sat with my sketchpad and drew another circle.

Inside it, I wrote: Who's watching who?

CHAPTER
SIX

THE WHISPER IN THE AISLE

My first day back after Donny's collapse started with a corporate audit—just not the kind anyone expected. Mike was no longer a mystery. His name appeared in bold black letters on the clipboard he carried, followed by the words "Federal Compliance Liaison." No one used the word "FBI," but everyone felt it.

People stared when he walked by. Employees scattered when he turned a corner. Ted wouldn't look him in the eye. Betsy kept trying to look busy, folding aprons that didn't need folding, restocking cups we weren't out of. Trina? She vanished for two hours in the middle of the shift.

I found her later, behind the warehouse doors, texting furiously in the shadows by the pallet racks. Her face was red, and her shirt was darker with sweat than usual.

"Everything okay?" I asked.

She flinched. "Fine. Just hot back here."

I didn't push. Yet.

The store was trying too hard to be normal. DJ Dennis played upbeat 2000s hits over the PA. Balloons had appeared in the bakery for no reason. Betsy hosted a pop-up tasting of new seasonal drinks by the kiosk.

"Try our new Lavender Matcha Fizz!" she said to a customer, flashing her press-on smile. "A touch of calm in every sip."

I watched her fake it while the entire store felt like it was holding its breath.

That afternoon, I was cleaning syrup nozzles when Lynn tapped my shoulder.

"You got a second?" she whispered.

She led me into the back hallway behind frozen foods, where the employee fridge buzzed like a warning.

"I heard something," she said. "About Donny."

I waited.

"Someone said he was trying to blow the whistle. Like, he saw something in the inventory logs. Something off. I don't know if it was money or shipments, but he was going to tell Mike."

My throat tightened.

"Who told you that?"

She shook her head. "Does it matter? Look around. Everyone's scared. But you're different. You ask questions. You listen. So I'm telling you. Watch your back."

After my shift, I walked the aisles pretending to shop. Watching. Listening. I turned the corner near canned goods and nearly bumped into Mike.

He looked at me, expression unreadable. "Be careful who you trust," he said, low and quiet. Then walked away.

That night, I added two more names to my sketchpad list.

Ted. Trina.

Then underlined them twice.

Before I left, I checked the logbook at the kiosk. Three entries were missing from the morning shift—temperature checks, waste tracking, and a drink label verification. All signed off by Trina.

I added a note to my pad: Missing entries = pattern. Cover-up or incompetence?

Out of the corner of my eye, I saw Mike again, near the endcap of cereal. He was pretending to read labels, but his eyes scanned the ceiling—checking for cameras. He wasn't here to audit prices. He was watching systems. Watching people.

And now I was watching him.

I passed Betsy near the floral section. She flinched when she saw me. Then smiled. "We're all good here, right Penny?"

"Totally," I said. "So good."

She moved on, her walk just a little too fast. Her belly was just starting to show—baby number five. But her nerves were louder than her heels.

Behind the kiosk, Trina was wiping the same counter over and over, glaring at anyone who came too close. I noticed she'd left her phone face-down near the register. When I passed by, it buzzed.

One notification glowed: TED: "Meet behind lot after close."

My pulse kicked.

Trina was meeting Ted? Again? Something more than gossip was brewing.

This wasn't just about poisoned drinks anymore.

This was a conspiracy.

And I was in the middle of it.

I made my way toward the breakroom but stopped short when I overheard Jorge talking to Dennis by the mop sink.

"She's been sniffing around a lot lately," Jorge said. "You think she's gonna report someone?"

"Penny?" Dennis lowered his voice. "I don't know. But if she's smart, she'll keep her head down. People are on edge."

I stepped back before they saw me and quietly turned toward the stockroom. There was an energy in the air I couldn't quite shake—like the moment before a storm when all the hairs on your arms rise.

Later, while taking out the trash, I spotted Mike again. He was standing near the dock, watching a pallet being delivered from a truck that wasn't scheduled. The driver looked unfamiliar. The label on the crate read Dry Goods, but the barcode didn't match the store manifest.

Mike scribbled something in his notes, nodded at the driver, and walked away.

I took a mental snapshot of the barcode. Something wasn't right with that delivery.

And something told me... Mike knew it too.

The next morning was brutal.

The line at the kiosk was out the door by 8:15, snaking past the floral department and into produce. I was on bar alone again—Trina was "running late"—and every drink order felt like a countdown to losing it.

The customers weren't helping. A woman wearing oversized sunglasses and a hooded sweatshirt stepped forward and slammed her hand on the counter.

"I was on Survivor, you know," she announced loudly. "And I'm about to survive this line if someone would hurry up."

It was Hannah. A former reality show contestant who now haunted Sunset Star like a curse with a caffeine addiction.

"I'm late for a doctor's appointment!" she barked. "Could you make my drink already?! This is ridiculous!"

"Just a moment," I said as calmly as I could.

But my hands were shaking. My nerves frayed. My jaw clenched.

This wasn't my real job. I wasn't trained to smile through tantrums and microaggressions from Z-list TV villains with control issues.

"I don't have all day!" Hannah yelled, making the customers behind her shift uncomfortably. "Is this how you treat people with actual jobs?!"

Trina strolled in fifteen minutes later, unbothered and reeking of old sweat and fabric softener that had clearly lost the battle.

"Rough start?" she asked with a smirk.

I didn't answer.

She parked herself behind the register and immediately started fiddling with her phone. I spotted it again—screen unlocked, a text from Ted open: "Don't forget the envelope."

My fingers itched. If I just leaned over slightly, I could read more.

"Need something?" Trina asked, turning suddenly.

I jumped back. "Just refilling syrup pumps."

She narrowed her eyes but didn't push it. Not this time.

Later, Betsy pulled me aside near the bakery.

"I don't need attitude from you," she hissed under her breath. "I've got enough problems right now."

"Then maybe stop creating them," I said without thinking.

Her eyes flared. She leaned closer. "You don't know who you're messing with, Penny. Stay in your lane."

I smiled. "Sure. Right after I wipe down this whole damn highway."

On my break, I stepped outside for air and caught sight of Trina slipping out the employee entrance near receiving. She didn't notice me—too focused on where she was going. I followed her at a distance, staying low behind the shopping cart corral until I saw her round the back of the building.

Ted was already there, leaning against the wall with his arms crossed. I ducked behind a pallet of shrink-wrapped toilet paper.

"I told you to be careful," Ted said, his voice hushed but firm.

"I am being careful," Trina snapped. "She's always watching me. Like a damn hawk. It's getting obvious."

"Then stop drawing attention. Don't text me during shifts."

They stepped further behind the dumpster. I crept closer, heart pounding, but just as I did, a cart boy slammed a string of buggies into the bay beside me, nearly giving me a heart attack. By the time I peeked out again, Trina and Ted were gone.

Later, back at the kiosk, I was wiping down the espresso machine when one of our regulars stepped up quietly.

"Rough day?" she asked.

She was older, kind eyes, always ordered a plain drip coffee with half-and-half.

"Something like that," I said, forcing a smile.

"You look tired."

I handed her the coffee. "Thanks. It's the lighting."

She didn't laugh. Just nodded and said, "Don't forget to breathe." Then walked away.

It hit harder than I expected.

I had been holding my breath. For days. Weeks, even. Everything was unraveling. Every step closer to the truth made the floor under me feel thinner.

But I couldn't pull back. Not now. I was in too deep, and the web was tighter than I ever imagined.

I took one long breath and stepped back into the rush.

It was time to push harder.

To dig deeper.

And maybe... to bait someone into making a mistake.

That evening, I did something risky. I left a fake inventory discrepancy in the logbook. Just a minor one—off by a couple of cups and a pound of espresso. Enough to be noticed by someone trying to cover tracks. I signed it with Trina's initials.

Then I waited.

When I came back from my ten-minute break, the page was gone.

Not crossed out. Not corrected. Ripped out.

I checked the trash. Nothing. Whoever had taken it didn't want to correct the record—they wanted it to vanish.

I logged it in my sketchpad: Fake log test: result =
hit. Someone's watching the records. Actively.

The noose was tightening, but I still didn't know
around whose neck.

And then there was Mike. Always two steps ahead.
Always scribbling. Always scanning. Watching me now,
too. Was he my backup—or someone else's handler?

Every answer only seemed to open more doors. And
I was running out of keys.

The next morning, I was called to headquarters for a
brief meeting with Gus.

He didn't waste time with pleasantries. "We got the
toxicology report," he said. "It was Raid. In his blood-
stream. Donny was poisoned with a pesticide—house-
hold stuff, but deadly in concentrated doses."

My breath caught.

"Raid?" I repeated. "As in bug spray?"

Gus nodded grimly. "Yep. And here's the thing—
it's sold in Alfie's. Meaning someone could've bought it,
or someone could've stolen it from the shelf. Either way,
we're running an internal inventory check. Every store
in the district. Corporate's bringing in a special unit to
sweep Sunset Star."

"They're looking for a can?" I asked.

"They're looking for the can. Prints, residue, anything. Until we find it, we don't know who had it, where
it went, or how it got into that drink."

I swallowed hard. "You want me to do anything dif-
ferently?"

"Keep your eyes open. Keep doing what you're doing. But Penny…"

He leaned in slightly.

"If you feel the heat's getting too close—pull out. I mean it."

I nodded, even though we both knew I wouldn't.

Because this wasn't just a store anymore. It was a crime scene.

As I left Gus's office, I passed through one of the upper corridors of headquarters and caught sight of Mike standing outside a conference room, talking with two men in suits. He didn't see me—or at least I didn't think he did.

But the sight of him there rattled me.

He was more embedded than I'd realized. I started to wonder: did he know about me? About my assignment? Was he monitoring me too?

If he knew, he was playing it cool. And if he didn't—what would happen when he found out?

Back at Sunset Star, the weight of Donny's absence hit me like a wave when I passed his locker. It was still decorated with a photo of his dog and a bumper sticker that read: Cheese Life Chose Me. Someone had stuck a single yellow daisy in the locker vent.

Joe, the Store Director, stood near the registers when I returned. Tall, bald, with a sharp suit and a silver chain that glinted under his collar—he looked like a retired gangster or a soap opera villain. He reminded me of Telly Savalas. He gave me a slow wink.

"Everything alright, sweetheart?"

I hated when he called me that.

"Peachy," I said, walking past him.

He used to be close with Donny. Promised Donny's family that he'd look out for him after he transferred from a different Alfie's location. Now Donny was gone, and Joe hadn't made a single announcement. Just kept walking around like nothing happened.

People feared him, that much was clear. No one questioned his decisions. No one called him out. He didn't need to raise his voice—his presence alone kept people in line.

And that wink? It wasn't charm. It was a message: Keep quiet, and you stay safe.. And someone in that store had weaponized something you could buy off aisle nine.

CHAPTER
SEVEN

HOT STUFF

They called him Hot Stuff.

Not to his face, of course—but between shifts, in whispers behind the breakroom door and over the milk frothing station.

He was the new armed security guard posted at the front of Alfie's. Tall, olive-toned skin—flawless, like he actually followed a skincare routine, and probably had opinions on under-eye cream. You could tell he took self-care seriously. He was in his early 40's, well built, lean muscle visible even beneath the layers of uniform and gear. A tattoo curled around one of his forearms—black ink with sharp edges, the kind of design that meant something, even if he never talked about it. And he had that kind of swagger that made even the frozen food aisle feel ten degrees hotter. His fitted uniform looked custom-made, his bulletproof vest snug beneath it. His utility belt was spotless—carrying a baton, handcuffs, a can of pepper spray, and a holstered firearm, the unmistakable weight of it never out of reach. Most armed guards had worked in law enforcement before, and something about the way he moved told me he probably had too. His hair—long but slicked back above the shoulders—was always perfectly in place. He had the posture of someone who had seen real things, someone who didn't flinch easily. A workaholic, by all signs, and he took the job seriously. He never left his post for more than a few minutes, rarely looked at his phone, and always kept an eye on the exits.

And yet—he was overly friendly. Playful. The kind of guy who could throw a wink at the bakery Manager while also clocking a suspicious exchange at register four. Secretive too. No one really knew where he was from, or how he ended up at Alfie's. But he had a way of making everyone feel like they knew him. Like he was in on the joke.

He was a full-on contradiction.

A full-on distraction.

I first noticed him while restocking lids at the kiosk. He walked past the kiosk with a slow, deliberate stride, scanning the store with that quiet intensity only guards or predators had. A few customers gave him second glances. I wasn't the only one who turned.

Lynn nudged me. "That's him. Hot Stuff."

"Is that his actual name?"

"No, but does it matter?"

It didn't.

He was confident, casual, and—most important-ly—new. Which meant he didn't know the politics yet. He didn't seem weighed down by the same tension or haunted by the whispered ghosts of poisoned drinks and conspiracy texts.

Not yet.

He came to the kiosk during his first official break. Ordered a cold brew, black—no frills, just like him.

"You must be Penny," he said.

My heart kicked. "How do you—"

"Name's on the board. I read the schedule."

"Efficient."

"Hot Stuff," Trina said under her breath behind me, too loud to be subtle.

He grinned but didn't respond. Just took his drink, gave me a playful fist bump—something he seemed to love doing with everyone—and walked off.

I didn't smile back. Not because I wasn't interest-ed—but because I didn't know who to trust anymore. And people who were too charming? They were either naïve... or dangerous.

Still, I found myself watching him out of the corner of my eye. The way he moved. The way people seemed to instantly like him. Even Joe gave him a shoulder pat one afternoon near the store's front entrance. That was rare.

Maybe too rare.

Later, during cleanup, I found a note tucked under the grinder drawer at the espresso station. Folded twice. No name. Just one line:

You're not the only one watching.

I froze.

Had someone seen me following Trina? Reading the logbook? Snooping around the storage manifest? Was it Mike? Was it Hot Stuff?

Was it Joe?

I tucked the note into my apron and kept my face neutral. But inside, my mind was already spiraling.

Whoever left it knew something.

And now, so did I.

The next time Hot Stuff came by the kiosk, it was after a commotion near the front registers. Some guy had tried to leave with a cart full of unpaid groceries. Hot Stuff had stopped him cold—didn't even raise his voice, just stood firm until the guy froze, then calmly escorted him out like it was nothing.

When he came to grab his usual cold brew, I already had it ready.

"That was impressive," I said, handing it to him.

He gave me that grin again and held out his fist.

"Gotta keep the peace. One cart at a time."

I bumped his knuckles, feeling the weight behind his calm demeanor. "You ever work in law enforcement?" I asked, casually.

He tilted his head, considering. "I've worked a few places. Big box, private, contract."

"Security?"

"Let's just say I've seen my fair share of nonsense." He sipped the drink. "Alfie's is different, though. Something's off here."

That caught me off guard. "Off how?"

He shrugged. "Too many eyes. Too many secrets. But hey—maybe I just like puzzles."

He tapped the counter once, then walked away.

I stood frozen, the hairs on my neck standing up. He noticed. He knew. Maybe not everything—but enough to raise red flags.

Hot Stuff wasn't just charming. He wasn't just watching.

He was looking. And maybe, just maybe, he was on my side.

The following afternoon, he stopped by again—this time not for a drink, but just to lean against the counter like he had nothing else in the world to do.

"Slow day?" I asked.

"Never," he said, with a wink. "But sometimes I make it look that way."

I laughed, surprising myself. It felt... natural.

"I'm still trying to figure you out," I said.

"You and everyone else," he replied. "Let's just say I've worked contracts for people who ask a lot of questions and expect even fewer answers. Private security gigs. Some government-adjacent. But when it got political, I stepped out. Now I'm here. And Alfie's?" He leaned in slightly. "It's got a scent to it. Not just fishy. Sour."

His words hung in the air longer than they should have.

I watched him as he scanned the room behind me. Not in a lazy way—in a tactical one. Counting people. Mapping exits.

"I take it you didn't come here just for the benefits package," I said.

"Nope." He grinned again, but there was something sharper beneath it this time. "And neither did you."

I didn't answer.

He let the silence sit for a moment before breaking it with a soft nod. "You've got good instincts. Just don't ignore them."

Then, as always, he gave me a fist bump.

And just like that, he was gone.

That night, I couldn't stop thinking about him. Not just the way he moved or the calm, practiced confidence he carried like armor—but the things he wasn't saying. The way his words dropped like riddles. The way his eyes swept a room like they were trained to find what didn't belong.

I looked him up in the security rotation binder the next morning. His name was Matt. Just Matt. No last name. No emergency contact listed. But his employee file had a note in red ink: External contractor – cleared.

That meant something. Something big.

When I saw him that day, I said his name out loud for the first time.

"Matt."

He turned like he'd been waiting for it. "Penny."

There was a pull between us now, and it wasn't just curiosity. It was recognition. Like we were circling the same fire from opposite ends.

"I think you know more than you're letting on," I said.

He smiled, slow and deliberate. "That makes two of us."

He reached for his drink, then held it mid-air. "Tell me something. What's the one thing you haven't told anyone since you got here?"

I blinked. "That I'm scared."

He nodded. "Good. That means you're still in control."

He bumped my fist again—this time softer, more deliberate. Then he added, "If anything ever feels off—really off—find me. No questions asked."

Then he turned and walked off again.

And this time, I wasn't just watching him go.

I was trusting him to come back.

The next time we crossed paths, it wasn't at the kiosk. It was in the back break room, past the stockroom and the flickering soda machine that never worked. I'd gone in to grab a granola bar from my locker and there he was—sitting in the corner, alone, reading what looked like a police incident report on his phone.

He looked up, mildly surprised. "Didn't expect to see you back here."

"I could say the same."

He slid his phone into his vest pocket. "I like the quiet. Too much noise up front."

I grabbed my snack and leaned against the locker door. "What were you reading?"

"Nothing official," he said with a smirk. "Let's just say I keep tabs on the neighborhood. Helps to know who's who."

Before I could respond, a call came through on his radio. There was an incident in the restroom—again.

He sighed and stood. "Third time this week."

By the time I wandered back toward the front, I saw him outside the restroom talking calmly but firmly to a woman in a torn dress and rainbow wig. She was pacing, ranting, high-strung and half-coherent. A regular—one of the unhoused trans women known to use Alfie's for a quick wash-up or an argument. She was clearly high, maybe worse.

"I don't need this right now!" she shouted. "I ain't doing nothing but putting on some lipstick, alright?!"

Matt held up both hands, his voice steady. "You're not in trouble. But you can't solicit here. You know the deal."

She waved a mascara wand at him like it was a dagger. "This store don't own me!"

"Nope. But I do need you to move along."

A pause. A twitch. Then she pointed at me, suddenly aware I was watching.

"Who's she? Why's she always looking at everybody?"

Matt stepped in, body angled to shield me. "She's nobody. Just doing her job."

I stiffened—but something about the way he said it told me we were playing the same game.

Eventually, she left, grumbling and tossing curses over her shoulder. Matt waited until she turned the corner before finally relaxing.

"Are you always this calm?" I asked as we walked back toward the front.

He chuckled. "Not always. But yelling back doesn't get you anywhere. People like her... they've been through too much to be scared of a badge."

I nodded. "Still. You handled it."

He shrugged. "That's the job. Keep the peace. Keep the place safe—even when it's falling apart from the inside out."

We shared a glance.

And just like that, the air between us felt different.

He wasn't just watching out for the store.

He was watching out for me.

I didn't see him for the next two days. And I hated how much I noticed his absence.

The tension inside Alfie's seemed sharper without him. Trina was more on edge, Betsy kept double-checking every logbook entry like she expected an audit, and even Joe had this twitch in his jaw that made everyone give him a wider berth.

By the time Matt reappeared—cool and calm, sipping his cold brew like nothing had changed—I felt like the whole store exhaled with me.

"You disappear or just hide really well?" I asked as he passed by.

"Little of both," he replied. "Had to check in on something off-site. You hold down the fort?"

"Define hold down," I said. "There was almost a blender-throwing incident in the kiosk, a bagger walked into the freezer and fainted, and someone wrote 'narc' on my locker."

He stopped walking. "You okay?"

"I'm fine."

"You sure?"

He didn't say it like a question. More like a check-in from someone who'd been trained to read blood pressure from tone alone.

"Yeah," I said. "I'm fine. Just... wish I knew which direction this was all heading."

Matt nodded slowly. "Sometimes the best way to find the target is to stop chasing it. Let it circle back to you."

I raised an eyebrow. "Is that a security philosophy?"

He smirked. "That one's free."

He bumped my fist again, but this time, his hand lingered just a second longer than usual.

I walked back to the kiosk trying to ignore the stupid flutter in my chest. Because Matt wasn't just sharp, trained, and completely unreadable.

He was starting to matter.

That evening, as I closed down the kiosk, Matt showed up again—this time off-duty. His vest was gone, replaced with a black hoodie and jeans, but he still carried himself like he was scanning for threats.

"You off the clock?" I asked, stacking the last of the cups.

"Technically. But I forgot something in the office. Figured I'd check in."

He lingered at the counter while I scrubbed the syrup tray, his eyes drifting across the empty store.

"Ever feel like this place is waiting for something to happen?" he asked.

"Yeah," I said. "All the time."

He looked back at me. "You want to grab a coffee sometime? Outside of here. No earpieces. No name tags."

It caught me off guard, but I didn't flinch. "You mean... like a date?"

His smile was slow and confident. "Only if you want it to be. Could just be intel sharing."

I laughed quietly. "Might be the first time I say yes to both."

He nodded, gently tapped the counter twice, then turned to leave.

Before he disappeared down the aisle, he glanced back and added, "You're not alone in this, Penny. Even when it feels like it."

The words settled in my chest like a warm truth.

He wasn't just an ally now.

He was becoming a reason to stay.

CHAPTER
EIGHT

BREWING TROUBLE

I didn't think anything could surprise me at Alfie's anymore.

But that was before the morning shift when I opened the kiosk to find the milk fridge wide open and half of the supplies missing.

The cold air spilled out in waves, and the thermometer blinked red.

Someone had tampered with it.

Not just forgotten to close it—deliberately opened it, removed things, and left the door ajar long enough for the dairy to spoil. There was no condensation on the handle. No trail. But something about the way it looked, staged and sterile, gave me a chill.

I snapped a picture for my log and immediately flagged it in the temperature book. Then I went looking for Trina.

She was nowhere to be found.

Shocker.

Matt wasn't on the floor yet, and I felt his absence in the pit of my stomach. The store was too quiet, the kind of quiet that made noises echo louder—the beep of the register, the drag of a cart, the steady drip of the leaky sink behind the coffee bar.

When he finally walked in, adjusting his belt and nodding at Joe, I felt the ground steady a little. I waved him down as he made his way past the bakery.

"Something's off," I said.

"When is it not?"

"No—I mean off-off. Fridge door open. Supplies gone. Feels staged."

His eyes narrowed. "Any cameras on that corner?"

I shook my head. "Conveniently not. Only angle is from register six, and the footage is grainy."

"I'll take a look."

He turned and walked away before I could say more.

I watched him go, already combing through his mental checklist, already investigating. He was sharp. Unshakable. But even the sharpest blade dulls if pressed too hard.

I just hoped this wouldn't be the moment he bent.

It didn't take long for the chaos to begin.

A customer slipped on a puddle near the floral department. A Barista missed a temp log entry. Then came the audit email.

Corporate was sending someone down. Not Mike. Someone higher.

Someone from above compliance.

Trina finally showed up halfway through the rush, sweaty and smug, carrying a smoothie from the place down the street like nothing was wrong. She blinked at the mess, the missing milk, the melted whipped cream tray.

"What happened here?"

"Ask yourself," I said.

She rolled her eyes and walked off without a word.

I wanted to follow her. Corner her. Scream. But I didn't. Not yet.

Because Matt had taught me something: sometimes you don't chase the snake. You wait for it to show its fangs.

And they always do.

I was restocking syrups when I spotted a familiar figure near the front entrance, just past Matt's post.

My stomach dropped.

Mauricio.

He wasn't in uniform, but I'd recognize that limp anywhere—the slight hitch in his right leg, the result of a bullet wound that ended his patrol career. His eyes scanned the aisles like he was looking for someone.

Like he was looking for me.

I ducked behind the back counter, heart pounding. He wasn't supposed to be here. No warning. No message from Gus. No heads-up.

I peeked around the espresso machine just in time to see Matt approach him. They exchanged a few words—Matt calm and unreadable, Mauricio clearly fidgeting.

He was going to blow my cover.

I texted Gus with shaking fingers: "Why is Mauricio here?"

No response.

Matt turned and started walking Mauricio toward the kiosk.

Panic surged.

I popped up and plastered on my best fake-customer-service smile.

"Hi there, can I help you?" I said, projecting the chirpy tone I'd perfected.

Mauricio looked at me, confusion flickering across his face before he got the hint.

"Yeah," he said. "Large cold brew, two pumps vanilla."

His voice was tight, like it hurt to play along. I turned and started the drink, fighting every instinct to grab him and drag him into the back room.

Matt stood off to the side, arms crossed, watching us both.

I handed Mauricio the cup. "Anything else?"

He leaned in slightly and whispered, "You okay?"

"Peachy," I said through clenched teeth.

He gave a curt nod, then disappeared into the crowd.

Matt waited until he was gone. "Friend of yours?"

"Something like that."

"He seemed... invested."

"Old history."

Matt studied me for a moment, then let it go.

I didn't breathe until both of them were out of sight.

Mauricio showing up meant one thing: Gus was nervous. Maybe the case was bigger than he'd let on. Maybe I wasn't the only one they'd sent in after all.

Or maybe I was about to be pulled out—and just hadn't been told yet.

Either way, I was running out of time.

And I wasn't done yet.

Matt found me an hour later in the breakroom, staring down at the logbook again.

"Your friend gone?" he asked.

"He shouldn't have been here. We used to train at the same gym. He was injured on the job a while back—bad one. And now? He's not supposed to be anywhere near this store. He wasn't supposed to show up."

Matt nodded slowly. "He seemed protective. Like he thought you needed watching—but didn't really understand what he was stepping into."

I sighed. "That makes two of us."

He leaned against the lockers. "I checked that grainy camera footage. You were right—it was staged. Whoever opened that fridge wanted it to look accidental, but they wiped the handle and kept out of frame."

"And you don't think it was Trina?"

"No. I think someone else did the dirty work for her. Or for Betsy. Or maybe both."

Just then, a commotion broke out near the back dock. Voices raised, something crashing. We rushed out just in time to see Joe yelling at the receiving clerk and a vendor hauling out cases of expired product—product that wasn't even scanned into inventory.

Matt pulled me aside. "This is bigger than just the kiosk. That's theft or laundering. Maybe both."

I nodded, my stomach twisting. "And someone's trying to create enough chaos to bury it all under mistakes and distractions."

He gave me a sideways glance. "You really go all in, huh? Most Baristas don't talk like this."

I gave a nervous laugh. "I pay attention. Too many weird things going on not to."

He looked at me for a second longer than necessary, like he was filing that away.

He didn't know.

And I needed to keep it that way.

Matt narrowed his eyes. "We're missing something. A link."

I looked around the store—at the too-clean corners, the forced smiles, the way everyone flinched when the PA buzzed.

Then something clicked.

"I think it's in the logs. Not just ours. The store-wide logs—back in Joe's office. Deliveries. Voids. Waste. Everything."

Matt gave me a look. "You want me to break into his office?"

"Not break. Borrow. Briefly."

He smirked. "You get five minutes. No more."

That night, while Joe was busy smoothing things over at the customer service counter, Matt distracted the floor supervisor and I slipped into the office. It reeked of cologne and stale coffee. His desk was locked, but the file drawers were not.

What I found made my blood run cold.

Duplicate invoices. Orders marked as delivered that never hit the shelves. And waste reports showing "spoiled" goods that had never passed through receiving. Dozens of them.

It was organized. Intentional.

And signed by Betsy.

Matt was waiting by the exit when I walked out, heart pounding, folder zipped into my apron.

"I got it," I said.

"Good. Because we just hit the next level."

I looked up to see a black SUV pulling into the loading bay. Suits. Not corporate. Not compliance.

"They're not here for a milk audit," Matt said.

He wasn't smiling anymore.

The next morning, the sabotage escalated.

The espresso grinder had been disassembled overnight—screws missing, burrs loose. The entire machine looked like it had been tampered with by someone who knew exactly what they were doing.

"Who would do this?" Lynn asked, clutching a cleaning rag, staring at the opened guts of the machine like it was a crime scene.

"Someone with keys," I muttered, already jotting down notes in the logbook. "Or someone who convinced someone with keys."

The milk order never arrived that day either. And the daily deposit from the kiosk's register—a sealed pouch—was reported missing by the time it reached the safe. No one had signed it in.

Matt appeared mid-morning with a printed spreadsheet tucked under his arm and his jaw locked tight.

"They're digging deeper than we thought," he said. "That SUV yesterday? Not just a higher-up. That was an internal investigative team. And they're not just auditing Sunset Star. They're auditing Joe."

I blinked. "You're telling me corporate is finally turning inward?"

Matt nodded. "They suspect he's running his own side operation. Overordering, fake waste, kickbacks—maybe even moving product through Alfie's. Sunset Star might just be his front."

I looked around at the staff—some of them laughing by the rotisserie chickens, others quietly dragging their feet behind the juice bar. Most of them had no idea. Or maybe they did.

"But if Joe's being watched…" I started.

"Then anyone close to him is vulnerable," Matt finished.

Including me.

Including us.

And the deeper we got, the less sure I was that we'd make it back out.

That afternoon, while reviewing a shipment log near the service deli, I noticed a small handwritten receipt tucked under the bottom of the clipboard. It wasn't recent—dated nearly two months back—but it listed an unusually large quantity of powdered protein drink mix, billed to Sunset Star, but shipped to a different Alfie's location across town.

I flagged Matt, who was patrolling nearby.

"Check this out," I said, handing him the receipt.

He scanned it and whistled. "This is a ghost order. Looks like a shell transfer—send it to a legit store, never receive it, funnel it through a third party."

"Why protein mix?" I asked.

He hesitated, lowering his voice. "That stuff's powdered, compact, and has resale value on the street. Some supplement blends are used to cut other substances."

"Like drugs."

He nodded slowly.

And then the twist hit me.

I'd seen Trina carting boxes labeled 'supplements' into the breakroom two weeks ago. She said they were samples from her cousin who worked in fitness distribution. No one questioned it. We never opened them.

I stared at Matt, dread curdling in my stomach. "What if the breakroom isn't just a breakroom?"

He looked at me for a long, tense beat. "Then we've been sitting on a distribution hub this entire time."

The sound of the espresso grinder sparking back to life behind us made me jump.

For the first time since arriving at Alfie's, I felt truly afraid.

Not for my cover.

But for what we were about to uncover.

Later that night, I stayed late to clean up the kiosk—partly for the closing shift, partly because I needed time to think. The hum of the refrigerator, the soft squeal of a cart wheel passing by, the clink of a spoon in the wash sink—all of it blurred into background noise as I wiped down the espresso machine again and again.

Matt showed up just before closing, off duty, dressed down in his usual black hoodie. He held up a paper bag with a chicken quesadilla from the taco truck in front of the store. "Thought you might've skipped dinner."

I took it with a quiet thanks. "You always know when to show up."

"Years of practice reading people. You're easy to read, you know."

"Dangerous thing to say to someone with a history of disappearing."

He smiled, but it didn't reach his eyes. We both knew this was bigger than either of us had originally signed on for.

"I'll stick close tomorrow," he said. "There's too much movement behind the scenes. Someone's going to slip soon. You can feel it in the walls."

I nodded, letting the silence stretch as I nibbled at the corner of the quesadilla. He sat across from me on an upside-down milk crate, eyes always scanning—even now, even off the clock.

"You ever scared?" I asked quietly.

"All the time," he replied. "But I don't let fear make my decisions."

I looked at him longer than I meant to. And for the first time, I let the idea settle that maybe I wasn't just fighting this alone.

Maybe I didn't have to.

CHAPTER
NINE

BAD INGREDIENTS

By the next morning, word had spread.

Someone in produce said they saw Joe being pulled into an unmarked vehicle. The service deli whispered that an entire shipment of rotisserie chickens was unaccounted for. By lunch, everyone had a theory.

Betsy paced more. Trina laughed less. And Matt? He hovered.

The black SUV hadn't come back, but its presence lingered like the scent of spoiled dairy. The regulars sensed it too—less chatter, more side-eyes. Even the music on the store playlist seemed off—slower, more ominous, like the system knew something had shifted.

I tried to focus. I checked logs, counted spoons, wiped surfaces that didn't need wiping.

But I couldn't stop watching the doors.

Matt showed up before his shift, coffee in hand, and tapped his knuckles on the counter. "Walk with me."

We cut through the back hallway, past crates of canned beans and soda syrup.

"Something's off with Trina," he said. "She's acting like she's already been caught. But she hasn't run."

"Maybe she can't. Maybe she thinks she's protected."

Matt stopped near the freight elevator and lowered his voice. "I checked the supplement boxes in the breakroom. There's something under the liners. It's not protein."

My stomach flipped. "Then we need to report it."

"Not yet. We don't know how high this goes. If Joe was just a puppet, who's the one pulling the strings?"

Before I could answer, a voice broke through the silence.

"What are you two doing back here?"

It was Betsy. Her arms crossed, her expression tight.

Matt turned, calm. "Just taking inventory."

"You've got no business being back here, sweetheart."

I smiled, sweet as syrup. "Neither do you, Betsy. Isn't your shift up front?"

She didn't answer. Just narrowed her eyes, then turned and walked off, muttering something under her breath.

We waited until her footsteps faded.

"She's sweating," I said.

Matt nodded. "Hard."

And that's when I knew—it was time to stop watching.

And start moving.

Matt and I returned to the kiosk just as the lunch rush hit. I worked the espresso machine like it owed me answers, each steam blast clearing the fog from my mind. I had to stay sharp. Focused.

Trina lingered more than usual that shift. She kept pretending to wipe counters but always stayed just close enough to overhear things. When Matt walked by, her eyes followed him like she was calculating something.

"You good?" Lynn asked as she grabbed a sleeve of cups from under the counter.

"Just tired," I lied.

"You don't blink when you lie, you know that?"

I blinked. "Damn."

She chuckled and moved on, but I caught a different look from her this time. Concern, not suspicion.

Mid-shift, I slipped into the storage hallway again. My hands shook as I reached for the breakroom keys clipped to my belt. Inside, the fluorescent light buzzed above as I crouched by the stacked supplement boxes.

Matt had peeled back a liner yesterday, but I hadn't seen for myself.

Now I did.

Wrapped beneath the first layer of foil packets were small vacuum-sealed bags—unlabeled, opaque, tightly packed.

Not protein.

Not legal.

I snapped photos with my burner phone, heart thudding. Then I heard footsteps.

Trina's voice, outside the door.

"Yeah, she's in there. I'm watching her now."

I froze.

A second voice—Ted.

"Don't let her leave with anything. We'll handle it after close."

I slipped the phone into my bra, shoved the liner back, and stepped out just as Trina pushed the door open.

"Looking for the coffee filters," I said, cool as ice.

She squinted at me, her smile forced. "They're not back here."

"I thought maybe they got put with the catering stuff."

Ted stood behind her, arms folded.

"I'll check up front," I added, brushing past them.

Once out of sight, I didn't stop. I beelined to the loading dock, took a left through the receiving hall, and burst through the emergency exit into the alley. My lungs burned with panic.

I dialed Matt.

He answered on the first ring. "Where are you?"

"I think they know. Ted and Trina. They were waiting outside the breakroom."

"I'm on my way."

Ten minutes later, he met me by the dumpster out back. I showed him the photos.

"That's enough to trigger a raid," he said.

"Then why does it feel like we're the ones being hunted?"

He looked over his shoulder, then back at me. "Because we are."

We stayed outside for a few more minutes, hidden in the narrow alley behind the store. Matt leaned against the brick wall, arms crossed, while I tried to calm the wildfire in my chest. The weight of what we'd found—and who was involved—settled in deeper with every passing second.

"We need to escalate this," I said. "Call it in. Give Gus the green light."

Matt hesitated. "We should wait until you're off shift. If Trina or Ted even sniff what's coming, this whole place could go dark before backup arrives."

I hated that he was right. But he was always right.

"I can get the rest of the photos," I added. "There's more in those boxes—I didn't get everything. And if there's anything else stashed, I need to find it."

Matt pushed off the wall. "I'll keep them occupied. You go back in. Act like nothing happened."

Back inside, Sunset Star buzzed with manufactured cheer. A line at the kiosk, music slightly too loud, the scent of bleach from a freshly mopped floor. Everything felt like a lie.

Trina was at the register, pretending to organize the tip jar.

"Everything good?" she asked, voice syrupy sweet.

"Peachy," I replied, tying my apron with a smile.

She held my gaze a beat too long.

I made it through another hour before slipping into the back once more. This time I opened a second box. Inside were more packets—some labeled as 'powdered turmeric' but none of them were sealed like anything legal. I took more photos, documented timestamps, even wrote a note in the Manager's logbook under a false shift name, just in case something happened to me before I could turn it in.

When I returned to the floor, Ted was waiting at the front of the kiosk.

"How's your shift going, Penny?"

I kept my voice steady. "Smooth so far."

He smiled, but it didn't reach his eyes. "Glad to hear it. Management's watching, you know. Always."

Was that a threat?

Matt appeared then, casual as ever, sipping a cold brew as if he hadn't just helped me document a felony. He bumped my shoulder gently as he passed.

It grounded me.

"Tonight," he murmured under his breath. "We bring it in. Be ready."

I was.

And I wasn't.

Because when you're undercover this long, you forget what it feels like to come up for air.

You forget the sound of your own name when it isn't a lie.

And part of me feared, once the truth came out—there might be nothing left to return to.

After my shift, I stayed behind, tucked into a corner of the upstairs employee lounge with a view of the parking lot. I needed the space, the air, and the illusion of distance. Below, customers moved in and out of Alfie's like nothing was wrong, like their coffee hadn't been served next to illicit shipments, like the smiling faces behind the counter weren't spinning in a vortex of deceit.

Matt texted me: "Stay put. I'm circling the back."

I tucked my phone back in my pocket and stared through the smudged glass. I could still feel the tension in my shoulders, the weight of pretending, the crackling truth that buzzed between every shift and whispered conversation.

A door creaked open behind me. Matt.

He closed it gently, carrying two coffees this time. "Thought you might need something warm."

I took the cup without a word. We stood there quietly, sipping and watching the world go on.

"You ready for what's coming?" he asked after a long silence.

"I have to be."

"You don't have to do it alone."

I looked at him then. Really looked.

He wasn't just the guy who watched my back on the floor. He wasn't just the one who pulled me out of the alley when I needed air.

He was the one I trusted.

And trust didn't come easy—not for someone living under a borrowed name.

"We move tonight," I said, setting my cup down. "No more waiting. We've got the photos, the time-stamps, the signatures. We've got motive, opportunity, and evidence. And if we don't act now, they'll bury it. Just like they tried to bury Donny."

Matt's jaw tightened. We'll take it straight to the top—quietly."

"But fast."

He nodded once. "Fast."

I exhaled slowly, the weight on my chest not gone—but lighter. For the first time since stepping into Sunset Star, I felt like I was standing on solid ground.

We weren't just Baristas and guards anymore.

We were the fuse.

And everything was about to explode.

I headed back down to the floor after Matt left, wanting to check the kiosk logs one last time before I clocked out. A double-entry from earlier caught my eye—one of my own. I'd logged the turmeric packets under two different aliases, too quickly, too nervously.

Sloppy.

I started deleting the duplicate when the office door creaked open.

Footsteps. Heavy ones.

Ted.

I closed the logbook and turned in my chair as he entered. "Everything alright?" he asked casually.

I nodded. "Just cleaning up. Thought I'd get a head start on tomorrow's prep."

He looked at the screen, then at me. "That's what we like to see. Team players."

I smiled thinly. My palms were damp.

"By the way," he added, leaning against the doorframe, "there's talk going around. Weird vibes. Maybe you've noticed."

I shrugged. "Can't say I've had time for gossip."

He studied me for a moment, nodded once, then walked out.

I let out a breath I didn't know I was holding.

On my way back to the breakroom, a customer stopped me.

"Hey," he said, holding a half-empty drink. "You work here a while, right?"

I nodded cautiously.

"You hear what they said on the radio this morning? About some 'distribution ring' being investigated in local grocery stores?"

My spine went cold.

"I don't listen to the news much," I lied.

He grinned. "Crazy world, huh? Anyway, thanks for the coffee."

I watched him walk away and thought—someone out there was already talking. And the storm was closing in faster than we thought.

I opened my locker and found something tucked between the folded apron and my water bottle.

A burner phone. Not mine. Clean. Brand new. No contacts. No history.

There was a note taped to the back:

Use this if yours is compromised. —M

Matt.

He thought of everything.

I slipped it into my apron, pulse steadying just slightly.

While I sat in the breakroom, pretending to scroll, a memory pushed through the noise of the day.

Donny, on my first day, handing me a perfectly labeled sandwich and saying, "This job's a circus, but hey—you've got the ringmaster look. Just don't let the lions bite."

I'd laughed. Now it felt like a whisper from the grave.

He hadn't deserved what happened.

And they were going to pay.

Back on the kiosk floor, Trina was restocking cups, her movements too slow, too precise. She looked up at me as I walked past. "You sure work a lot of late shifts, Penny."

I kept moving.

Then I stopped.

Turned back.

"You ever feel like this place is one spark away from burning down?"

She tilted her head, smile tight. "That depends. Who's holding the match?"

I held her gaze.

Then smiled.

"Guess we'll find out."

CHAPTER
TEN

THE TIPPING POINT

It was nearly midnight when I slipped the envelope into Gus's gloved hand behind the grocery store loading dock. A manila folder thick with evidence: photos, forged invoices, a USB drive with security footage and audio from my burner phone. It was everything we had. And it was just enough to set fire to everything they'd built.

Gus looked over his shoulder, then back at me. "You're sure you weren't followed?"

"No," I said, honest. "But I didn't see anyone."

He nodded and tucked the envelope inside his coat.

"Tomorrow," he said. "You won't need to come in."

The idea hit harder than I expected. After everything, this place had become more than a cover. It was a storm I'd grown used to standing in.

"Is Matt looped in?" he asked.

"He's ready."

Gus gave me a long look, the kind that says more than words. Then he disappeared into the dark.

The next morning felt like any other.

Sunlight slanted through the windows above produce. The bakery cranked out cinnamon rolls. DJ Dennis played his usual 2000s throwbacks. Trina chatted with customers. Betsy pretended to organize receipts.

But underneath it all, something pulsed. An edge.

Matt stood near the floral aisle, nodding to me subtly as he checked his earpiece. Backup had arrived.

And it was showtime.

But before anything went down, I needed to be absolutely sure of one thing: what Trina and Ted were really hiding.

Matt and I hadn't found the source yet—not the one responsible for initiating the movement of whatever was being pushed through Alfie's. The packets, the forged orders, the missing cash deposits—it was all too clean, too organized.

There had to be a ringleader.

And I had a theory.

Someone no one wanted to name. Someone who hadn't shown their face in weeks, but whose initials appeared at the bottom of every major transfer log dating back four months: C.V.

Cynthia Vazquez. Regional Director. Based out of the Northridge Alfie's location.

She hadn't been seen in Sunset Star in over a month. But she was still signing off high-level approvals.

Matt and I split up. He headed toward the receiving logs to cross-check deliveries. I circled through dry goods, found a quiet spot behind the wine section, and texted Gus.

"Any word on Cynthia Vazquez? Is she being looked at?"

He replied seconds later.

"Her name is flagged, but no official investigation yet. Thread carefully."

Thread carefully.

Back near the kiosk, I found Lynn finishing her shift, wiping down the espresso machine.

"You okay?" she asked. "You look like you saw a ghost."

I almost laughed. "Something like that."

She hesitated. "Listen, I don't want to be in your business... but you know Trina's been watching you, right? Like—really watching. She thinks you're gunning for her job."

I blinked. "Her job?"

Lynn shrugged. "People like her—paranoid. She doesn't know what you're doing, but she knows it's not just lattes."

I thanked her, then made a mental note: Trina might try something soon. Something desperate.

And if I wasn't ready for it, she could blow everything.

I checked the clock. Three hours left in my shift.

Three hours to finish the job.

Three hours before this place either burned to the ground—or I did.

I found Matt near the breakroom, his posture easy but his eyes scanning like always. We hadn't had more than five minutes of quiet since the beginning of this whole mess.

"Got a second?" he asked, voice low.

We slipped into the alley behind the store—the same place we'd handed off evidence the night before. He leaned against the wall, eyes soft now, hands tucked into his jacket pockets.

"After all this is over," he said, "I still owe you that coffee. A real one. No aprons. No comms."

I looked at him, heart thudding. "You remember that?"

He gave me a small smile. "I remember a lot of things about you."

For a moment, I didn't respond. I wanted to say yes. I wanted to say finally. But the truth was, Matt didn't know everything.

He didn't know that Penny Padlock wasn't my real name. That I wasn't just a sharp Barista with a gift for spotting lies. That my whole life—my real life—was back in a safe house file, classified under Raven McCool.

He didn't know about the ex-husband. About Josh.

Josh, the too-handsome real estate mogul from Beverly Hills, who used to call me the most dangerous woman on the Westside. Not because I carried a weapon. But because I didn't need one.

Our marriage hadn't ended because of infidelity. It ended because I kept secrets. Big ones. Long missions. Undercover identities. There's no room for love when your life's built on lies, even noble ones.

Matt wasn't Josh. But he had that look—the strong jaw, the quiet confidence, the fire under control. And what can I say? I had a thing for beautiful men with secrets.

"I want that coffee," I finally said.

Matt's smile turned real. "Good. I'll bring the good kind."

We met up the next night.

Off duty. Off the radar.

Matt picked a quiet coffee shop in Los Feliz, tucked between an old record store and a vintage bookstore that looked like it hadn't changed since 1987. No uniforms. No comms. Just him in jeans and a thermal shirt, his hair pulled back but looser than usual, and me, finally out of my brown work hoodie.

It felt like meeting a stranger I already knew.

We sat outside under a heater lamp, two steaming mugs between us. He ordered black, of course. I went with a chai. Something warm. Something indulgent.

For the first ten minutes, we talked about nothing—music, the weirdest drinks I've ever served, the difference between LA fog and smoke. It felt easy, almost too easy.

Then came the quiet moment.

"You ever think about what comes next?" he asked. "After Alfie's?"

"After this case. After all of it."

I hesitated, staring into my mug.

"I used to," I said. "But the truth is... I'm not good at the afterward. I get stuck in the middle of things."

He nodded, like he understood that in his bones.

"I'd like to see you afterward," he said, quiet but clear.

I didn't answer right away. I was still Raven McCool under it all, and this wasn't supposed to happen. Not again.

But I reached across the table and tapped my knuckles lightly against his. "Then let's make sure there is an afterward."

We stayed until close. He walked me to my car. We didn't kiss, but the air buzzed like we had.

That night, I got a message from Gus: "Matt's being reassigned temporarily. Special detail. One week."

Just like that, he was gone.

No warning. No goodbye. Just an empty kiosk stool and a silence that pressed harder than usual.

And something didn't sit right.

Not because I didn't trust Matt—but because I did. Too much.

And the timing was too perfect.

If he was reassigned now, it meant either someone wanted him gone—or something was about to break wide open.

And I'd be standing in the middle of it alone.

The next few shifts dragged like molasses. I kept my head down, stuck to my duties, and tried not to look like a woman one spark away from combusting. Trina was quieter, but in that dangerous, prowling way—like a storm cloud circling the breakroom. Ted barely made eye contact with anyone. And Betsy? She'd suddenly taken an interest in doing her own deposit runs again. I made a note of each one.

I started noticing details I'd missed before. Who always took the trash out. Who lingered by the backroom after hours. Who locked the cabinet that supposedly had broken cash drawers. I tracked time stamps, signatures, faces.

And I waited.

Without Matt around, everything felt a little less certain.

During my shifts, I worked the register like it was a lifeline. Customers lined up, asking for lattes with almond milk, matcha with extra foam, and americanos that had to be exactly 120 degrees. I took every order with a practiced smile, nodding, marking cups, calling out names. But every name echoed a little longer, every drink felt like one too many.

The other Baristas were running on caffeine and instinct. Lynn moved like a blur between machines, calling out, "Double cap for Jessie! Vanilla cold brew to the left!"

Jordan, our youngest, kept forgetting the difference between ristretto and regular shots, and I had to quietly correct him twice before Trina noticed. I didn't want her sniffing around.

There was a rhythm to it all—a dance that masked the chaos underneath. On the surface, we looked like just another overstressed coffee team. But I saw it now: how Betsy always turned up just before a shipment arrived, how Ted hovered near the kiosk anytime the registers got busy.

Even when I was pouring milk, I was watching. Listening.

And every drink I handed over felt like a countdown to something I couldn't yet see.

I checked his locker once. Empty except for a folded coffee sleeve and a rolled pair of backup gloves. That made me sadder than I expected.

By day four, customers were starting to act strange again. One woman asked if Sunset Star was "under new management." A man in a suit who claimed to be a Yelp reviewer asked me three different times what brand of chai we used. It was off. I reported it to Gus.

His reply: "Hold steady. Operation is live. You're not alone."

That helped. For five minutes.

Then, just before closing, I spotted a figure I hadn't seen before.

A woman in a long gray trench coat, standing near the frozen pizzas. She wasn't shopping. She wasn't even pretending to. She was watching. Watching me.

And when I caught her eye—she nodded.

Like she knew me.

Like she knew what I was doing.

I turned to grab my phone. When I looked back, she was gone.

And just like that, I knew.

This wasn't just going down.

It had already started.

After the woman disappeared, I tried to shake the feeling, but it clung to me like static. Every aisle I walked, every corner I turned, I expected her to reappear. Or worse—someone else entirely.

I finished my shift on autopilot, restocking syrups, wiping down counters, and keeping my tone light with customers even though my heart wouldn't slow down. My brain worked faster than my body, calculating risks, memorizing faces, wondering if I was being followed.

Lynn approached me near closing. "You okay? You're even quieter than usual."

"Just tired," I said.

She handed me a protein bar. "Eat something before you pass out. I don't care how tough you are, you run on fumes too long, you crash."

I smiled and nodded, pocketing it.

Trina lingered too long near the napkin dispensers, not even trying to look busy. Our eyes met. Hers narrowed.

The tension between us was no longer subtle. It had shape. Weight.

I slipped into the breakroom to clock out. My hands moved on muscle memory while my mind raced. I knew what I had to do. If tomorrow brought what I thought it would—raids, arrests, exposure—I needed to be two steps ahead.

Before I left, I opened the breakroom freezer. The one no one ever touched.

Inside, beneath a fake bag of ice, was a folder I had hidden weeks ago.

Backup.

Everything I'd copied—just in case. Duplicate USBs. Printed receipts. Time-coded transaction logs. A secondary phone.

I slid it into my bag and zipped it tight.

If tomorrow was the end, I'd be ready.

But tonight, I'd sleep with one eye open.

I paused before heading out the door, taking one last glance around the breakroom. My reflection in the vending machine glass caught me off guard—worn out eyes, hair pulled tight, shoulders heavy with secrets. I didn't recognize her. Or maybe this was the real me all along.

Before stepping into the night, I scribbled a note and slid it behind a stack of old schedule printouts: If found, tell Gus it's under the freezer. Trust no one but him. A last resort.

Outside, the city buzzed like it always did. Sunset Boulevard never truly slept. Neon signs flickered above traffic, sirens wailed somewhere in the distance, and for the first time in a long time, I felt the full gravity of being undercover—not just as a cop, but as a person drifting between two lives.

No matter what happened tomorrow—who got arrested, who ran, who talked—someone would be exposed.

And I wasn't sure anymore if I was ready for what that meant.

I adjusted the strap of my bag, pulled my hoodie tight, and walked into the night like a woman carrying fire in her hands.

CHAPTER
ELEVEN

BEHIND THE BEANS

The next morning, Sunset Star smelled like bleach and citrus.

The store had been cleaned overnight—too thoroughly. Floors gleamed unnaturally. Counters were buffed to a mirror sheen. Even the pastry case sparkled like it had never held a single croissant.

It felt like someone was trying to scrub away the sins.

I walked in through the front entrance instead of the employee elevator. Just to see it. Feel it. Smell what had changed.

And I wasn't the only one who noticed.

Lynn was already at the kiosk, her hair tied back in a high ponytail, staring at the prep sink like it had just whispered a confession. Jordan arrived seconds after me, earbuds in, hoodie up, and blinked at the freshly mopped floors.

"Did someone die?" he asked.

I almost laughed. Almost.

"No," I said. "Not yet."

Trina hadn't arrived. Betsy was late. Ted was on the floor, looking like he'd slept in the produce freezer.

I knew something was coming. I just didn't know when—or how loud it would be.

And when the delivery guy rolled in with four sealed crates marked SPECIAL INVENTORY – INTERNAL USE ONLY, I felt my heart punch into my throat.

They were here.

And it wasn't just about caffeine and pastries anymore.

I told Lynn I'd handle the freezer pull. She looked relieved. Said the cooler had been giving her the creeps all morning.

The back hallway was quiet. Too quiet.

I opened the freezer door and stepped into the cold.

And immediately stopped.

Voices. Low. Urgent.

Then—movement. A shifting of shadows behind the stacked crates.

I took one more step and saw them.

Trina's hair.

Ted's belt halfway undone.

They didn't see me. Not right away. But I saw enough.

My stomach turned. The air felt even colder, like it was icing over my skin.

Trina's hand flew to her mouth. Ted fumbled with his zipper. Neither of them spoke.

"Wrong crate," I said flatly, grabbing a tub of frozen oat milk like it was all I came for.

And I walked out.

They scrambled behind me, whispering something sharp and frantic.

But it didn't matter. I had confirmation. Not just about the affair—but the way they protected each other, covered for each other. Every forged log, every missing deposit, every shipment that went somewhere it shouldn't.

They were in it together.

Neck deep.

I just hoped they'd keep their mouths shut long enough for justice to kick in the door.

Back on the floor, things were already starting to feel different. Customers were edgier, more impatient. The music overhead switched from indie folk to corporate pop like someone behind the scenes was trying too hard to project normalcy.

Lynn gave me a look when I came back, a silent question hanging in the air. I just shook my head slightly. Not here. Not now.

At the register, a woman ordered an oat milk mocha and asked if "anyone else had gotten sick from the almond milk lately." I smiled and assured her everything was up to code, but inside, the question gnawed. Had someone already figured something out? Had word slipped beyond our walls?

Behind me, Jordan dropped a ceramic mug and cursed under his breath. The crash was loud—too loud. Customers flinched. Ted stepped out from behind the counter with forced authority, acting like he hadn't just been pants-down in a freezer. Trina was nowhere to be seen.

Then the door alarm buzzed.

Two men in black coats entered the store.

They didn't look like customers. They didn't even try.

One of them made direct eye contact with me and gave a tiny nod.

Not yet. But soon.

I turned back to the register, heart steady, hands calm.

Everything was in motion now. All I had to do was hold it together long enough to watch it unravel.

That's when Lupe strutted in like she was walking a red carpet down the frozen foods aisle. Lupe—the Sales Manager who wore ambition like perfume and cleavage like a weapon. Everyone adored her. At least, they claimed to.

She was built like a fantasy, all curves and confidence, with a bosom that practically introduced itself before she did. Her makeup was flawless, her hair always teased just enough, and her scent—some expensive gardenia thing—arrived five seconds before she did.

She giggled as she passed the kiosk, tossing me a too-sweet smile and glancing at the two men in coats like she already knew their life stories.

"Morning, Pen-Pen," she cooed, a nickname I never approved. "The boys come in yet for my tea?"

Speak of the devil.

Two older Latino regulars approached the register, leaning slightly on the counter with greasy charm.

"Lupe's tea, mija," one of them said with a wink.

I nodded like I hadn't heard this routine a hundred times. Extra hot, splash of oat milk, three pumps of cinnamon syrup. It wasn't tea. It was Lupe's brand of attention.

She gave her signature laugh—a little high-pitched trill like a wind-up toy with lip gloss—and twirled her badge lanyard like it was a sash.

Lupe pretended not to like Betsy, but her real disdain was for me. I'd seen the side-eyes when Matt used to linger near the kiosk. The way she got quiet when I walked into the breakroom.

Lupe was all smiles on the surface, but under that perfect foundation was someone who collected grudges like handbags—and I was her latest accessory.

The men took their drinks and thanked her like she was royalty. She gave them a tiny wave, then turned to me with a smirk.

"Some of us have fans," she said, sipping her drink like it was the last drop of relevance.

I smiled. "You certainly do."

Lupe strutted off, hips swaying like she was trying to hypnotize the aisle.

I watched her go, wondering how many faces you could wear before one of them cracked.

Lupe had been around forever, the kind of employee whose roots went deeper than the building's foundation. Rumor had it she and Joe had a fling back when she was still a cashier, and he was just climbing the ladder. That was Joe's thing—"promote from within," he used to say with a wink. Everyone knew what that really meant.

Lupe played the team player card well—always the first to volunteer, always the one clapping loudest at store meetings. But when push came to shove, she'd throw you under the bus with a smile and a wink, then bring cookies the next day to cover the tire marks.

She didn't trust Betsy, but she didn't need to. And as for me? I was new enough to be a threat and too observant for her taste. Especially when Matt was around. I could feel her sizing me up every time he leaned on the counter. It wasn't jealousy. It was strategy.

Lupe wasn't just playing the game. She was betting on the dealer.

And if this investigation didn't move fast enough— she'd find a way to come out on top, no matter who she stepped over to get there.

I kept an eye on her the rest of the morning, watching how effortlessly she floated from department to department, dropping compliments and half-hugs like party favors. She flirted with vendors, scolded baggers, and somehow managed to pull off authority with a pout.

Around noon, I caught her in the stockroom, talking low and close to one of the back office clerks—a guy named Ruben who handled internal reports. She smiled as she spoke, but I caught the edge in her voice, the way her perfectly manicured hand rested a second too long on his forearm. Ruben laughed nervously, nodded, and scurried away.

I didn't miss the glance Lupe shot over her shoulder to make sure I'd seen it.

She knew.

Not everything. Not who I really was. But enough to sniff danger. Enough to stir it.

And that made her dangerous.

More dangerous than Betsy. Maybe even more than Trina.

I made a mental note to flag her to Gus.

Because in a building full of suspects, the most polished player was sometimes the most poisonous.

The pressure didn't ease up after lunch. In fact, it thickened, like the store was holding its breath.

I caught Ted pacing near the floral department, pretending to be on his phone. His eyes kept darting toward the entrance. Toward the coats. He knew something. Or at least suspected.

Betsy finally arrived, her usual swagger dulled. She headed straight for the office and didn't come out for nearly forty-five minutes. When she did, she looked pale. Like she'd seen a ghost—or maybe just a copy of the shipping logs I'd slipped into Gus's file.

I went on break and took the long way to the rooftop lot, passing the service elevator and catching a glimpse of Lupe again. This time she wasn't smiling. She stood with her back turned, talking to someone I didn't recognize. A tall man in a suit, face sharp, posture military. He held a clipboard and wasn't wearing an Alfie's badge. Lupe laughed—too loud—and touched his shoulder briefly before walking away.

The man stayed behind.

Taking notes.

That's when it hit me.

The takedown wouldn't be loud at first.

It would be quiet. Precise. Paper trails. Silent signals. Smiles hiding subpoenas.

And when it landed—it wouldn't just shake Sunset Star.

It would drop the entire block.

Fifteen minutes later, I spotted a familiar figure entering through the sliding glass doors near customer service.

Cynthia Vasquez..

The elusive Regional Director. So rarely seen in person, most employees believed she was just a signature on the bottom of payroll memos.

Today, she wore an eggshell blazer and tortoise-shell sunglasses. Hair swept back. Clipboard in hand. She looked like she was headed to a TED Talk, not a grocery store takedown.

She didn't speak to anyone right away. Just made a slow, calculating sweep of the floor. Her gaze passed over me, paused for half a second, then moved on.

Lupe practically materialized beside her, all smiles and perfume, offering a loud, fake laugh at something no one said. They started a tour of the store together, pausing dramatically at the bakery, at the dairy case, at the floral department like they were filming a promotional video.

I slipped away from the kiosk and headed for the back. Something wasn't right. I opened my locker, needing to check my backup flash drive—only to see the combination lock slightly twisted.

Someone had tried to open it.

My pulse spiked.

Everything was still inside. Untouched. But that was the point.

A warning.

When I returned to the kiosk, Lynn handed me a slip of paper from the tip jar.

"This was in there. Don't know who dropped it."

I unfolded it slowly.

Just one line, scrawled in thick black ink:

"They know."

I folded the note back up and tucked it in my apron pocket, nodding at her like everything was fine.

But nothing was fine.

The house was on fire.

And the match was already lit.

Still, I had a shift to finish.

I returned to the register and smiled at the next customer, a woman in workout gear ordering a green tea latte like she was late for a yoga cult. I made her drink without flinching. Call it reflex. Call it survival. Every move, every pump of syrup, every scribbled name on a cup kept me anchored—because if I stopped pretending for even a second, I might lose the thread completely.

Behind me, Jordan knocked over another stack of lids. Lynn muttered something under her breath about mercury retrograde. And all the while, the hum of corporate tension settled in over the store like fog.

Lupe passed the kiosk again, Cynthia trailing behind her this time, both of them laughing too hard at something that didn't sound like a joke. Lupe shot me another look—this one smug, knowing, rehearsed.

I returned a blank stare. Calm. Measured.

She didn't know what I knew.

Not yet.

But I was getting the sense that the feeling was mutual.

Somewhere in the maze of security cameras and employee files and whispered secrets, we were all watching each other. Testing boundaries. Taking notes.

And at some point soon, someone was going to make a mistake.

I just hoped it wouldn't be me.

Around 4:30, just before the dinner rush, the PA system cracked and whined like someone bumped the mic.

Then, silence.

And then—"Attention Alfie's team, we'll be conducting a brief systems check in ten minutes. Please ensure all handheld devices are synced and logs are finalized."

Lynn looked up from her cleaning rag. "They never say that over the PA."

She was right. Announcements like that usually came from management directly, in person, whispered between departments, not broadcast like a warning.

I looked over at Ted. He was staring at the ceiling like he could read the subtext in the drywall.

Trina reappeared, suddenly helpful, suddenly upbeat. She offered to restock the grab-and-go sandwiches and refill the cold brew urn. Everyone was playing a part.

Everyone was trying to look innocent.

Cynthia and Lupe stood in the frozen section, quietly watching a new team of visitors in Alfie's polos move into the back hallway.

Not suits. Not investigators.

Internal security.

The ones who didn't wear jackets or sunglasses.

The ones who just showed up when things were about to blow.

I felt it in my bones.

The countdown had started.

CHAPTER
TWELVE

PUMPKIN SPICE OOH LA LATTE

I t was 8:37 a.m. when Penny Padlock first noticed the man ordering eight shots of espresso. Not two, not four—not even a respectable six. Eight. He didn't blink, didn't yawn, just stared straight ahead like he was preparing for combat or small talk at a high school reunion.

She scribbled the order on the cup—JACK / 8 ESP—and watched him shuffle down the bar, earbuds in, hoodie up, eyes fixed on the floor.

"Jack's got demons," she muttered under her breath.

"Or finals week," Trina whispered beside her, sliding a tray of pumpkin-themed drinks down the bar. "Or maybe both."

The smell of pumpkin spice clung to the air like fog on an October morning. It was Day Two of the Pumpkin Spice Ooh La Latte launch, and it had already turned Sunset Star Coffee into a sugar-dusted battleground. Every other drink had cinnamon, whipped cream, and seasonal optimism.

"Hi, can I get... um... one of the pumpkin things? With the... you know, the fluff on top?" said the next customer, a woman in oversized sunglasses who pointed vaguely at the overhead menu.

Penny held back a sigh. "Do you mean the Pumpkin Spice Ooh La Latte, the Pumpkin Fog, or the Pumpkin Cold Foam Dream?"

The woman blinked. "Which one has, like, that pumpkin taste?"

"They all do."

"...What's the difference?"

"One is hot, one is iced, and one is like a cloud in a blender."

"Oh. Uhhh... iced?"

"Got it," Penny said, tapping the screen.

But the woman wasn't done. "Actually, no... maybe hot? Or—wait, does that one come with almond milk?"

Penny's smile strained. "It can. Everything can."

Five minutes later, after three add-on changes, one dairy consultation, and a debate about cup size, Penny passed off the drink and braced herself for the next customer.

A man stepped up and stared at the pastries like they were a crime scene. "What's that?" he asked, pointing at the chocolate croissant.

"A chocolate croissant."

"And that?"

"An almond croissant."

"And the one next to it?"

"A blueberry muffin."

He paused. "What's in it?"

Penny blinked. "Blueberries."

She could feel her patience thinning, like stretched caramel under a torch. She reminded herself to breathe, to stay undercover, to smile, but good grief, the social ineptitude. How did people survive in the wild?

The line moved. Barely.

A girl ordered a drink entirely from TikTok terminology: "Can I get like, a venti... double pump, cold foam on top, but like not whipped, and a splash—not a pour—of oat? Also a caramel drizzle in a spiral? Not zigzag."

Penny stared. "Sure. That'll be $6.87 and six years off my life."

Behind her, Trina laughed. "You need a drink?"

"More like a lobotomy," Penny muttered. "Or a nap. Or both."

"You could just throw your apron at the wall and run out the back door."

"Tempting."

Then the automatic doors whooshed open and in rolled Ruthie.

Literally rolled. Purple roller skates, elbow pads, and her signature chaos energy. Her sparkly red T-shirt read

I'M NOT TIRED, YOU'RE TIRED and she was absolutely a menace in motion.

Right behind her was Mary—iced tea queen, story repeater, and probably one of the nicest people in the building.

"Security said she's fine!" Mary called cheerfully to no one. "She knows the route—bakery to cereal, and back again!"

"Ruthie," Penny said, "are you skating or solving mysteries today?"

"Both!" Ruthie called, veering wildly past the registers. "I'm gonna find secrets!"

Her mother Mary stepped up, holding her glittery reusable tumbler.

"Large iced tea, sweetened," she began, "I don't drink coffee. Gives me the jitters. When I met my husband Harry at a Jewish singles event in San Francisco years ago; we were the only ones there drinking tea instead of coffee. I knew he was my soulmate right then."

Penny looked up with a warm smile, already filling the cup with ice. "Yup. I remember."

Mary laughed. "I say it every time, don't I?"

"Just means you're consistent."

Penny never minded hearing it. In fact, she found it comforting. The predictability. The sweetness. It gave the day a kind of grounding—like the universe still had space for love stories and happy coincidences."

Mary tapped her card and swiped her straw dramatically into place.

Penny turned to prep the next order, but Ruthie reappeared with a screech of wheels, holding something high above her head.

"I FOUND KEYS!" she yelled.

Sure enough, a clinking set of keys with a squid keychain. Lost near the cereal aisle, just like she predicted.

"You're a legend," Penny said. She reached beneath the counter and pulled out a chocolate chip cookie. "For your Detective work."

"YESSSS," Ruthie declared, grabbing the cookie and zipping off into the produce section like a sugar-fueled comet.

Late morning brought the usual mix of regulars, newbies, and caffeine zombies. Penny was in the zone—pour, steam, swirl, smile, repeat. The worst part wasn't even the drinks. It was the dialogue. The exhausting, pull-teeth-to-get-an-answer exchanges.

People couldn't decide if they wanted hot or cold. People didn't know how to say "latte" without second-guessing. One woman kept whispering like she was at a funeral, and Penny had to lean over the register just to hear her say "vanilla."

Penny felt like a human translator. Like she needed to create a new universal language just for coffee. She kept imagining herself writing a manual: "How to Order a Drink Without Causing Your Barista Existential Dread."

Then the intercom buzzed.

"Attention, Alfie's guests and associates. We have a Code Adam in progress. Repeat, Code Adam. A child is missing. His name is Oliver. He is three years old, brown hair, blue shirt, red shoes. Last seen near aisle four."

Penny froze.

Her cop instincts snapped awake. Muscles tense, vision sharpened. She scanned the store—entrance, exits, blind spots, security posts.

Her hands hovered over the bar.

But she didn't move.

She couldn't. Not without risking everything.

This wasn't her op. Not directly. Her cover mattered more than one impulse.

So she stayed. Behind the counter. Watching. Listening.

Shoppers slowed. Murmurs rippled through the aisles. Someone near the juice bar asked if they should lock the doors. A dad near the bananas picked up his toddler instinctively.

Then came the calm.

Matt.

He strode in from the employee entrance, sleeves rolled up, hair perfectly tousled like he'd just left a photoshoot for Grocery Store Monthly. Penny barely breathed as she watched him take in the situation.

Security pointed him toward the last known location.

Without hesitation, Matt moved.

Straight down aisle five walking past the freezer section to the back of the store. Calm, confident, quiet.

Penny tracked every step.

Three minutes later, he returned—holding Oliver's hand. Apparently, Oliver had made his way to Receiving on his own and was stuck in the service elevator after pressing every button like it was a game.

The boy's mother let out a strangled sob and collapsed to her knees, pulling her son to her chest.

Matt bent low and said something Penny couldn't hear. The mom nodded, eyes wet, clutching her boy like he might disappear again.

Penny's throat tightened. Not from emotion. From restraint.

She should have helped. She wanted to help. But she couldn't afford to.

Matt glanced toward the coffee bar. Their eyes met. Just briefly.

He nodded once.

Penny didn't smile. But her heart did something strange.

But Penny didn't get to ride that soft hum all the way to clock-out.

Mid-afternoon, just as she was wiping down the espresso machine for the third time, Betsy's voice cut through the bar like a sneeze in a library.

"Penny, I need you in the back. You're scheduled for your computer modules."

Penny blinked. "What? Now?"

"Now. Corporate compliance. You're behind. They're required. Three of them."

Penny felt her jaw tighten. She glanced around the bar, scanning the customers, the corners of the café, the flow of energy. She didn't want to leave. Didn't want to miss something.

But undercover agents didn't get to protest training videos.

She peeled off her apron and marched toward the grim little break room, where a sluggish desktop computer waited for her like a digital dementor.

The modules were a special kind of soul death. The first was on proper food temperature maintenance—what constituted the "danger zone," how long items could sit out, and the importance of thermometers in daily checks. The second module covered cleaning up spills throughout the store, complete with a cartoon banana peel and a jingle about mop safety. And the third—and longest—was on active shooter scenarios: identifying exits, locking down safe rooms, and what to do if chaos came through the front doors.

Each module ended with a quiz. Each quiz had questions that felt like riddles written by bureaucrats.

Penny sat through all three, shoulders hunched, bouncing her leg with impatience. Every tick of the clock was a missed moment back at Sunset Star. What if Betsy made a weird move? What if Matt said something revealing? What if Ruthie skated into the walk-in freezer?

By the time she finished the final quiz and got her "Certificate of Compliance," she felt like she'd aged a month. Three hours had been stolen from her shift. Three hours of valuable observation.

She returned to the café and immediately noticed the disarray. Whipped cream canisters half-full. Syrup rings on the counter. A lonely cup marked "LISA / HALF CAF PSL" sitting abandoned.

Trina handed her a rag without looking up. "Welcome back, Soldier. We barely made it."

Penny grumbled. "I passed my test. I know how to mop now."

"Ooh, careful, we might promote you."

But Penny wasn't joking. She felt the ache of disconnection. Every second she wasn't behind that counter was a second she wasn't catching clues.

And this place—this seemingly simple coffee bar tucked into a Hollywood grocery store—had more secrets than the staff handbook had typos.

Even as Penny jumped back into her Barista duties, she couldn't shake the feeling that something was brewing under the surface. Betsy had been lurking around the storage area more than usual, and Matt's perfectly timed arrival during the Code Adam made her wonder yet again what exactly his story was. He wasn't just a friendly face with great hair—there was precision in his movements, calm under pressure. Traits that usually pointed to experience... the kind of experience Penny was trained to spot.

She wiped down the bar with a little more aggression than necessary.

The customers kept coming. Some familiar, some seemingly dropped into the store by alien lifeforms unfamiliar with Earth culture. A man in a suit asked if "decaf still had caffeine," then asked what 'latte' meant, then asked if his drink could be "extra warm but not hot"—whatever that meant. A woman handed over a crumpled receipt from two months ago and insisted it was a coupon for a free latte because it had the word 'latte' printed on it. And a teenager stood frozen in front of the pastry case for ten whole minutes, brows furrowed like he was negotiating a hostage situation, before whispering: "...I guess... cake pop."

One woman ordered, then backtracked, then re-ordered, then asked if she had ordered the first thing or the second thing—and when Penny repeated it to her, she frowned and said, "That doesn't sound like me." Another customer scrolled on her phone for her entire turn, then looked up and said, "Wait, what do you sell here again?"

By the fifth time someone asked, "What's in the chai latte?" Penny found herself answering: "Mostly regret."

Trina nearly dropped a pitcher laughing. "Girl, you need a nap and a margarita."

It was exhausting. And Penny couldn't even rely on her breaks to recover.

Any time she tried to sneak away for a ten—or the sacred, elusive thirty-minute break—she was intercepted. A customer would stop her near the refrigerated cases: "Do you know where the good yogurt is?" Another flagged her near floral: "Where do I find tarragon? Is that an herb or a spice?"

Sometimes, they didn't even ask questions. They just hovered, trailing behind her like lost puppies, waiting to be rescued from their own confusion.

Penny learned fast that knowing the store layout wasn't just helpful—it was survival. If she could say, "Aisle four on the right," and keep walking, it saved her precious minutes. If she had to lead someone across the store looking for chipotle mayo, her break disappeared faster than the last chocolate croissant.

And when she did make it to the break room, there was no guarantee she wouldn't be called back early.

Still, somewhere in the tedium, Penny found her rhythm again.

And not just behind the espresso machine. She was juggling two roles now—Barista at Sunset Star and general floor worker for Rock n'Roll Alfie's. It meant that on any given day, she could be restocking organic granola bars in the health aisle, sweeping up shattered olive oil jars near the checkout lanes, or directing someone to aisle 12 while holding a milk jug in one hand and a broom in the other.

It was chaos. Controlled chaos. Corporate chaos. But chaos all the same.

She'd made it her mission to memorize the entire store layout. If she could tell someone exactly where the tahini was without turning her head, it bought her time. Precious seconds. She had developed a mental map like a secret agent memorizing blueprints. From produce to pet care, she knew the terrain.

Because every time she had to escort someone to pickles or paper towels, it chipped away at her break. Her actual break. The ten or thirty minutes of semi-freedom that allowed her to breathe, recalibrate, and stay sharp. And staying sharp was key.

Missing even one beat could mean losing track of Matt. Or Betsy. Or a new detail in the murder investigation.

So Penny played the long game. Navigated aisles and registers like she belonged there. Answered customer questions with a trained patience and an unshakable poker face. All while collecting clues and connections like espresso shots—quick, hot, and potentially explosive. Trina cracked a joke about pumpkin being the true national currency, and Ruthie reappeared once more to show off a sticker she got from produce that read "Organic Hero."

The neighborhood weirdness, the tiny victories, the human quirks—it was maddening and sweet and very, very alive.

And that was what made it worth it.

Even the undercover stuff. Even the training modules. Even the three-hour corporate detour.

Because underneath the burnt espresso shots and sugary foam was something real. Something worth protecting.

And Penny was getting closer.

Closer to the truth.

Closer to the heart of it all.

Even if she had to smile through 800 more pumpkin lattes to get there.

Trina handed her a cup with an absurd drawing on the side: a Barista-cat with laser eyes and a nametag that read Agent Purrlock.

"This is how I picture you," Trina said. "You know, if you had a tail."

Penny smirked. "Very professional."

"I try."

She wiped down the bar one last time and looked toward the store entrance.

Ruthie was being guided out by Mary, still holding her cookie wrapper and proudly spinning her skates. Oliver was safe. Betsy was pretending to be helpful. Matt had disappeared again like smoke.

Penny exhaled.

One more day undercover.

One more step toward the truth.

And still, the biggest mystery might not be the murder... but what kind of man Matt really was.

CHAPTER
THIRTEEN

STARS, LATTES, AND HOLLYWOOD MAGIC

Penny had seen a lot of weird things working in Hollywood. She once saw a man walk a ferret wearing sunglasses through the frozen foods aisle. Another time, a woman in stilettos demanded to see the Manager because her avocado wasn't emotionally ripe. But nothing—and she meant nothing—could have prepared her for what happened at 3:14 p.m. on a random Wednesday.

Taylor. Swift. Walked. In.

Not just Taylor Swift, but Taylor Swift with her mom, brother, and a close friend. No entourage. No paparazzi. Just them. Walking into Alfie's like it was any old grocery run.

Penny was wiping down the espresso machine when she saw her. At first, she didn't believe it. She blinked twice. Did a quick internal reboot. But there she was. Tall, graceful, and somehow normal. Not the stadium-selling icon, not the glittering goddess of music videos—just a sweet, smiling woman in a sweatshirt and sneakers, chatting softly with her mom and scanning the pastry case.

"I'll be damned," Trina whispered from beside her. "That's her, right?"

"Yup," Penny said, too stunned to blink. "That's her."

When Taylor stepped up to the counter, she leaned forward with a warm smile and said, "Hi! Could I get a blended Pumpkin Spice Ooh La Latte, please?"

Penny stared for half a second too long before snapping into action. "Of course! Grande?"

"Grande's perfect," Taylor said. "And can I add one for my mom too? She's obsessed."

Her mom laughed softly and waved. Her brother picked out a muffin. The friend asked about cold brew.

They were... just people. Kind, funny, courteous. Taylor even complimented Penny's sparkly enamel pin. By the time the drinks were handed off, Penny was borderline floating.

"Thanks so much," Taylor said, reaching for the tray.

"No," Penny said without thinking, "thank you for existing."

Taylor grinned. "That's the nicest thing anyone's said to me all week."

And just like that, they disappeared into the store, grabbing cart wipes like regular humans.

The second they were out of earshot, Trina fanned herself with a napkin. "Did we just serve Taylor Swift?"

"Yup."

"And she ordered a PSL."

"Blended."

"I'm gonna need to lie down."

Penny had barely recovered when Jeremy Renner appeared an hour later, loading bags of produce into a shopping cart. According to one of the cashiers, he was doing a drop-off for a local food bank. He wore a hoodie and looked like someone who just wanted to be useful and get out. Penny admired that. Quietly heroic. Way more refreshing than the influencer who tried to film herself giving a banana to a stranger and made them redo the moment twice.

Rock n'Roll Alfie's was a celebrity magnet. That was the deal when you were a grocery store on Sunset Boulevard. Soap opera stars came in with sunglasses and hats like they were in disguise but hoped you'd still notice. Instagram models posed in front of the kombucha fridge. One guy who played a vampire on a streaming show kept asking if the sushi was fresh.

It was absurd. And amazing. And part of why Penny loved it here.

Because behind the glitter, the egos, and the oddities, this town was real. Messy and surreal and alive. Just like the people in it.

She wasn't just serving coffee. She was watching the world swirl around her—celebrity sightings, grocery meltdowns, romantic reunions, awkward first dates—all happening at the Sunset Star counter.

And every once in a while, someone like Taylor Swift would show up and remind her that even icons like pumpkin spice.

Hollywood magic.

Served with whipped cream.

The thing was, working at Alfie's wasn't just about serving lattes or stocking shelves. It was about becoming part of a surreal tapestry that only existed in a place like L.A. You didn't just clock in—you signed up to witness the whole spectrum of human drama unfold between organic apples and canned soup.

One time, Penny saw a B-list actor loudly argue with his personal trainer over the macros in almond milk. Another time, a former child star accidentally dropped a bag of frozen peas, and when they scattered, he whispered, "Just like my career," and walked off solemnly.

Some celebrities were low-key and polite—buying frozen pizza and eye drops like everyone else. Others walked in with tiny dogs and the energy of someone expecting a standing ovation just for picking out a melon. Penny had learned to spot them all. She didn't get starstruck often anymore.

But some still surprised her.

Like the time she handed an oat milk cappuccino to a guy who looked vaguely familiar. Only later did

Trina scream into her apron, "THAT WAS THE GUY FROM EVERYTHING'S A DISASTER! HE PLAYS THE HOT DAD!"

"Oh," Penny had replied. "He tipped five bucks."

Then there was the soap opera actress who cried real tears in the dairy aisle, holding a container of Greek yogurt, while muttering lines to herself. Penny had circled back twice just to confirm it wasn't a breakdown. It was a rehearsal.

"I swear, this store is half produce, half film set," Trina once said.

"Don't forget the podcast corner," Penny added. A YouTuber was currently recording life advice in the juice bar seating area. He'd brought his own ring light.

Not that Penny minded. The circus-like quality of the place helped her blend in. No one questioned why a Barista might be paying extra attention. Everyone was nosy. Everyone had something to hide or show off. It made things easier.

And honestly? It made the job fun.

Like that time two rival influencers came in at the same time and raced each other to the selfie mirror by the flower stand. Penny watched from behind the espresso machine, pretending to wipe a counter while quietly ranking their poses. The taller one won. Better angles.

Or the guy who tried to impress his date by ordering in Italian—only to mispronounce macchiato so badly that Trina asked if he was having a medical episode.

Not every shift came with celebrity sparkle. But the potential? It was always there. And that kept things electric.

Which was important, because the rest of Penny's life was anything but glamorous. Between double shifts, secret notebooks, and late-night intel reporting, she barely slept. Her world was part cover story, part caffeine, part calculated guesswork.

Sometimes she forgot what day it was. Sometimes she forgot her own name.

But she never forgot the mission.

And if that mission happened to involve spotting character actors in aisle 9 or serving PSLs to pop royalty... well, she'd take the perks.

Besides, celebrity sightings were great cover.

People got distracted. Talked. Gossiped. Dropped their guard.

That's when she listened most carefully.

It wasn't just the celebrities. It was the chaos they created in their wake—the buzzing chatter, the sudden crowding near the bakery, the employees scrambling to act cool while peeking through shelves of crackers. During those moments, people talked. Really talked. Gossip spilled like cold brew on a hot counter.

She overheard snippets of everything: romantic affairs between coworkers, tension between the assistant Manager and a vendor rep, rumors about Alfie's maybe going corporate and changing their name to something "more brand-forward."

One guy in produce was convinced Betsy had been there during a major scandal at another store. "She disappeared for six months," he told someone over the bananas. "No one knows why." Penny tucked that away.

Then there was the afternoon a mid-level TV producer came through the line, bragging on his phone about a new docuseries he was greenlighting—about criminal coverups in community spaces. Penny perked up at that one. She remembered his face, his company name. She'd look him up later.

It was intel wrapped in espresso steam and pop culture noise. And Penny was there for every beat.

Even when she was exhausted.

Even when her feet felt like bricks and her hands smelled permanently like caramel syrup.

Because somewhere in all the glamour and grind was the pulse of something real. A truth humming beneath the sparkle.

And Raven McCool—alias Penny Padlock—was getting closer to it with every shift.

The investigation into Donny's death had hit another frustrating wall. The can of Raid found behind the store had been confirmed as the poison source. It had traces of the same chemicals found in the drink he'd consumed. But when forensics came back? Inconclusive. Too smudged, too many overlapping prints. Nothing clear enough to hold anyone accountable.

Penny had stared at the report on her burner phone screen in the dark of her car, jaw tight. So close. And yet, they still didn't have enough to move on Betsy.

It made every shift harder. Every latte she handed over felt like a delay. But the mission had to be airtight. She couldn't blow her cover over impatience. Still, it gnawed at her.

At least Alfie's never ran out of characters to distract her.

Like the Rocker.

White guy. Long, greasy white hair. Always wore band tees from groups no one under 50 remembered. He claimed to have played drums with five different bands in the '60s and '70s—some names real, some she was pretty sure he made up. According to him, he now performed on Hollywood Boulevard, banging on buckets and cymbals for spare change.

He spent most afternoons at the three tables parked near the Sunset Star kiosk, sipping free water and staring a little too long at the Baristas.

"Morning, ladies," he'd say with that overly cheerful tone that made your skin crawl.

"Good afternoon," Penny would correct him, keeping her smile tight.

He never bought anything. He just lingered. Sometimes talking to himself. Sometimes to customers who didn't want to be talked to. He told stories that danced between reality and delusion—how he once opened for

Janis Joplin, how he turned down a record deal because it was "too corporate," how he used to party with Bowie.

"Guy lives in his car," Trina whispered one day. "Pretty sure he sleeps in the lot."

"Which lot?" Penny asked.

"Exactly."

Creepy or not, he was part of the landscape. Another fixture in a place that blended the bizarre with the brilliant. Another person with secrets. Just like everyone else at Rock n'Roll Alfie's.

Penny stayed alert. One hand on the coffee grinder. The other on the pulse of the city.

Because eventually, someone was going to slip.

And she'd be right there when they did.

Sometimes Penny found herself reflecting on what it meant to live a double life in a place already full of people performing different versions of themselves. Sunset Star Coffee was both her stage and her hideout. She wondered if the customers had any idea that the girl smiling behind the espresso machine had once tackled suspects in alleys, or spent nights listening to wiretaps.

She missed that world. Missed the adrenaline and purpose of it. The clarity. Here, everything was fogged in frothy sweetness and celebrity gloss. But the crime was no less real. Donny was dead. And someone inside this building—this store full of smoothie bowls and smiling influencers—had poisoned him.

The weight of it settled heavily on her as she cleaned the espresso machine that night, her reflection warped in its chrome surface.

Trina yawned from across the bar. "You ever think we're all just extras in someone else's movie?"

"Every day," Penny said.

A pause. Then Trina added, "But if this were a movie, you'd be the lead. You've got that mysterious main character thing going."

Penny smirked. "Plot twist: I'm actually an undercover cop."

Trina laughed. "Right. And I'm a secret heiress to a vegan cheese empire."

They both chuckled. But only one of them was kidding.

Outside, the city glittered as night fell. Lights from the Sunset Strip bounced off the windows, merging with the buzz of Hollywood after dark. Another shift done. Another day deeper into the mystery.

Raven McCool wasn't just undercover.

She was running out of time.

Even after closing, the store didn't sleep. Stockers wheeled crates down aisles, music pulsed quietly through the speakers, and the air smelled faintly of floor cleaner and cinnamon. Penny stayed a little longer than she needed to—tidying up, double-checking supplies, pretending to be busy while her mind raced.

She noticed things when it was quiet.

Like how one of the ceiling cameras near the service hallway had been bumped—tilted just enough that the exit door wasn't fully visible. She logged it mentally. Could be nothing. Could be important. Could be someone inside had done it.

She wandered to the break room for her bag, passing by the community bulletin board. A new flyer had been pinned up—something about a "Poetry Open Mic Night" happening in the juice bar next week. Another perfect distraction.

She knew the kind of people those events attracted. People who shared too much. People who liked to be seen. People who didn't realize they were being watched.

Before she left, she took one last slow loop around the perimeter. The Rocker was asleep at the outside table, his head on his arms. A security guard was gently nudging him awake.

Inside, the last light flicked off behind the deli. A couple holding hands walked out laughing, unaware of how close they were to something dark.

And Penny—Raven—slipped into the night, silent, invisible, and determined.

Because someone had killed Donny.

And she was getting closer to finding out who.

The night air hit her like a soft slap—warm and restless, filled with exhaust and faraway music. She walked past a group of tourists trying to spot stars on the Walk of Fame, and a man in a cowboy hat singing Elvis covers badly off-key. Hollywood was never quiet.

She passed a street artist sketching caricatures, a group of dancers filming a TikTok, and a tarot reader with a fold-out table and a neon sign that read: "Your Future is Waiting."

For a beat, Penny paused.

She let the thrum of the boulevard settle into her bones, the strange electricity of it all. This city was full of masks. Glamour and grit stitched together with ambition and denial.

It was the perfect hiding place.

She tucked her hands into her jacket pockets and kept walking, already planning her next move. She needed to dig deeper into the security footage from the morning of the poisoning. Cross-reference who had access to the back prep area. And she still needed to pay closer attention to Betsy's routine.

Tomorrow, she'd slip into conversation with that new overnight stocker—he'd mentioned something weird about a cleaning checklist being tampered with.

And maybe she'd finally talk to Matt again. Really talk. Because if anyone else had secrets around here, it might be him.

But not tonight.

Tonight, she faded into the rhythm of Hollywood, where nothing was ever what it seemed—and everyone was pretending to be someone.

Just like her.

Back at her car, Penny sank into the driver's seat and let her head fall back against the rest. She stared at the roof of the car, letting the last threads of the day unravel.

She thought about Taylor Swift's kind smile. About the soap opera actress rehearsing lines in the yogurt aisle. About the Rocker and his worn stories. About the poisoned can of Raid and the fingerprints that didn't tell her what she needed to know.

She pulled out her phone and typed a few quick notes into her secure app—timelines, shifts, possible patterns. Names. Triggers. Things she'd overheard.

In the background, a couple argued two rows over about whether or not to go to Runyon Canyon the next morning. A skateboard clattered by.

Hollywood was so loud, even at its quietest.

But Raven McCool was listening.

Always.

CHAPTER FOURTEEN

POINTS OF NO RETURN

The next morning, Penny arrived at Alfie's early. She didn't need to. Her shift didn't start for another forty-five minutes. But sleep had been pointless, her mind too wired with late-night theories and flickers of memory. She'd dreamt of coffee cups marked with secret symbols, faces with no names, Betsy's clipboard turning into a dagger.

She needed to be here.

Last night's dream was still lingering in her mind like the scent of over-pulled espresso.

It started with a red bed. Not just any bed—a talking one. Its name was Freddy, and it had the voice of a cheerful game show host and the energy of a caffeinated squirrel. In the dream, Freddy zipped through the aisles of Alfie's on wheels, playing a bizarre game of cat and mouse with her.

"Come on, Penny! Keep up!" Freddy had laughed as he darted between cereal displays and rolling carts. "Danger's rising like un-proofed dough!"

The dream had felt both ridiculous and disturbingly real. Freddy paused in front of the bakery department, bouncing with cartoonish anxiety.

"There! Trouble's proofing in the ovens! But also... someone's baking more than bread, sweetheart. Biola's back. Or maybe she never left."

Biola.

Betsy's mom.

Penny hadn't heard her name in weeks. The last she'd known, Biola was "traveling," according to Betsy—a vague explanation Penny never quite bought.

"Freddy, what are you saying?" Penny had asked the talking bed.

"I'm saying someone's up to something sticky! And I'm not just talking about the cinnamon rolls. Speaking of which—can I have one? Please? With extra glaze?"

Then he'd vanished. Just poofed into a display of day-old scones.

She woke up with the sound of Freddy's laughter echoing in her ears and the inexplicable urge to check the bakery department.

It unsettled her more than she cared to admit. She wasn't used to sitting still. Sunset Star, with its narrow footprint and constant bustle, made her feel stuck. Like a bird in a display case. She liked motion. Momentum. She solved problems by doing, and right now she was chained to espresso machines and chit-chat.

How could she find out what Biola was doing—or if she was even here—when she barely had time to step outside the kiosk?

She needed eyes. She needed allies. Or maybe she needed another dream.

The store was just waking up. The fluorescent lights buzzed like sleepy bees overhead. The early crew was still dragging through the opening checklist, yawning over boxes of croissants and bagged lettuce.

It was the calm before the daily symphony of chaos.

Near the front end, Jorge—the front-end Manager with a permanent Bluetooth in his ear—was already giving his daily store tour to the latest batch of new hires. Penny had seen this a dozen times. Jorge talked with flair, gesturing dramatically toward the floral department, produce displays, and customer service desk like he was guiding them through a five-star resort instead of a grocery store.

"Here at Alfie's, we believe in three things: service, smiles, and systems!" he declared.

The newbies nodded along, their polos stiff with fresh creases.

It would've been funny if it wasn't also slightly eerie. People came and went constantly. Baristas transferred. Stockers reassigned. Overnight workers replaced midweek with no warning. Coworkers who were there one day were suddenly gone the next.

No explanations. No goodbyes. Just Jorge's tour continuing as if nothing had changed.

Penny had started keeping track. She was up to six people in the last two weeks who had disappeared from their schedules without a trace.

She had a feeling at least one of them hadn't transferred at all.

Something was shifting beneath the surface of Alfie's. And the more Penny watched Jorge's overly enthusiastic finger guns and rehearsed lines, the more she wondered how much he actually knew—or how much he was pretending not to.

Penny took advantage of the quiet to make a lap around the perimeter. She checked the outdoor seating, scanning for any new signs of life. The Rocker's usual spot was empty—for now. A lone napkin fluttered under the table like a forgotten thought.

Inside, the produce section was half-staged for a citrus display. She passed a crate of lemons and noted a clipboard someone left behind—blank, except for a note scribbled hastily across the top corner: "check with AM re: cleaning log discrepancy."

Cleaning log.

That made her pulse jump.

She snapped a photo with her burner phone and tucked the clipboard back into place.

By the time she returned to Sunset Star, Trina was just unlocking the syrup cabinets. "You're early," she said.

"I wanted to beat the rush," Penny replied, slipping on her apron.

Trina side-eyed her. "You okay?"

"Just tired."

They didn't say more, which was good. Penny wasn't in the mood to lie today.

By 9 a.m., the store was in full swing. The usual mix of morning zombies and Hollywood hopefuls lined up for caffeine and validation. Penny made drinks, watched faces, and listened hard. Everyone seemed like a suspect. Everyone had something to say—about a canceled audition, a breakup, a casting director who didn't text back.

But no one talked about Donny.

It was like he'd never existed.

And that made Penny angry.

In between orders, she glanced toward the break room hallway. She'd need to access the cleaning logs. Cross-reference who was on duty that day. And she still hadn't followed up with the overnight stocker.

Too many loose ends. Too many open questions.

But she'd get there.

One coffee. One lead. One step at a time.

The day had just barely kicked off and already Alfie's was its usual circus of caffeine-deprived customers, neon signage, and '70s rock anthems blasting at borderline inappropriate volumes. "Sweet Emotion" pulsed through the speakers as Penny restocked pastry bags and tried not to judge the guy asking for a triple ristretto in a reusable Hello Kitty cup.

Then the doors whooshed open and everything—*everything*—shifted.

Barbara had arrived.

Leopard-print flats hit the polished tile with purpose. A pair of white linen pants somehow remained perfectly crisp despite Los Angeles' spring humidity. Her turquoise blouse caught the light, matching her beaded necklace, clip-on earrings, and her Alpha Rewards clipboard—which had a rhinestone-studded "VP" sticker slapped onto the back like a badge of honor. Her brown hair, streaked with bold caramel highlights, bounced with intention.

And the perfume—*oh, the perfume.* Floral. Expensive. Loud enough to clear out the citrus display.

"Is that Steven Tyler I hear?" she trilled. "Oh, *this* is going to be a fabulous day."

A customer dropped his organic ginger root. The produce clerk looked like he wanted to crawl into the mushroom bin. But Barbara didn't notice—or she did and simply didn't care.

She marched straight to her usual spot: the small front-of-store space just past the carts, where a folding table, helium tank, Alpha Rewards swag, and a tangled banner waited.

"Oh no no no," she scolded to the air. "Who folded the tablecloth like its laundry? This isn't a PTA bake sale—it's branding, people. We're building loyalty, not flipping Tupperware!"

From behind the espresso bar, Penny watched with a frown. "Who *is* that?"

Trina didn't even look up. "That's Barbara. VP of Loyalty. She shows up like... four times a year to throw glitter on the Alpha Rewards program."

"She works here?"

"She works *life,*" Trina said. "She's Ted's stepmom. Her husband—Ted's dad—passed away last year. And let's just say the Will didn't exactly leave Ted clapping."

"Oh," Penny murmured, looking at Ted, who'd just appeared near the vitamin aisle. His smile evaporated the second he saw her. Barbara caught his eye, gave him a saccharine wave, and then—just to twist the knife—blew him a kiss.

Penny narrowed her eyes. "Yikes."

"She's... a lot," Trina said. "She doesn't *need* this job. Does it for fun. Says it keeps her connected to the people. Also rescues dogs. Has a cat. Don't trust her."

Barbara suddenly appeared in front of the coffee bar like a mirage made of linen and confidence. "You must be Penny!" she beamed. "I'm Barbara. VP of Loyalty and unofficial queen of Alfie's. We're *so* lucky to have you here."

"Thanks," Penny said cautiously.

"I'm a big animal lover," Barbara declared without prompting. "Three rescue dogs—one poodle with anxiety, a mutt who only likes jazz music, and a pit mix who eats throw pillows. And a cat named Smokey who tolerates me. I keep pictures. Want to see?"

Barbara was already flipping through her phone. "That's Bruno. He only drinks filtered water. Can you believe it? Anyway, I'm just here to brighten up the day, hand out some coupons, and catch up with the locals. You'd be amazed what people confess over camembert."

She paused, her expression softening as her gaze flicked over Penny with an assessing sort of warmth. "You've got sharp eyes, sweetheart. I like that. You see things. Just... be careful who sees *you* seeing things, okay?"

Before Penny could respond, Barbara leaned in and lowered her voice.

"And if I forget to say goodbye later..." she whispered, slipping a dog-shaped sticker onto the espresso machine, "just know—I'll be back."

With a wink and a flip of her hair, she turned and strutted off toward the cheese wall, already asking a customer if they preferred aged gouda or family secrets.

Penny watched her go, slightly stunned.

"She's exhausting," Trina muttered.

"She's *dangerous,*" Penny said. "In heels."

Just before her lunch break, a woman with a small dog in a designer bag stepped up to the counter and ordered a triple-shot matcha latte with honey, lavender, and 'vibes only.' Penny didn't even blink. She nodded, smiled, and went through the motions.

But she was getting more frustrated by the minute. She wasn't built for standing still. She was trained to move, chase, question, solve.

"Sometimes I wonder if this is what purgatory looks like," she muttered to Trina while restocking lids.

"You mean the coffee bar?"

"I mean being this close to the truth and not being able to reach for it."

Trina looked at her for a beat, then handed her a clean rag. "You need to clean the pastry case. Minnie said someone sneezed on it."

So she cleaned. She scrubbed. She stared into the case at the cinnamon rolls and thought of Freddy the dream-bed. "Danger's proofing in the ovens!"

Could Biola really be back? Was Betsy hiding her in plain sight? Was it possible Biola had something to do with the poison, or was she just another distraction?

The rest of the shift dragged like syrup. Penny fielded customer complaints about lukewarm oat milk, rearranged the napkin holders for the third time, and politely declined a flirty actor's offer to run lines from his new pilot.

On her break, she wandered toward the bakery department. She didn't need anything. She just needed to look.

A new employee was working the counter—a girl she hadn't seen before. Tall, with slicked-back hair and a face like she had better places to be.

"Hey," Penny said casually. "You new?"

The girl shrugged. "Third day. I'm temping. They pulled me from Studio City."

"Cool. Busy back here?"

"Not really," the girl said, eyeing her. "Why?"

"No reason," Penny said, and walked off slowly, eyes scanning everything.

A list was taped to the side of the warming cabinet. Names. Shifts. Biola's wasn't there—but Penny still had a weird feeling in her gut.

Maybe Freddy was onto something after all.

Back at the kiosk, a customer dropped a full extra-large caramel macchiato onto the floor, and Penny jumped back just in time to avoid a caramel splash to the knees.

"Five second rule?" the man joked.

"I'm gonna pretend I didn't hear that," Penny said dryly, grabbing the mop.

The truth was, she felt it. The pressure building. The clues stacking. The cracks in Betsy's story starting to show.

She just had to stay patient a little longer.

Harder than it sounded.

As she mopped up the caramel, Penny heard the low rumble of a snare roll coming from outside. Sure enough, the Rocker had returned. He was sitting at his usual table near the front of the store, tapping on an upturned plastic container with two drumsticks, lost in his own rhythm.

She watched him from a distance. His grungy T-shirt was torn at the collar, and his pale hair frizzed out like a halo of static. He wasn't always there at the same time, but when he was, he stayed for hours. Sometimes silent, sometimes rambling about the good ol' days.

He'd once told Penny he'd toured with Jefferson Airplane, then in the next breath claimed to have played a set with The Beatles at a house party. She never knew what to believe, but there was a melancholy consistency to him—always eager to talk, always alone, and always watching.

"Think he sleeps in that chair?" Trina whispered.

"I think he sleeps in the parking lot," Penny replied. "And I think he sees more than we realize."

"He gives me the creeps. You ever catch him just... staring?"

"All the time."

Still, Penny couldn't help but wonder—if he really was always around, had he seen something? Heard something? She made a mental note to find a way to talk to him off the record, maybe slip him a hot drink and a few questions.

She was already plotting out the next phase of her investigation when the radio crackled to life.

"Team lead to front bakery. Repeat: team lead to front bakery."

Her ears perked up.

Penny glanced across the store. The new temp was no longer at the counter. The Manager on duty—Gerald, a gentle but scatterbrained guy—was already walking over.

She didn't know what was happening, but her instincts were on high alert.

She set the mop aside and casually wandered over to the edge of the kiosk, wiping down the counter as an excuse. Something was going on in the bakery. And Penny/Raven wasn't going to miss it.

Before she could get too close, Lupe, the always-hurried Sales Manager, flagged her down.

"Penny! Can you help in bakery for a bit? We're short. One of the temps just walked out. Gerald said you've worked food service, right?"

Penny blinked. "Uh... yeah, of course."

She didn't love being yanked off bar duty, but this was perfect—finally a way into bakery without drawing suspicion.

The moment she stepped behind the counter, she could feel something off. The air was different—too careful. Too controlled. The new girl had vanished. Gerald handed Penny gloves and pointed her toward the back where trays of pastries were cooling.

"Just help wrap and restock, okay?"

"Got it," she said, tying on an apron.

As she moved toward the prep station, she noticed something strange near the boxes of baking supplies. One container, labeled "Powdered Sugar," was sealed tight and taped with two thick strips of clear packing tape—more secure than any other box.

She squinted at it.

The texture didn't look right. The powder inside wasn't as fine, and the label had a faint sticker residue like it had been peeled off and relabeled.

Her gut twisted.

A few minutes later, a well-dressed woman in over-sized sunglasses strutted up to the counter and asked specifically for the cinnamon cake with "extra vanilla cream" topping. Her voice was low, discreet—too polished for a bakery run.

A minute after her, a man in a tracksuit and flashy watch walked up and said the exact same thing.

Penny's eyes narrowed.

She had seen that pattern before. Sketchy men. Beverly Hills women. All ordering the same specialty items like they were part of a hidden menu.

Her stomach churned.

They weren't just selling pastries.

Someone was using the bakery to push drugs.

Disguised as baking powder.

Freddy had been right.

And Penny? She had just stepped into the oven.

She kept her cool. That's what she was trained to do. But her mind raced as she wrapped cinnamon rolls and handed over biscotti with an even smile. She took note of every face, every name on a shift list, every odd order that came through.

Two more customers came in with the same coded pastry order. One of them, a lanky man in his sixties with a Bluetooth headset, tapped the counter twice after saying "extra vanilla cream," then gave Penny a nod like they shared a secret.

She logged it.

Later, while stocking the refrigerated display, she heard Gerald whispering to Lupe in the back prep room. Something about "Betsy running this part quietly." That alone made her stomach tighten.

Betsy. Again.

She was in deep—deeper than Penny originally thought. Penny always assumed Betsy's involvement in Donny's death was rooted in control, power, or vengeance. But now? It might've been about business. Dirty, criminal business.

As the end of her bakery shift neared, Penny slid a small piece of parchment paper into her pocket. On it, she'd written the last five names on the bakery pickup list—coded, vague, but still traceable. She'd dig into them later.

When her replacement arrived, Penny peeled off her apron and made her way back to Sunset Star. Her arms ached. Her head buzzed. But she knew something critical now.

The bakery was a front.

And the deeper she got, the closer she came to the truth.

There were secrets baked into every corner of this store.

And Penny? She was finally learning the recipe.

She didn't clock out right away. Instead, she lingered at the condiment station, pretending to organize stir sticks and sugar packets. She was watching. Listening. Taking note of who interacted with whom. Who disappeared into the back room and returned empty-handed. Who looked over their shoulder too many times.

She also made mental notes of customers who left without purchasing anything but had spent more than a few minutes loitering around bakery—or worse, speaking in vague code to employees.

At one point, the Rocker strolled by again, humming something that sounded suspiciously like "Sympathy for the Devil." He gave her a long, knowing look. She nodded once.

"You ever get the feeling," he said, not stopping, "that something sticky's rising in the heat?"

He was gone before she could respond.

Later that night, Penny sat in her car in the parking structure's top level. She scribbled notes into her black leather notebook by the glow of a weak dome light.

Donny. The Raid. Betsy. Biola. The cleaning logs. The coded orders. The mysterious temp. The woman in sunglasses. The man with the Bluetooth.

She'd have to start connecting the dots.

The deeper she went, the more dangerous it became. But it was too late to pull back now. The scent of cinnamon and conspiracy was thick in the air—and she wasn't backing down.

She reached into her glove compartment, pulled out a protein bar, and chewed it slowly while watching a raccoon crawl across the far edge of the lot. It paused, stared directly at her, then scurried off under a cart corral.

Even the wildlife in Hollywood was shady.

Penny smirked.

Tomorrow, she'd dig deeper. Maybe it was time to look into the financial side of things. Follow the money. Follow the cake.

Because the closer she got to the center of this sugar-coated operation, the clearer it became:

The bakery wasn't the only thing operating under the radar. The entire store was in flux. People were shifting like pieces on a chessboard. And she couldn't ignore how often Jorge—always with his Bluetooth and boundless energy—was front and center, guiding new faces around the store while old ones disappeared like ghosts.

One week, Ruby from deli was there every morning prepping cold cuts; the next, she was gone without a word. No goodbye party. No "Ruby's Last Shift" cake. Just a blank space on the schedule and a shrug from Jorge.

"You know how it goes," he'd say with a grin. "People get moved. We're one big family!"

But families didn't transfer you without warning. Families didn't erase your name and pretend you never existed.

Penny knew better. These weren't random movements—they were strategic. Quiet. Too clean.

She had to stay one step ahead before she became the next name wiped from the board.

Lately, that fear had been clawing its way closer. What if she was transferred? What if someone—Betsy, Jorge, even upper management—decided to move her out before she finished her assignment? Before she got the evidence she needed? Before she figured out how Donny died and who was behind the bakery front?

It wasn't just paranoia. It was gut instinct. And her instincts had never failed her.

Worse, she was starting to feel something else too. Something messier.

Matt.

He was supposed to be a background character. Just another employee. But the way he moved during the Code Adam, the way he looked at her like he saw her, not just the Barista mask she wore—it stuck with her. He'd been kind. Capable. And maddeningly mysterious.

She hated that she found herself scanning the breakroom every time she passed by, hoping for a glimpse of him. She hated that he made her heart stumble a little when he smiled.

Raven didn't do distractions. Raven didn't do attachments.

But Penny?

Penny was slipping.

And that scared her more than anything else.

That night, as she tossed in bed under the faint glow of a streetlamp bleeding through her blinds, she tried to shut her thoughts off. But Matt kept showing up in her mind. His voice. His timing. His way of deflecting with dry humor while still stepping up when it mattered. She hated the way it made her feel vulnerable. Seen. Even comforted.

She tried replaying the day like surveillance footage in her mind—scrutinizing every word, every face, every misplaced box of 'powdered sugar.' But his smile kept interrupting the tape.

She rolled onto her back, eyes tracing the ceiling like a map she could never fully decipher.

What if he was innocent? What if he wasn't? Either way, she was getting pulled into something deeper than intel and mission briefs.

This wasn't supposed to happen.

But maybe it had to.

Someone in Alfie's was using pastries to bury secrets.

And Raven McCool was ready to crack the recipe wide open.

CHAPTER
FIFTEEN

OLD GROUNDS, NEW TENSIONS

The morning crowd had started to mellow, the line curling gently instead of spiking chaotically like it did during peak hours. Penny was grateful. Her hands moved almost without thought, steaming milk, swirling syrups, tapping out drink stickers like she was composing a symphony in whipped cream.

Trina hummed beside her, bopping to an imaginary beat, whisper-singing lyrics to a song that had been playing overhead twenty minutes ago.

Then he walked in.

Tall. Polished. Smug as ever.

Josh.

Penny's ex-husband.

She almost dropped the milk pitcher.

He looked like he always did before a showing—tailored slacks, overpriced blazer, sunglasses that probably cost more than her monthly rent. He was on the phone, of course, barking some directive about keys, locks, and "making sure the ficus looks alive."

She hadn't seen him in over a year.

He was showing a house in the Hollywood Hills, naturally. Josh specialized in luxury listings and superficial charm. His idea of connection was commenting on how shiny someone's shoes were or pretending to care about feng shui.

Penny ducked slightly behind the espresso machine. She wasn't ready. Not for this. Not here.

But then he stepped up to the register.

And she had no choice.

He didn't recognize her right away.

"Large black coffee. No sugar, no room. Just hot. Like a real cup of coffee. Not whatever oat-choco-frothy mess you guys sell."

His voice.

The condescension.

It hadn't changed.

Penny straightened. Quietly keyed in his order.

Then he looked up.

Their eyes met.

A flicker of confusion.

Then realization.

He blinked. "Raven?"

She smiled, tight and professional. "It's Penny now."

"Penny? What on earth are you—"

"Working."

He scoffed, like it was a punchline. "Behind a coffee bar? That's where you ended up?"

Trina raised an eyebrow and took an aggressive sip of her green tea.

"I like it here," Penny said coolly. "Plenty of character."

He gave her that look—the one he used when she told him she wanted to stay in law enforcement instead of joining his real estate empire. The one that said, You're wasting your potential.

"I'm surprised," he said. "I figured you'd be halfway to a federal promotion by now. Still chasing crooks?"

"Not at the moment," she lied.

"Must be a humbling change," he added, voice slick with faux-sympathy. "But I guess not everyone's cut out for the big leagues."

Trina stepped forward. "Here's your coffee," she said, her tone sharp enough to slice drywall.

Josh took it with a nod, then turned back to Penny.

"Nice seeing you," he said, though it clearly wasn't. "Try not to spill anything."

Penny didn't respond. Just watched him walk away, sipping his coffee like it proved something.

The door whooshed shut behind him.

Trina turned. "That was him, wasn't it?"

"Yeah," Penny said quietly.

"The ex?"

She nodded.

Trina frowned. "What a tool."

Penny exhaled slowly. Her hands shook a little as she wiped down the bar.

That was Josh.

All polished arrogance and hidden cruelty. The same man who belittled her for working cases that didn't make headlines. Who resented every hour she spent at the precinct. Who couldn't understand why helping people meant more to her than country club brunches or matching Teslas.

He hadn't changed.

But she had.

And she wasn't going to let him rattle her.

Not now.

Not when she was this close to the truth.

Still, the encounter left her feeling like she'd been doused in cold brew. Memories bubbled up like a shaken can—arguments about schedules, the nights she came home late after a stakeout, his passive-aggressive remarks about how her job wasn't "ladylike."

He never understood why she did what she did. Why helping victims meant something. Why justice wasn't a career move, but a purpose.

She took a breath and reached for the next cup, her hands steadying as the rhythm returned. Steam. Pour. Swirl.

Josh might have walked away smirking, but he didn't know the whole story. He didn't know she was here by choice. Undercover. Digging into something that actually mattered.

Trina handed her a fresh rag. "If he ever comes back, I vote we serve him decaf and tell him it's espresso."

Penny smirked. "Tempting."

They shared a grin, and for a moment, the tension loosened.

Then the next customer stepped up to the counter and ordered the cinnamon cake with "extra vanilla cream."

Penny's smile dropped.

Another one.

This wasn't over—not by a long shot.

Later that afternoon, Penny tried to lose herself in the rhythm of the rush. She made foam rosettas and oat milk hearts, but her mind kept skipping like a scratched record. Every face that came to the counter was suspect. Every cake order sounded like a code.

The Josh encounter had lit a slow burn in her chest. She couldn't shake the things he said—or worse, the way he said them. Like her career had been a phase. Like her choices were all mistakes.

And yet here she was, undercover in a grocery store that moonlighted as a criminal front, sipping bad drip coffee and pretending to care about whether someone's whipped cream was organic.

The bakery orders hadn't slowed. If anything, they'd picked up. Four separate customers—none of whom looked like regular shoppers—had come in asking for the same suspicious pastry by name. And the new girl in the bakery? Gone again. Supposedly 'called to another location,' which was starting to sound a lot like code for something else.

Penny needed air.

She tapped out from the kiosk, grabbed her coffee, and walked out to the loading dock behind the store. She sat on an overturned milk crate that had become her unofficial thinking chair.

Back inside, the store had its usual afternoon hum. But something was different.

Taurus was behind the bar again.

The seasoned Barista—always quick to remind everyone he'd worked for Sunset Star for twenty years—though no one quite believed him considering he barely looked thirty-five. He wore his badge with pride and his ego even louder. Taurus had an air about him, like he knew the inner workings of the espresso machine better than the person who built it.

He was obsessive about bar cleanliness. He'd once scolded a new hire for leaving two sugar packets slightly askew. Penny found it oddly comforting—if anyone noticed tiny things out of place, it was Taurus.

Unfortunately, he and Trina clashed constantly. Her tone toward him veered too often into something bitter, even hostile. Penny had caught her muttering once about Taurus being "a quota hire," and it made her stomach turn. Trina liked drama—liked pitting coworkers against each other like it was a sport. And Taurus, with his routines and meticulous nature, made an easy target.

But despite the tension, Taurus had her back.

A few days ago, he'd leaned in while checking the steamed milk pitchers and whispered, "You ever notice how inventory doesn't match? Like someone's baking off books?"

Penny had nodded, but said nothing.

Taurus didn't know the full picture. But he was paying attention. Like a lot of people here, he was starting to notice things. Drop hints. Reveal pieces.

And Raven? She was there to catch them all.

A new armed guard was walking the floor. Young—barely out of academy, if Penny had to guess—and clearly eager to prove himself. He was trailing Matt like a shadow, nodding at every comment Matt made, adjusting his belt every few steps as if to remind everyone he had one.

Trina leaned over the bar. "Who's the new puppy?"

"Don't know," Penny said. "But he's got that 'just unwrapped' energy."

A commotion erupted near the service deli. Two men were arguing in hushed but sharp tones, one of them clutching a hot rotisserie chicken like he'd just won it in a fight.

The rookie sprang into action, rushing over like he was responding to an armed robbery.

Matt followed behind him with a calm, steady pace.

Penny and Trina watched as the rookie confronted the two men—customers, clearly trying to slip out with stolen chickens. One was already halfway to the express lane when the rookie cut them off.

"Gentlemen," the young guard said, voice too loud for the situation. "You planning to pay for those?"

The chicken thief froze. The other guy tried to bluff his way out of it.

Matt stepped in smoothly, de-escalating before things could turn into a scene. He spoke low, calm. Directed the men toward the front desk. Told them they could walk out clean if they just returned the merchandise and left.

The rookie looked disappointed not to use his radio or tackle anyone.

Penny shook her head with a smile.

"That guy's going to burn out in a month," Trina said.

"Or start a fire," Penny replied.

She flipped open her notebook and jotted a few details:

Josh sighting, unplanned. Don't let it rattle you.

Same coded cake order—third one today.

Look into supplier invoices for bakery items (ask Trina if she knows where records are kept).

The page was getting crowded. So was her brain.

Just then, a voice startled her.

"Hey there, Penny for your thoughts?"

It was Matt. Casual, holding a sandwich and an orange sports drink. He leaned against the loading ramp rail like he belonged there—and maybe he did.

Penny tucked her notebook away quickly. "Just... decompressing."

"Break time blues?"

"Something like that."

Matt unwrapped his sandwich, took a bite, and chewed thoughtfully. "That guy earlier—the tall, too-perfect real estate dude—you looked like you'd seen a ghost."

Penny considered lying.

Instead, she said, "My ex-husband."

Matt paused, mid-chew. "Ah. That explains the whole 'kill-me-now' vibe."

Penny smirked. "He thinks I'm wasting my life making coffee."

"Then he clearly doesn't get it."

She looked at him.

Matt shrugged. "Coffee saves lives. Or at least saves people from themselves. Plus, this place would be a lot duller without you."

It wasn't flirtatious—it was honest. And that made it more dangerous.

Penny felt a warmth crawl into her chest she didn't ask for.

"Thanks," she said softly.

He tapped his drink against her cup. "To undercover Baristas everywhere."

She gave a soft laugh, and for a moment, the weight of everything lifted just a little.

But only for a moment.

Because when she returned to Sunset Star, she found an anonymous note wedged between the syrup bottles.

All it said was:

"You're getting close. Watch your back."

She stared at it for a long beat, the world narrowing to the slip of paper in her hand. Her heartbeat picked up, pounding behind her ears. Someone was watching her. Someone knew.

The timing wasn't random. It came after the encounter with Josh, after the rotisserie chicken scuffle, after her break with Matt.

Penny folded the note carefully and slid it into her apron pocket.

No one had ever warned her off unless she was onto something real.

And now? She was certain of it: this went deeper than bakery fraud. There were layers. Players. Patterns. And someone in the store was beginning to feel threatened.

Good.

Let them sweat.

She adjusted her ponytail, straightened her apron, and turned back to the espresso machine.

"Let's make some damn coffee," she muttered.

Because nothing covered suspicion better than a good foam pour and a practiced smile.

And Penny? She was just getting started.

Before closing, she did one last slow lap of the store. To anyone watching, she was just a tired Barista taking a stroll before clocking out. But in reality, she was scanning—checking angles, security mirrors, blind spots the cameras didn't quite cover.

Near the greeting cards, she paused just long enough to watch Taurus chat with one of the bakery regulars. The woman—mid-fifties, pearls and perfect posture—wasn't holding any pastries. Just standing too close, speaking low. Taurus didn't seem fazed, but something in his body language flickered: a shift in stance, a glance toward the bar.

Penny took a mental snapshot.

Back in the breakroom, she pulled out her burner phone. She opened the secure messaging app and typed out a single line to her handler:

"Escalation confirmed. Suspect internal. Note received. More soon."

She hesitated for a second before hitting send.

Then she turned off the phone, slid it into her boot, and headed out to the parking lot with her keys in hand.

The streetlights buzzed overhead. The city never slept. Neither did the truth.

And tomorrow, she'd be one step closer to exposing it.

CHAPTER

SIXTEEN

NORA KNOWS

Penny arrived earlier than usual. The store hadn't opened yet, and the fluorescent lights still flickered with that sleepy buzz. She walked through the double doors and found Nora already there, dragging out the black anti-slip mats with one hand and humming a salsa tune under her breath.

"Hola, Penny!" Nora called, flashing her familiar crooked smile.

"Good morning, Nora," Penny said, grabbing one end of a mat to help. "You're early."

"I always early," Nora declared proudly. "No drama. Only mop."

Penny smiled. Nora was a custodian and sometimes a bagger—mid-sixties, tiny, with wiry strength and the energy of someone half her age. She didn't speak much

English, but she didn't need to. Nora read people like novels and remembered everything. She also did an uncanny impression of nearly everyone in the store, including Taurus.

"Oye," Nora said, nodding toward the bakery. "You know Joe? Him too slow. Always phone. Always flirting with that lazy girl."

Penny blinked. "The other custodian?"

"Sí, sí. Her name is... eh, I call her Sleepy. Always hiding. No help. Just lipstick. Pfft."

Penny chuckled. "You two not best friends then?"

Nora slapped the air. "Please. She steal my hours. Say she work, but she hide in the back. I tell Lupe—no one listen. I mop! I clean! She pose like flower."

The image was too good. Penny laughed out loud.

Nora leaned in. "But you—" she said, tapping Penny's arm, "You smart. You watch."

Penny nodded slowly. "You see anything strange lately, Nora?"

Nora raised her eyebrows dramatically, then mimed someone slipping a small bag into their pocket.

"Near the bakery?" Penny asked.

"Yes. Fancy woman. Glasses. White shoes."

That matched the vague description Penny had in her notes. And Nora just confirmed it—without even knowing what she was doing.

They finished setting up the mats and stood in comfortable silence for a moment.

Then Nora spotted Richie walking toward the back with a tray of caramel drizzle bottles balanced like a circus act.

Nora perked up. "He sing! You hear? Like angel and Beyoncé."

Penny grinned. "Yeah, he's got talent."

"He make me happy. I call him Mi Cielo."

As Richie passed, Nora gave him a big wave. "Hola, mi estrella! Sing for me today, sí?"

Richie did a playful twirl. "Only if you promise to clap!"

"Always!" Nora called.

Penny shook her head, warmth blooming in her chest. In a store full of secrets, Nora was the heartbeat. Loud, unfiltered, and impossible not to love.

And she was watching everything.

Which made her more valuable than anyone realized.

Later that morning, Nora passed by the coffee kiosk again, this time holding a mop and a bottle of lavender-scented cleaner like a sword and shield. She stopped in front of Taurus, who was mid-rant about someone rearranging the sugar packets.

"You move my bins again, Taurus?" she asked, hands on hips.

Taurus sighed. "Nora, I told you—it's not me. Someone keeps putting the empty racks on the wrong side of the dish basin. I have a system."

"You have too many systems," she shot back. "You need girlfriend."

Penny nearly spit out her sip of coffee. Taurus, to his credit, just blinked and said, "I need a cleaner backroom."

Nora turned to Penny. "You tell him. Clean brain, clean life."

"Clean espresso machine, clean mission," Penny added with a wink.

Taurus raised an eyebrow. "What mission?"

"The mission of not losing my mind before 10 a.m.," she replied smoothly.

"Mmhm," Nora muttered, walking off with a grin. But not before giving Trina—just arriving for her shift—a wide berth.

Penny noticed. Trina didn't even say hello.

Nora whispered in passing, "She think she boss. She not boss. She bored."

Another clue. Another thread.

The store wasn't just a front for something shady—it was a stage. And people like Nora? They saw the whole show.

Every act. Every slip. Every curtain drawn just slightly too late.

Nora kept proving it, too. That afternoon, she came up to Penny near the café ice machine, muttering something under her breath in Spanish before switching to English.

"Too much talking in the freezer," she said.

Penny paused. "What freezer?"

"Back bakery. Big one. The walk-in," Nora whispered. "Three people go in. Only two come out right away. I wait. The third? He stay long time."

That made Penny straighten.

"Did you see who it was?"

Nora squinted. "Big man. Hat. No name tag. Not Alfie's worker. I think he pretend."

That matched a theory Penny had scribbled down weeks ago. Outsiders using back-of-house areas for un-monitored exchanges.

"You're amazing, Nora," Penny said.

Nora waved it off. "Pfft. I mop and I see. That's my job. I don't wear tie. I wear eyes."

It was true. Nora's eyes missed nothing. She swept floors, wiped down carts, organized bins—and in be-tween, she logged the true heartbeat of the store.

She leaned closer. "You be careful, Penny. You too smart. They notice. People don't like smart in the dark."

Penny nodded. Her throat tightened.

Nora patted her arm. Then marched off to scold someone for leaving an ice bucket on the wrong shelf.

But not before throwing one last jab over her shoul-der.

"Trina and Ted," she muttered with a dramatic eye roll. "Always disappear. Think I don't notice? I notice. They hide. They whisper. Always same time. Like tele-novela."

Penny blinked. "Trina and Ted? You sure?"

Nora nodded firmly. "She act like she boss. He act like he busy. But I see! They go poof—like magic trick."

It was a small thing. But in Penny's world, small things added up. Especially when whispered by someone with a mop in one hand and a perfect view of every back hallway in the store.

"You hear from me first," Nora added with a proud nod. "But you didn't hear from me."

Penny smiled. "Wouldn't dream of it."

Nora knew.

She might not know everything—but she knew enough.

And for Penny, that made her more than just a custodian.

It made her a silent ally in the shadows of the store.

Later, while wiping down the café tables during a lull, Penny caught Nora doing an impersonation for one of the overnight stockers. It was unmistakably Trina—arms crossed, nose scrunched, muttering something sarcastic about people not knowing how to do their jobs. The stocker howled with laughter.

Penny raised an eyebrow as Nora shuffled past, still mid-performance.

"You think Trina funny?" Nora asked.

"She's... unique," Penny said carefully.

"She rude," Nora said bluntly. "Act like she queen, but she no do nothing."

She looked both ways, then leaned in again.

"And Ted—he always help her 'move boxes.' Boxes, boxes, always boxes! Nobody see these magic boxes."

Penny nearly choked on her sip of iced tea.

"You keep watching," Nora added, wagging a finger. "Not everyone who smile is sweet. And some sugar go bad if you leave it out too long."

Penny nodded, absorbing every word.

That was the thing about Nora—she didn't just see everything. She remembered it. Logged it. Performed it, even.

And while most people laughed off her impressions, Penny was beginning to realize they were closer to confessions.

Truth told sideways, in character.

Clues wrapped in comedy.

Later that week, Nora started wearing a button on her apron that read "Mop Boss" in glittery, handwritten letters. Penny had no idea where she got it, but it suited her perfectly. She wore it like armor.

"You see this?" Nora said proudly. "Now they know. I see all. Mop sees all."

She made it her new catchphrase. Whenever she caught someone slacking, she'd point to her badge and mutter, "Mop sees all."

Richie, ever the performer, began doing a dramatic slow clap every time she said it.

"Somebody give this woman a trophy," he'd say, bowing low. "Or at least a good broom."

Nora loved the attention, but more than that, she loved the rhythm of routine. She swept through the store like a Detective with a cleaning cart. And every so often, she'd drop another breadcrumb for Penny to follow.

"I see the Sleepy Girl again," she said one morning. "But now she not with Joe. She talk to Lupe. Too close. Maybe she tell secrets. Maybe she make trouble."

Penny's ears perked. Lupe and the other custodian had always been background noise. Now Nora was suggesting they might be something more.

"I just clean," Nora shrugged. "But I clean everywhere. Even where I not supposed."

It was the most useful job in the store—and the most underestimated.

And Penny was starting to realize Nora's mop wasn't just cleaning up messes. It was uncovering them.

One morning, as Penny was prepping syrups and restocking espresso lids, she spotted Nora crouched under the back counter near the dish area—not mopping this time, but inspecting something. Her face was serious. Focused.

"You okay, Nora?" Penny called.

"One minute," Nora said. She emerged a moment later holding a torn corner of a receipt with something scribbled on the back.

She handed it to Penny. "You like puzzles, sí?"

Penny took it. The handwriting was messy, almost rushed. It looked like a time and initials: "4:30pm - T + L."

"I find it near bakery back wall," Nora said. "They leave trash, but maybe it not just trash."

Penny's brain lit up. T and L. Trina and Lupe?

"You're a wizard, Nora."

Nora beamed. "I'm mop boss, remember? Mop see all."

Then she turned and marched toward the front with her cart, leaving Penny with the slip of paper and a rapidly growing list of suspects.

Every day, Nora pulled a new thread.

And with each thread, Penny could feel the whole web tightening.

The next day, Nora approached Penny in the middle of a midday rush, her mop still dripping and a determined look in her eyes.

"I see something again," she said in a low voice.

Penny was in the middle of steaming milk, but she paused. "Go on."

"Boxes," Nora said, pointing with the mop handle. "But not normal boxes. Bakery boxes. Heavy. One of them go in—Trina. She come out fast. Then Lupe go in. But the box? Not come back out."

Penny felt her heart skip.

"Where were they taking them?"

Nora shook her head. "Not back. Not front. I think... under."

"Under what?"

"Storage. The weird room near wine. Locked most times. I mop close once. I hear buzz—like machine. But no fridge there. Not supposed to be."

Penny blinked. That was new. A locked room. Buzzing.

She jotted it into her notes later in the breakroom, circling the phrase: WINE ROOM—STORAGE—BUZZING.

Nora wandered in behind her and sat on an overturned bucket like it was a throne.

"You ask questions, Penny. But you also listen. People like you."

"I listen because people like you talk."

Nora smiled. "We both smart. You find truth. I sweep path."

They sat for a beat in companionable silence.

And then Nora muttered, half to herself, "One day, this whole place? Boom. Truth fall out like rotten melon."

Penny didn't laugh. She just nodded.

Because she could feel it too.

And Nora? Nora would be there, mop in hand, to witness every drop.

That evening, long after her shift officially ended, Penny stayed late under the pretense of helping Taurus wipe down the espresso machines. Really, she was watching the movement around the wine storage room. Just as Nora had said, there was something unusual about it. The door wasn't labeled, and yet it had a keypad lock. She hadn't noticed it before.

As she stood near the coffee grinders, pretending to restock syrup pumps, she saw Lupe approach the area with a clipboard and a tote bag. Seconds later, Trina appeared from the other side of the store, holding a bakery box and a forced smile.

They exchanged no words. Just nods.

Then both of them disappeared into the room.

The door clicked shut.

Penny's pulse picked up.

She noted the time. 7:06 p.m.

When Lupe emerged five minutes later, her bag looked fuller. Trina never came back through that hallway—at least not while Penny was watching.

She texted one word to herself in her burner phone: Confirmed.

Back in the breakroom, Nora passed her with a bag of cleaning cloths slung over her shoulder like a sash. "They think I clean. But I see," she said simply.

Penny smiled. "You do more than that."

Nora winked. "You too. We keep sweeping. They slip eventually."

And Penny believed her.

Because the truth wasn't just beneath the surface anymore.

It was leaking through the cracks.

The next morning, Nora greeted Penny with a warm croissant and a folded napkin that had something scribbled on the inside.

"Today, I mop the truth out," she said with a grin.

Inside the napkin, Penny found another puzzle: a floor map Nora had drawn in blue pen, highlighting the corner between the bakery and wine aisle. She had drawn tiny stick figures, one labeled 'T,' one 'L,' and an arrow pointing down.

"Trina, Lupe," Nora said quietly, pointing. "They move like clock. Always same time. I see pattern."

Penny tucked the map into her notebook, heart beating faster. Nora wasn't just witnessing things—she was tracking them.

Later that day, Penny saw her crouched near the frozen foods aisle, pretending to scrub gum from the floor while eyeing the side hallway that led to dry storage.

She was undercover in her own way. A cleaner with instincts. A Barista with a badge.

As the afternoon light filtered in through the automatic doors, Penny caught her own reflection in the pastry case glass. Behind her, Nora mopped.

But their eyes met for a second—and in that brief glance, Penny knew she wasn't alone in this.

Not anymore.

She had Nora.

Mop Boss. Truth whisperer. Comedian. Spy.

And in this store full of lies, Penny was finally start-ing to believe she could clean house—with the right crew behind her.

CHAPTER
SEVENTEEN

UNDER THE FREEZER

I f anyone had told me that Tuesday morning would end with me crawling under a walk-in freezer in a corporate grocery chain while wearing a name tag that read "Penny Padlock," I would have ordered a venti-sized reality check and called in sick.

But here we were.

I had come in early, earlier than usual, because Trina had texted the night before in her all-caps dramatic style:

"YOU MIGHT WANT TO SEE THIS BEFORE THE MORNING CREW ARRIVES."

I didn't know what to expect. Trina had a flair for drama, and 80% of the time, her "emergencies" ended in nothing more than a mystery pastry gone stale or an overstock of oat milk. But the way she said it—no emojis, no sarcasm—meant this one was different.

I slipped in through the back dock door just past five-thirty. The store smelled like disinfectant and old bananas. The lights buzzed low overhead, the floor machines, still groaning faintly from the night crew's half-hearted attempt at cleaning.

Trina stood near the freezer with her arms folded and her eyebrows raised like she was about to drop a mic.

"Please tell me this isn't about a frozen croissant," I said.

"I wish." She gestured behind the shelf where we stored the almond milk and half-frozen cookie dough balls. She pulled aside a rolling cart and bent low, tapping a section of the wall. A piece of trim shifted slightly.

"It fell off when I was cleaning last night. I wasn't even trying to snoop, but then I saw that edge pop out—so I tugged. Look."

Behind the trim was a shallow panel, just big enough for someone to wedge open. The latch was covered in grime, and it took both of us pulling to pop it loose. What we found wasn't a door exactly, but more like an access panel that dropped into a crawlspace.

The smell hit us first—cold, metallic, and slightly sour.

"You go first," I said.

"You're the one with the badge," she shot back.

So, I went.

The space wasn't big. Just enough to crouch in, maybe four feet tall at its highest point. A concrete tunnel, lined with broken crates and old storage bins. At the far end, a flickering lightbulb dangled from a wire like something out of a horror movie.

We crawled in together, neither of us willing to be left out. The tunnel curved slightly to the right and then opened into a wider room—a sort of forgotten sub-basement below the back storage area. There were boxes labeled ALPHA AIRWAYS and ROYAL ALPHA VOYAGES in faded marker, some with reward program brochures dating back a decade.

"What is this place?" Trina whispered.

I recognized one of the folders. Alpha Rewards. The same branding Barbara had been handing out at Rock n' Roll Alfie's. I flipped it open. Inside was a list of member IDs and points breakdowns—but some were flagged. Annotations in red ink next to names, like "ACQUISITION PRIORITY" and "DO NOT CONVERT."

"Okay, this is officially weirder than that time Betsy tried to host karaoke in produce," I muttered.

One of the folders was half-charred. As I reached for it, I noticed a business card wedged between the boxes. I pulled it out. It was smooth, slick, and almost holographic.

Barbara Templeton, VP of Loyalty Systems

On the back, in tiny font: "We're not watching. We're listening."

Trina read it. "That's creepy, right?" she said.

"Oh yeah," I said. "Peak corporate dystopia."

But it wasn't just creepy. It was proof.

Proof that Barbara's little side show in the front of Alfie's wasn't just a PR stunt. The rewards system was being monitored, tracked—and curated.

Curated for what? I didn't know yet.

But I had a feeling I was about to find out.

When we emerged from the crawlspace, my phone was already buzzing. Gus.

GUS: "You weren't supposed to find that."

ME: "Then maybe you should've picked a better hiding place."

GUS: "It's not just Alfie's. It's bigger."

Before I could reply, Matt appeared near the stockroom with a clipboard and two coffees—one for me. He raised an eyebrow as he handed it over.

"Rough morning?"

"You have no idea," I said, our fingers brushing for just a second too long.

He smelled like cinnamon and danger. I didn't want to admit it, but being around Matt felt like getting a perfectly pulled shot of espresso after hours of decaf.

"You, okay?" he asked.

"Working on it."

I looked at him. Really looked. He knew something, too.

Not everything. But enough.

"If you ever need to talk about... whatever this is, I'm around," he said.

"Thanks," I murmured. "Same goes."

He nodded once, then walked off.

Trina poked me in the side. "You're blushing."

"Shut up."

<hr>

By mid-afternoon, the store had filled with tension you could cut with a latte knife. Betsy was all nerves and clipped instructions. Trina was glued to my side like a detective's apprentice. And I was starting to piece together a picture that didn't quite make sense—yet.

The poisoning wasn't random.

The loyalty program wasn't harmless.

The freezer crawlspace was a clue—but to what?

I had a list of flagged Alpha Rewards names. I had Barbara's card. I had an increasing sense that the walls were closing in.

And I had one undeniable truth:

If I didn't solve this soon, someone else was going to get hurt.

Still, despite the chaos, the hidden crawlspace, and Barbara's unsettling message, I wasn't going to lose focus. I looped Charles in quietly, asking him to cross-check a few of the flagged Alpha Rewards names with any internal changes in HR or sudden transfers—anything that might scream 'cover-up.' He didn't ask questions, just gave a small nod and said, 'Give me twenty minutes and a strong macchiato.' Gus had warned me to let it go—for now. "Forget about it," he'd said. So, I nodded, tucked everything away, and pretended to follow orders.

But I didn't forget. I just filed it away in a folder labeled 'future reckoning' in the deepest drawer of my brain—right next to 'awkward crushes,' 'unfinished revenge plots,' and now, apparently, 'subterranean corporate corruption.'

CHAPTER
EIGHTEEN

SUNRISE SUSPICIONS

By 7:00 a.m., the chaos had already begun. Penny was behind the espresso machine wiping down the steam wand when Joe appeared at the register. Just like clockwork. Mumbled his order, half to himself, half toward the pastry case.

"You said... a drip or a latte today?" Penny asked, already knowing he'd change it.

He smirked. "I said hot. Not cold. And not too much milk this time. Unless it's not real milk. Then no milk. You people always mess that up."

Joe never said good morning. Never smiled. Always treated his order like a test Penny was destined to fail.

And yet, there he was. Every day. 7 a.m. sharp.

Sometimes with the meat department Manager—a red-faced, loud-talking man named Glenn—and other times with a stoic, silent produce lead who only ever gave a curt nod.

Together, they were like a morning parade of scrutiny and ego. If they all showed up together, it usually meant Penny's day would be laced with snide remarks and confusing special requests.

Unlike Ted, who was blissfully predictable. Nonfat latte. Every. Single. Time.

"Nonfat," he'd declare. "I'm allergic to everything else. If it touches almond milk, I die."

He said it with the same flat seriousness every morning, even if no one had offered almond milk in the first place.

Then there was Pierre.

Overnight supervisor. Serious as a tax audit. If the coffee wasn't hot and ready when he clocked out, he'd report you faster than you could press the brew button.

"You know the rules," Pierre once said when Penny handed him a drink that was one minute late. "We do things on time, or we don't do them at all."

No one knew what Pierre did overnight, but the man ran the backroom like a ship captain facing a storm.

The combination of Joe, Glenn, the produce posse, Ted, and Pierre all between 6:30 and 8 a.m. was its own kind of espresso-fueled endurance challenge. A test of memory, speed, diplomacy, and the patience of a saint.

Penny passed it all with a cool smile. But behind her calm, she was watching.

Because in that crowd of complaints and caffeine, someone was hiding more than just a bad attitude.

And she was going to find out who.

The morning crew wasn't the only source of chaos. By 6:45 a.m., the delivery driver would roll in—always wearing the same faded hoodie and a baseball cap with an old Lakers logo. His name was Nico. He delivered pastries and dairy products to the store three times a week and made it a point to order four cheese danishes and an extra large iced coffee with half and half every time he stopped by.

But his order wasn't the only reason he showed up.

He had a not-so-subtle crush on McKenzie, one of the newer Baristas at Sunset Star. Young, stylish, with a nose piercing and a constantly evolving collection of pastel hoodies, McKenzie was a part-time employee who juggled classes and coffee with practiced ease. Richie had referred her, mentioning they lived in the same building—"She's cool, reliable, and doesn't judge me for singing in the shower."

McKenzie had a soft laugh, a quick wit, and a not-so-secret vape habit she tried to hide in the backroom. Nico, smitten from day one, asked for her number after a few weeks of lingering conversations by the ice machine.

She gave it to him.

At first, it was harmless. A meme here, a "good morning" there. But when her school schedule changed and she started working fewer morning shifts, Nico didn't take the hint.

He began asking about her constantly.

"Is McKenzie in today?"

"When's she working again?"

"Tell her I brought extra danishes this time."

His texts became more frequent. A little too persistent. And McKenzie, sweet but firm, started ignoring them.

But he kept coming.

And Penny noticed.

She made a note of the way Nico's smile didn't quite reach his eyes. The way he lingered near the pastry case just a little too long. The way he looked disappointed when she handed him his coffee instead of McKenzie.

In a store full of quirks, he didn't stand out at first.

But now?

Now Penny had her eye on him too.

That morning, Richie noticed too. He slid up beside Penny at the espresso machine during a lull and leaned in conspiratorially. "Nico's giving off clingy ex energy," he whispered.

Penny nodded. "He asked me if McKenzie's shifts are 'locked in.' That's not a coffee question."

"I told her to be careful," Richie said, suddenly serious. "He's not just lingering—he's lurking."

Penny made a mental note to check the security footage from the past two weeks. Just to see how long Nico had been hanging around.

THE BRASS BELL ON THE COUNTER GAVE A SINGLE, polite *ding*.

Penny looked up from restocking lids to see a woman standing at the register—composed, calm, and stylish in a no-fuss kind of way. She wore a soft wool coat over a gray sweater, hair pulled into a low twist, with a simple leather crossbody slung over her shoulder. There was nothing flashy about her, and yet she had that unmistakable presence—the kind of woman who walked through a space like she already knew how it worked.

"Med Bomb," the woman said, voice smooth. "Extra honey. Steamed lemonade hot, not lukewarm."

"You got it," Penny replied, grabbing a cup.

The woman pulled out a Sunset Star gift card and placed it gently on the counter. "One of my tenants gave me this. A thank-you, I think. Or maybe a bribe. I didn't ask too many questions."

"You must be doing something right," Penny said with a smile.

"I try," the woman said. "I'm Amira. Property Manager for Mashcole. I handle two buildings just up the street."

"Penny. Barista-slash-newbie."

"I figured. You're still smiling like you mean it."

That got a soft laugh out of Penny as she started pumping honey into the cup. "You know your way around this drink."

"I should," Amira said. "This is the only legal substance keeping me functional during cold season. Tenants don't care if you're sick—they'll still call at midnight because their neighbor's blender is 'possessed.'"

"Yikes."

"Mm. And don't get me started on plumbing. I've seen things, Penny. Things that haunt me."

Penny grinned. "Sounds like you need a frequent flyer card for this place."

"Right? You'd think after thirty-seven Med Bombs someone would name a booth after me."

As Penny steamed the lemonade, Amira leaned in just slightly, eyes scanning the room with an ease that said she noticed *everything*—from the broken pastry case hinge to the couple fighting softly near the sugar station.

"Oh—and while you're adjusting to the regulars," she added, lowering her voice, "keep an eye on Tommy."

"The bagger?"

Amira nodded. "Petite guy, dirty sneakers, always has gum in his mouth. Too quiet, but not in a good way."

Penny paused. "What's his deal?"

"He's got a foot thing," Amira said simply, then took a sip of her tea as Penny blinked. "Tells women they have 'elegant arches,' offers to help them with their bags, and then transitions the conversation into how good he is at pressure points. One of my tenants said he tried to show her reflexology diagrams on his phone while loading her trunk.”

“That’s… next-level creepy.”

“It is,” Amira said, unbothered. “He hasn’t crossed a physical line that I know of, but I’ve made it very clear if he ever tries with me, he’ll be walking home barefoot.”

Penny laughed but felt the edge of truth in Amira’s words.

“Thanks for the heads-up.”

“Of course,” Amira said, standing straighter. “You’ve got that ‘people trust me’ vibe. Which is lovely. But it also attracts weirdos. Protect your energy.”

Penny handed over the finished drink. “Here you go. Piping hot and hopefully medicinal.”

Amira took the cup, wrapped her hands around it like it was gold. “The Med Bomb is the cure for everything except annoying neighbors and busted elevators. But it helps.”

“I’ll have to try one,” Penny said.

“Wait until the throat tickle starts. You’ll remember my voice telling you to order it.”

Penny smiled. “I think I already will.”

“See you around,” Amira said, then added with a knowing look, “You’re going to do fine here. You listen before you speak. That’s rare.”

And with that, she walked out the front doors, calm and steady. No big goodbye, no theatrics. Just someone who knew the neighborhood, the people, and maybe even Penny a little better than a stranger should.

Meanwhile, the rest of the morning parade rolled on. Glenn, the meat Manager, spilled hot sauce on the napkin dispenser and laughed like it was a comedy special. The produce team blocked the path to the café fridge while arguing about cucumber pricing, and Pierre returned to bark about the new thermal carafe not being calibrated to the exact temperature standard.

McKenzie arrived halfway through the madness, eyes bleary but hoodie on point.

"Morning," she mumbled, clocking in with one hand and pulling a vape pen out of her hoodie pocket with the other.

"You know Pierre's gonna write you up if he sees that," Penny warned.

"Pierre's afraid of my pineapple mango cloud," McKenzie said with a smirk, taking a hit and blowing the scent toward the breakroom vent.

The regulars didn't stop. Ted ordered his nonfat latte with his usual doomsday milk allergy warning. Joe complained that his cup felt "too light."

By 7:55 a.m., the air was thick with caffeine, vape clouds, cheese danish crumbs, and passive-aggressive tension.

Penny wiped down the bar with a precision that came from practice—and pressure.

Because beneath the early morning chaos was a steady hum of something deeper. Something colder.

And she wasn't going to miss it.

What she also couldn't miss—no matter how much she wanted to—was Lynn.

Lynn had been a part of the Sunset Star crew longer than most. She wasn't fast, and she certainly wasn't subtle, but she had a way of lingering like the smell of burnt espresso: strong, distinct, and impossible to ignore. Lately though, Lynn had been... off.

She complained more than usual. Muttered to herself while sweeping. Gave customers the death glare for asking about sugar-free syrup. There were rumors floating around that she'd been trying to get transferred—or worse, was about to quit in some dramatic fashion.

"She's been in rare form," Richie said one morning. "Told me yesterday she's going to 'burn her apron and vanish like Houdini.'"

McKenzie chimed in from the milk fridge. "She said she's only staying because she wants to see Trina trip over her own ego first."

Penny didn't know what Lynn's exact breaking point would be—but it felt imminent. The woman carried herself like she was one customer complaint away from pulling the fire alarm and marching out the back door.

If she left, there would be drama. Guaranteed.

And if she stayed? Well... that might be even messier.

Either way, Penny added her to the mental watchlist.

Because in a store like Alfie's, even the exits came with plot twists.

That morning, the vibe was extra combustible. The produce team had spilled a crate of lemons near the café seating, and no one had picked them up. Penny nearly slipped carrying two hot drinks.

"Floor's a death trap," Richie muttered, side-stepping a rogue lemon like a landmine.

Ted complained that his nonfat latte had "too much foam," then added, "It's probably because I said something critical yesterday." He sipped it anyway.

Pierre was unusually quiet, which somehow made it worse. He stood by the door for five minutes, watching, then turned on his heel and disappeared without a word.

"Silent Pierre is the scariest Pierre," McKenzie said under her breath.

Penny nodded, jotting it all down in her head.

And then there was Lynn—moving slowly near the straws, rearranging them with unnecessary aggression.

"The straws don't need alphabetizing," McKenzie teased.

Lynn didn't look up. "Everything should be in order. If the company can't do it, someone has to."

That was when Penny knew—it wasn't a matter of if Lynn was leaving.

It was just a matter of when and how big the explosion would be.

And in that messy, caffeinated storm of personalities and power plays, Penny stood still, centered.

She could feel the shift coming.

And whatever happened next, she'd be ready.

At exactly 8:01 a.m., the first drink complaint of the day rolled in—somehow a minute late and right on time. A regular customer, frazzled and over-accessorized, slammed her iced vanilla latte on the counter.

"This is not what I ordered. I said light ice, not glacier!"

Richie swooped in. "We'll remake it right away."

Behind him, McKenzie snorted softly. "Glacier's the new house pour."

Penny remade the drink without missing a beat, eyes still tracking the morning circus. Joe returned to complain he didn't get a receipt. Glenn spilled a second packet of hot sauce. Ted hovered near the hand sanitizer, muttering about dairy conspiracy theories. Pierre had returned and was silently examining the new milk labels like he was decoding national secrets.

Then Nico popped back in.

Again.

He hadn't even made a delivery this time. Just sauntered over to the counter and ordered another iced coffee.

"McKenzie in today?" he asked, casual but not really.

"She's in the back," Penny replied without looking up. "Busy."

He looked disappointed. His fingers drummed on the counter.

"Tell her I said hi?"

"I will."

She wouldn't.

By the time 8:15 hit, Penny had mentally clocked every face, every tone shift, every passing glance.

And somewhere in the tangle of steaming cups and whispered warnings, the truth was percolating.

She could feel it.

And it was nearly ready to pour.

At 8:17 a.m., the last café table became the battlefield of the moment. Glenn, hot sauce-stained and huffing, slammed his lunchbox down at the same time the produce lead dropped his half-eaten banana. A passive-aggressive standoff ensued.

"We rotate," Glenn growled.

"You had it yesterday," the produce lead snapped.

Neither sat. Both stood in rigid silence, glaring. Eventually, Glenn surrendered, muttering something about "favoritism in fruit."

Two minutes later, Lynn dropped a full tray of cold foam pitchers. They exploded like dairy grenades across the floor.

She stared at the mess like it was a personal betrayal.

"Of course," she whispered, grabbing a rag with fury.

"Hey, no big deal—" McKenzie started.

Lynn cut her off. "No. Big. Deal? Try juggling 200 things while your shift lead watches like a hawk and you're running on one hour of sleep. Try that and tell me what's no big deal."

The kiosk went silent. Even Richie stopped mid-syrup pump.

Penny moved to help, but Lynn waved her off.

"I got it. I always got it."

Behind her, Pierre and Joe were having a hushed conversation near the condiment cart.

"I told you it's getting sloppy," Joe muttered.

Pierre didn't respond, just nodded slightly. His eyes flicked toward Penny's direction, then back.

She looked away quickly, pretending to grab more sleeves.

McKenzie, sliding next to her, whispered under her breath. "You catch that?"

"Every word."

McKenzie leaned in, lowering her voice even further. "I think something weird's going on."

Penny's grip tightened on the cup.

"You're not wrong," she murmured. "And I think we're standing right in the middle of it."

CHAPTER
NINETEEN

CRACKS IN THE SHIFT

Penny was still riding the tension from the morning rush as the store settled into its mid-morning lull. Or what passed for a lull at Rock n' Roll Alfie's—music still blaring through the overhead speakers, a few regulars hunched over scones and lukewarm lattes, and Managers buzzing like caffeinated bees.

She glanced at the floor. Still a few rogue lemon peels near table four. The aftermath of produce's breakfast battlefield. Nobody had bothered to pick them up yet.

Trina appeared beside her like a gossiping shadow.

"You see Lynn? She's been stomping around like she just found out her shift was canceled. Again."

Penny didn't answer. Trina kept talking.

"You ask me, she's milking the drama. Probably wants everyone to beg her to stay. Classic Lynn."

Penny tamped espresso with a little more force than necessary.

At the far corner of the café, she spotted Tommy—the bagger Amira had warned her about, loud and nosy, often seen corralling carts in the parking lot—sitting alone, sipping a coffee he definitely didn't pay for. He was talking to Rebekah, the overnight stocker, their heads close together. Penny couldn't hear what they were saying, but their body language was tight. Controlled. Like people used to hiding in plain sight.

Tommy's voice—naturally loud—slipped through the hum of the café. "You just have to be smarter about it, that's all I'm saying," he muttered, jabbing the lid of his coffee cup like it had wronged him.

Rebekah didn't look up. "I am smart. You're just reckless."

Tommy leaned in closer, still half-shouting. "We've gotten away with worse, and nobody noticed. Nobody cares."

Rebekah's eyes flicked toward the front counter. "Someone cares. You need to stop talking so loud."

Tommy leaned back and gave a low chuckle that didn't reach his eyes. "You worry too much. It's just carts and coffee. Nothing illegal about those."

But something in the way he said it made Penny's skin crawl.

She could see Rebekah's fingers tightening around her paper cup.

They weren't talking about carts or coffee.

And Tommy knew exactly what he was doing.

She took a deep breath and jotted another note into her pocket log:

Tommy + Rebekah — corner table, whispering. Check camera 4.

Then she saw something stranger: Joe standing at the edge of the frozen aisle, watching them.

Not browsing.

Just watching.

And for the first time, Penny realized Joe wasn't just a cranky regular.

He was paying attention too.

Joe wasn't exactly trying to hide it either. His arms were crossed, his jaw tight, and his gaze didn't waver from Tommy and Rebekah. Penny watched his eyes narrow just slightly when Tommy leaned too close. When Rebekah pulled back, Joe shifted his weight, as if bracing for something.

Then he glanced around, caught Penny watching him, and for a split second, their eyes locked.

She didn't flinch. Neither did he.

But something passed between them—unspoken, sharp. A flicker of mutual suspicion, or maybe a warning.

Joe broke the stare first, disappearing down the frozen aisle like nothing happened.

Penny exhaled slowly. If Joe knew something—and it seemed more likely every day—he wasn't just observing. He was monitoring. Possibly protecting something. Or someone.

And that made things even more complicated.

She scribbled again in her log:

Joe — watching Tommy & Rebekah. Intentional. Possibly involved. Or security-adjacent?

Every shift, the web thickened.

And Penny was right in the middle of it.

That's when Ayeda showed up.

It was like watching a sorority president crash a coffee seminar—energy too bright, confidence too loud, a scent trail of designer perfume and polished ambition. Ayeda, the Store Manager of the corporate Sunset Star location on the corner of La Brea and Sunset, strutted into the kiosk like she owned every coffee bean within a five-mile radius.

She wore a full face of makeup, a high ponytail, and a clipboard she didn't actually write on. Her white sneakers sparkled unnaturally in the overhead lights.

"Heyyy Baristas!" she called out in a singsong voice. "Corporate check-in! How's everyone feeling today?"

McKenzie groaned under her breath. Richie vanished behind the espresso machine.

Ayeda's eyes landed on Penny. "You're newish, right? Penny, was it?"

Penny gave a practiced smile. "Yep. Just getting into the groove."

Ayeda leaned on the counter like she was offering friendship bracelets. "You've got a clean vibe. I like it.

You ever think about transferring? We've got room at the La Brea store. Bigger operation, better hours, tons of growth potential."

Penny blinked. "Oh wow, that's... nice to hear. I'll think about it."

She wouldn't. Not for a second.

Ayeda smiled a little too brightly, already turning to evaluate the syrup pumps. "Let me know! We're always looking for energy that pops."

When she left, McKenzie muttered, "If 'pop' means cheerleader in a caffeine cult, she's nailing it."

Penny jotted another note:

Ayeda — Corporate Manager. Entitled. Pushy. Possibly watching more than just latte art.

Later, while restocking napkins behind the bar, Taurus leaned in close.

"Watch your back with Ayeda," he muttered under his breath.

Penny raised an eyebrow. "Yeah?"

Taurus nodded, his tone unusually serious. "She's two-faced. Acts all sparkle and sunshine when corporate's watching, but she'll throw anyone under the bus if it makes her look good. I've seen her do it twice. Once to a lead who trained her."

That explained the clipboard. And the way she kept scanning the kiosk like it was a set she was auditioning for.

"Good to know," Penny said.

"She's all about image," Taurus added, pulling back. "Doesn't mean she's not dangerous."

Another note for the mental files.

Ayeda wasn't just annoying.

She was a threat hiding behind a trademarked smile.

Taurus added one more thing before walking off to wipe down the counter. "I knew her type back when I worked at the corporate Sunset Star locations. That La Brea shop? Pure politics. Ayeda thrives in that world. But this place? The kiosk at Alfie's is a franchise—it's different. Less rules. More chaos. She doesn't really have power here, but she still acts like she does."

That made sense. Ayeda's presence was performative. Flash without substance. But people like that could still cause real damage if you weren't careful.

Penny filed the info away. She had enough enemies inside the store already. She didn't need a corporate-climbing caffeine queen adding to the mix.

And yet, Ayeda lingered.

She circled the café like a peacock in platform sneakers, chatting with customers, nodding at Managers, and taking faux notes on her clipboard. She even tried correcting McKenzie on how she steamed milk, which earned her a full-eye-roll and a sassy, "You wanna clock in and show me?"

Ayeda didn't take the bait. She never did. She just smiled wider.

Trina, of course, flocked to her like a moth to fake glitter.

"Ayeda! You look so fierce today. Is that a new gloss?"

Penny watched it all play out with the same neutral expression she used when cleaning syrup pumps. But inside, she was thinking: if Ayeda really had no power here, why did everyone still treat her like she did?

Maybe that was the secret. Not about having power, but convincing everyone you did.

She added a final line in her notes:

Ayeda — Influence unchecked. Dangerous only if underestimated.

It was moments like these that reminded Penny how much of the store operated on vibes. Not policies. Not systems. Just layers of personality and tension and noise. Every department had its own orbit. The café was the planet of its own people, but gravity still pulled in characters like Ayeda. And Tommy.

She looked around the café. A toddler was trying to drink whipped cream straight from a cup. Lynn was mumbling curses while taping a pastry label that wouldn't stick. Taurus muttered to himself while organizing the tea sachets by country of origin. And McKenzie, wearing an oversized hoodie and mismatched socks, performed a perfect latte pour while vaping out the back door. It was chaos. Beautiful, cracked, caffeine-fueled chaos.

And still, the rhythm carried. The soundtrack of Alfie's wasn't the overhead music—it was the background noise of personalities colliding. Penny had learned to tune in to the dissonance.

That morning, she'd even seen Ted trip over a display stand while lecturing a customer on soy intolerance. The customer laughed. Ted did not.

Everyone at Alfie's was a character with quirks bordering on caricature. But Tommy... Tommy had started veering into something else.

Because horror didn't always come with fangs and fog machines.

Sometimes it came with a clipboard, or a Manager's smirk.

Sometimes it came with a friendly face and a fixation you couldn't unhear.

Just before the end of her shift, Penny caught Tommy lingering near the paper goods aisle, talking animatedly to a young woman juggling two frozen dinners and a 12-pack of soda. He wasn't even bagging or helping—just hovering, too eager, too close, pretending to be helpful while clearly pushing for a longer conversation.

The young woman smiled politely but kept inching away. Tommy didn't seem to register the discomfort—or didn't care. She couldn't hear the words, but the tone—the overly familiar chuckle, the way he leaned in—sent a flicker of discomfort up her spine.

"He does that a lot," McKenzie muttered beside her, eyes narrowing as she restocked the cold brew bar.

"What?" Penny asked, even though she already knew.

"That thing where he offers to walk people to their cars. Especially women. He acts like he's just being nice, but it always feels... off."

Richie slid in behind them with a stack of clean cups. "He once offered to help a lady 'unload her groceries and her stress.' Like, who says that?"

McKenzie rolled her eyes. "She was so creeped out, she left her basket behind."

Penny's jaw clenched. That tracked. And it explained the lingering energy she kept picking up from him. Friendly on the surface. Prying underneath.

She made a mental note to check the exterior camera feeds around cart return.

That's when Tommy reappeared, this time lingering near the counter without a drink in hand. He leaned in a little too close.

"You ever wear those flip flops again?" he asked, voice low but grinning like it was a compliment. "Saw you once off-shift, in the parking lot. Nice toes. Real clean. That's rare."

Penny froze.

She didn't respond immediately. She'd learned to mask shock with neutral professionalism, the same way she masked suspicion.

Tommy chuckled, seemingly unbothered by the silence. "Don't worry, I'm harmless. Just appreciate nice feet. Always have. Ask my wife—she thinks I'm just being helpful. I even offer foot massages. You know, as a gesture."

He winked.

Penny forced a tight smile and excused herself to grab more straws, heart thudding as she turned.

There it was. The thing she couldn't unhear. The kind of red flag you circled three times in your notebook. He didn't even hide it.

And she was willing to bet this wasn't the first time.

She added one final note before clocking out:

Tommy — Foot fixation. Inappropriate comments. Following customers to cars. HIGH PRIORITY.

She snapped the notebook shut.

This shift might have ended, but Tommy's story was just beginning.

CHAPTER
TWENTY

NOT JUST CARTS AND COFFEE

Penny didn't sleep much that night. The echo of Tommy's voice haunted her long after she'd scrubbed the smell of espresso from her hands.

"Nice toes. Real clean. That's rare."

It wasn't just gross—it was targeted. Calculated. And too casual to be the first time he'd said something like that. What disturbed her more was the way he said it—as if he genuinely thought he was giving a compliment. As if he thought she should be flattered.

She ran the conversation on loop while staring at the ceiling of her studio apartment. Tommy's foot fetish wasn't the issue on its own—it was how emboldened he'd become. How he walked the store like it was his own personal hunting ground.

And now, she had to decide how to move forward. She could file an anonymous report, but that might trigger HR without results. She could tell Amira, but Amira already had one eye on Tommy for unpaid rent. She could talk to Lupe—but Lupe was inconsistent at best, and suspicious in her own right.

No. She needed more.

Documentation. Witnesses. Patterns.

If Tommy was doing this to her, and had done it to others, someone else had to know.

She flipped open her notebook and underlined three names:

McKenzie — witnessed behavior. May have more stories.

Richie — overheard things. Trustworthy.

Nora — sees everything. Likely has her own intel.

This wasn't about one creepy comment.

It was about uncovering a pattern—and stopping it before it got worse.

Penny took a deep breath, closed her notebook, and checked the schedule for her next shift.

She'd be ready.

Tommy wasn't just a bagger.

He was a problem.

And Penny had just made him her new priority.

But as she stared out the window of her apartment, the city humming below, Penny—Raven—couldn't help but reflect on what she'd become.

Being undercover had its costs. Her real name had all but vanished from her lips. Raven McCool felt like a memory, a whisper she only heard in the quiet hours of early morning. Everything else was Penny now—the girl with the apron, the routine, the notebook.

And despite the chaos of the store and the swarm of characters she interacted with, she'd never felt more alone. The weight of secrecy, of being always slightly apart from everyone around her, was starting to wear her thin.

She'd uncovered so much already. Micro-crimes. Creeps. Red flags. But was she veering off track? Losing sight of the bigger picture?

Donny's poisoning wasn't why she was there. But the case felt buried under layers of café politics and side scandals. Was someone counting on that?

She thought about Gus, her direct supervisor. He always played it straight, but something about his overly neat clipboard and vague answers made her wonder: Could he be trusted? Did he know more about Donny's death than he let on?

Maybe it was time to check in with Sergeant Butler. Butler always had a soft spot for Raven. She was sharp, old-school LAPD, and always gave just enough rope for Raven to do her job while keeping a hand on the other end.

And then there were the beat cops—Annie Sterling and Sonia Delgado—assigned to patrol Sunset Blvd.

Annie, composed and cerebral, a former rowing champion with a near-Navy trajectory before pivoting to the LAPD. Sonia, physical and impulsive, with a sharp wit and a low tolerance for nonsense. Both attractive, mid-20s, and always arriving in perfect sync like something out of a buddy cop show.

Annie had history with Raven. Something unspoken. A friendship? A rivalry? Penny wasn't sure anymore—she just knew that whenever Annie looked at her, it was like she saw more than she was supposed to.

Penny closed her notebook and leaned back.

Too many stories were unfolding at once.

It was time to focus.

And maybe... time to make a call.

The next morning, Penny woke up with a singular focus: gather evidence, stay sharp, and start pulling threads without getting pulled under.

Her shift started at 9 a.m., and by 8:45, she was already behind the bar at Sunset Star, reloading cup lids and trying not to appear like she was watching every corner of the store. But she was. Every face. Every pause. Every glance.

McKenzie showed up ten minutes late, hoodie half-zipped and vape in hand.

"Rough night?" Penny asked casually.

"You don't even know," McKenzie muttered, then lowered her voice. "Nico tried to follow me again after my class. He texted 'Just wanted to make sure you got home okay.'"

Penny felt her jaw tense. "You okay?"

"Yeah. I blocked him. But he's weird. Too quiet all of a sudden."

One more name for the log.

While McKenzie restocked syrups, Penny asked lightly, "Tommy ever say anything creepy to you?"

McKenzie blinked. "Only like every other shift. Last week he asked if I wanted to model toe rings. Said I had 'gemstone potential.'"

There it was.

"Think you'd write a statement?" Penny asked.

McKenzie hesitated, then nodded. "If you're building something, yeah. I'll back it up."

They didn't say more.

At 10:12, Betsy strutted into the café with Joe two steps behind her. She was wearing her usual platform sandals and a zip-up hoodie embroidered with "Assistant to the Manager" in rhinestones.

"I really think it's time Trina stepped up," she said loudly, looking around as if half the store were supposed to agree. "She's already doing the work."

Joe nodded, distracted. He looked sleep-deprived, chewing the inside of his cheek like he was rehearsing something.

Penny took note.

Trina had power aspirations. Betsy was giving her a platform. That combo was more volatile than a broken steam wand.

And Gus? Nowhere in sight.

She made a mental note to reach out to Sergeant Butler before the day was done.

Because things were accelerating—and she'd need someone watching her back.

At 10:37, Gus finally appeared. Clipboard in hand, crisp as always, with the kind of energy that suggested he'd been up since dawn doing pushups and perfectly aligning his sneakers. Penny intercepted him near the backroom.

"Hey, Gus," she said, keeping her tone casual. "Heard anything new on the Donny situation?"

He blinked. Too long. Then shrugged. "Still being looked into. Corporate's handling it now."

"You sure?"

Gus didn't meet her eyes. "It's above my pay grade."

He turned before she could follow up.

It wasn't nothing. That pause. That redirect.

It meant something.

She clocked it in her mental log.

Just as she stepped back toward the kiosk, the front doors opened and in walked Annie and Sonia, the Sunset Blvd beat cops.

Annie was cool and unreadable as ever, her uniform crisp and posture impeccable. Sonia, a step behind, was chewing gum and scanning the pastry case like she hadn't eaten since Tuesday.

"Caffeine and protein," Sonia announced, pointing at a turkey cheddar sandwich. "In that order."

Annie smirked. "You going to arrest the sandwich or just interrogate it?"

Sonia winked. "Depends on if it answers my questions."

Penny gave them a nod, and Annie returned it with a flicker of something warmer—recognition, maybe. Or memory.

"Hey, Penny," Annie said, like it meant something more.

It did. But not here. Not now.

They placed their orders, chatted with McKenzie, and drifted toward the lobby.

Penny watched them go, heart ticking up a beat.

More players. More clues.

More pressure to connect the dots before the next shoe dropped.

Later that night, back in her apartment, Penny collapsed on her couch without even turning on the lights. Her limbs ached, her mind spun, and for the first time in weeks, she allowed herself to admit something: she wanted a day off. Just one day to be Raven again. No apron, no kiosk drama, no notebook.

She picked up her phone and stared at the last message she'd sent Matt.

Hey, hope your shift went okay. Want to grab coffee on our day off?

No reply.

It had been two days.

She bit her lip, debating whether to send another message. Was he ghosting her? Or was this just Alfie's shift chaos making it impossible to connect?

Ted had also stopped crossing paths with her. At first she thought it was just bad timing, but now she'd seen the schedule—and it had clearly been changed. Ted had asked to be switched. So had Matt. It was subtle, but deliberate. They no longer had overlapping shifts. Not even once.

It was one thing to be ghosted by a guy. It was another to have your entire rhythm recalibrated like you were being avoided.

She didn't know what had shifted between her and Matt. They'd shared a moment. Several, actually. There was something there. So why was he backing away now? Was it Trina? The investigation? Had she misread everything?

The question sat heavy on her chest.

Coincidence? Or coordinated silence?

Everything felt just out of reach—every connection, every clue.

She tossed her phone onto the couch cushion beside her.

What was she even doing this for? The case? The mission? Or the feeling that she still mattered, still had control?

The silence in the room only answered her with more questions.

She needed backup.

She needed clarity.

She needed answers.

And she was starting to realize—she might need them sooner than she thought.

The silence in her apartment wasn't peaceful. It was haunting. The kind of silence that hummed with unfinished thoughts and unspoken fears. Penny walked to the tiny kitchenette and poured a glass of water just to break the stillness.

Her eyes landed on the evidence wall she'd started behind her closet door—a messy grid of sticky notes, scribbled names, timelines, receipts. Every time she thought she was making progress, new layers emerged. New distractions. New dangers.

She stared at Tommy's name. Circled in red.

Beside it: Trina, Betsy, Gus, Ayeda, Joe.

A rogue's gallery.

But what if none of them were the core? What if she was spending her energy chasing down all these side stories while the real story—the real danger—was still in the shadows?

Her phone buzzed. She lunged for it.

But it wasn't Matt.

It was a shift reminder.

Sunset Star. Tomorrow. 7 a.m.

Penny let out a dry laugh. She was chasing criminals, writing reports, building cases—and she still had to be up early enough to mop syrup off the floor.

She grabbed her notebook one last time that night and added one more line beneath Tommy's name:

Tomorrow: follow the patterns. Watch who protects him. Watch who looks the other way.

She tucked it back under her pillow.

Sleep wouldn't come easy. But she'd be ready for whatever came next.

CHAPTER
TWENTY-ONE

PATTERNS EMERGE

Penny woke up before her alarm. Again.

Her body was running on instinct now. Coffee shop hours. Criminal investigation hours. Sleepless worry hours. They all blurred together until she couldn't remember what it felt like to truly rest.

She slid out of bed, dressed quickly, and walked out the door before the sun had even warmed the sidewalk. The city was quiet in that strange Hollywood way—still humming but not yet roaring. Her shoes clicked softly on the pavement as she approached Alfie's.

Today wasn't about reaction.

Today was about watching.

And documenting.

By 6:52 a.m., she was behind the kiosk counter, logging into the register while the espresso machine hissed to life. McKenzie shuffled in with two paper bags and a giant iced matcha.

"Breakfast and caffeine," she said, handing one of the bags over. "We're gonna need it."

"Thanks," Penny said. "You heard from Richie yet?"

"He's in at seven. Said he saw something weird on camera 2 last night—he's pulling the footage."

Perfect.

Penny had already made a mental checklist:

Check in with Nora

Watch Tommy's movements

Observe interactions between Betsy, Joe, and Trina

Confront Gus if he dodges again.

The door chimed. First customers.

Among them was Tommy, carrying a small pastry box he clearly wasn't assigned to deliver. He was too cheerful for the hour, practically bouncing as he approached the counter.

"Morning, ladies," he beamed. "Just helping out this morning—figured I'd drop this off before grabbing carts."

McKenzie side-eyed him. "You working bakery now?"

"Nah," he shrugged. "Just being nice."

Penny met his gaze, smile tight. "You always this generous, or just on Fridays?"

Tommy chuckled but didn't answer.

He was already on her list.

And now, the patterns were starting to show.

But for once, there was something else buzzing behind the counter besides suspicion.

That morning, the Sunset Star team was scheduled to try the new lineup of seasonal drinks and pastries. A cheerful flyer had been taped to the breakroom door the night before:

NEW MENU SAMPLING – For Baristas Only! Try the Banana Bread Latte, Mint Irish Iced Coffee, Pink Lotus Latte + Pumpkin Roll, Raspberry Pastry Braids, Peach Thyme Mini Galettes & Chocolate Babka!

The excitement was unusual for the team, but real. Even McKenzie perked up when she saw the tray being wheeled out.

"Finally," she said, grabbing a babka slice. "Something soft and sweet in this hellscape."

Richie, who had just arrived, added, "If the Mint Irish tastes like mouthwash, I'm suing."

Penny watched them with a smile, letting herself enjoy the moment. Even Nora joined in, taking a dramatic bite of the galette and moaning like it was a Michelin-star tasting.

"Betsy, of course, was the first to bring up the contest. She floated into the kiosk mid-sampling, latte in hand, and her tone full of sugary leadership energy. "You know what this means, right? Contest time! The Bahamas drink competition!"

McKenzie groaned quietly. "Here we go."

"I think Trina should enter," Betsy said, beaming. "She's so creative—she's got that pumpkin spice mind. It's her favorite, after all."

Richie raised an eyebrow. "She thinks putting cinnamon on everything counts as innovation."

"And Lynn? She's got the skills," Betsy continued, ignoring him. "Real flavor knowledge. Taurus is fast and accurate, but he doesn't exactly scream 'Bahamas.'"

Then her eyes landed on Penny.

"What about you? You're new, but sometimes new blood surprises people."

Penny gave a polite smile. "I don't know if that's my thing."

Nora, from the back, chimed in while chewing a chunk of babka. "Don't sell yourself short. You got instincts. You blend like someone who sees stories in flavor."

Penny laughed nervously, brushing it off. "I think I'll leave that to the pros."

But inside, the idea lingered—like the aftertaste of the Pink Lotus Latte.

Still, she knew the truth.

She couldn't enter. Not without drawing too much attention. Not with what she was hiding.

Even if—just for a moment—she wanted to.

But the lightness of the morning didn't last long. As the last pastry crumb was swept off the counter and the team settled into the first wave of caffeine-hungry customers, Penny refocused. Her checklist came back into sharp relief.

Tommy had dropped off the pastry box, but hadn't returned to carts. Instead, he lingered again—talking to a customer near the frozen aisle, a woman alone, pushing a half-empty cart. Penny's stomach tightened. She couldn't hear the words, but the posture, the over-eager gesturing, the way he stepped just a bit too close—it all painted the same picture.

She tapped McKenzie on the shoulder. "You see him?"

McKenzie followed her gaze and immediately frowned. "Again? He's not even on break."

"Grab the time. I'll talk to Nora."

Nora was sweeping near the dairy case. When Penny approached and asked if she'd seen anything, she nodded solemnly. "Tommy talk too much. Always same. Too nice. Fake nice. I see this before."

"You think he's bothering customers?"

"I think he follow. He wait outside sometimes. I don't like."

Penny jotted it down.

She needed more than just suspicion. She needed enough to build a case—not just to protect herself, but to protect every woman walking into the store thinking they were just there for groceries.

She looked across the store to where Tommy was now laughing with the woman by the almond milk.

It was time to get serious.

No more side trails. No more letting him slip through.

The patterns weren't just emerging—they were becoming undeniable.

CHAPTER
TWENTY-TWO

A KISS BEFORE THE REVEAL

Penny didn't expect to see Matt again—at least, not that morning. Not when her focus was so tight on Tommy, not when her energy was still wrapped in suspicion and surveillance.

But there he was.

Walking in just before her first break, the same confident stride, the same slightly lopsided smile that had thrown her off the first time they met. He wore his security uniform like it belonged to someone on the set of an action series—not a grocery store.

Their eyes met.

He gave her a cautious wave. She nodded back.

"Hey," he said, sliding up to the kiosk during a lull.

"Didn't think I'd see you here," Penny replied, watching him carefully.

"Schedule switch. Got pulled in for morning coverage."

There was a pause—uncomfortable, then softening.

"Want to grab dinner tonight?" Matt asked. "I was thinking Santa Monica. Low key. Good food. Better air."

Penny blinked. Part of her wanted to interrogate him—why the cold shoulder, why the avoidance—but instead she said, "Yeah. That sounds... good."

The shift before dinner had been brutal. Between dealing with a broken syrup pump, a health inspection surprise visit, and Betsy micromanaging every drink order that passed through the kiosk, Penny was running on fumes. She spent most of the day dodging Trina's smug glances and fielding Lynn's slow-burn sarcasm.

By the time she clocked out, her feet ached, and her ponytail felt like a vice tightening around her scalp. She got home, kicked off her shoes, and collapsed for a twenty-minute nap that stretched into forty-five. When she woke up, it was panic.

She rushed to the bathroom, splashed cold water on her face, and stared at herself in the mirror. Her reflection didn't help.

What would Penny wear? What would Raven wear?

Was she Penny tonight? Or was she Raven?

She tore through her closet, trying on three different outfits. One felt too serious. Another too casual. The third—jeans and a soft cream blouse—was a compromise. She didn't want to look like she was trying too hard. But she wanted to feel... something.

Nervous, full of anticipation, she checked her phone twice before Matt even arrived.

She hadn't been on a date since her divorce from Josh. And even if this was just a brief flicker of normalcy, she didn't want to mess it up.

Matt picked her up outside her apartment building. His own car was in the shop, so he'd borrowed his brother's—an older model sedan that smelled faintly of pine air freshener and gym socks.

As Raven stepped out of the lobby, she spotted the car idling at the curb. She hesitated for half a second—just enough time for Anselmo, the building's maintenance guy, to catch her eye as he stepped out of the side entrance with a toolbag in hand. He lived in the building with his wife and teenage kids and always greeted Raven with a polite nod or a knowing smile.

Tonight, he smiled, but his eyes narrowed slightly as he glanced at Matt's car.

"Big plans?" he asked casually.

"Just dinner," Penny said, offering a soft smile.

Anselmo gave her a thumbs-up, though he lingered at the curb for a second longer than necessary. Concern flickered across his face before he disappeared back into the building.

Matt leaned over from the driver's seat and opened the door. "Hey," he said, that same crooked smile pulling at the corner of his mouth. "Hope you're hungry."

Penny smiled despite herself. She slid into the passenger seat and buckled in. As they pulled into traffic, she tried to keep the nerves at bay. But Matt was coming off as... too smooth. Too practiced. Every compliment, every smile—it all landed just a little too perfectly. It wasn't that she didn't believe him, it was that it felt scripted. Like he was reading from a date-night manual.

Was this who he really was? Or just the version he brought out when he wanted something?

She reminded herself not to spiral. But her thoughts were stacking, louder than the soft playlist Matt had queued up on the car stereo.

She hadn't been on a date since Josh. Not a real one. Not one where she had to care what she wore, or whether someone was looking at her like she was more than background noise. And now here she was, a swirl of identities, trying to figure out if she was Penny—the Barista with the vague smile—or Raven, the woman chasing criminals and buried truths.

The truth was, she didn't know how to be either right now.

She felt the walls closing in, the pressure of being seen when all she wanted was to blend in. To stay unnoticed. But there was no hiding from Matt's gaze.

And worse? Part of her didn't want to.

But that realization—letting herself want something, someone—shook her more than she expected. She'd spent so long keeping everything in its compartment, locking away her hopes and instincts, that the thought of slipping—of caring—terrified her.

Matt was charming. He was easy. Maybe too easy. And she didn't know what scared her more: that he could be genuine, or that he could be hiding something too. Everyone hid something in Hollywood.

She shifted in her seat, crossing her legs and uncrossing them again. Her heart wasn't racing, but it wasn't calm either. She hated that she felt this exposed—and not from what he said, but how little he had to say to make her feel seen.

And it was the seeing that scared her.

She was so used to being invisible, to blending into the backdrop of cafes, grocery aisles, and surveillance cameras. Being seen meant being known. And Penny wasn't sure if Raven was ready for that.

Was this vulnerability? Or just loneliness, wearing a nicer outfit?

She wished she could slow it all down—her heart, the layers of doubt, the weight of feeling something again. The swirl of uncertainty she'd buried since her divorce now surfaced in full force. She hadn't let anyone in since Josh. And even then, toward the end, it hadn't been real. Josh never asked questions she didn't want to answer. He hadn't noticed when she stopped showing up emotionally.

Matt noticed everything. And it scared the hell out of her.

Every part of this night felt like it existed in a parallel timeline, one where she wasn't undercover, one where she didn't wake up every morning calculating moves and motives. She longed to fall into that version of herself, the one who wasn't afraid to be seen, who could wear a simple cream blouse and laugh about awkward first dates without wondering what it might cost her later.

But Raven was still in the room, still watching from the inside, tapping her foot, reminding her this wasn't safe. That real emotions weren't in the job description. That letting her guard down—even a little—could be the kind of distraction that got people hurt. On the ride over, the silence between them wasn't uncomfortable—it was charged. Penny stared out the window, half-lost in thought, half-watching Matt's reflection in the windshield.

She hadn't brought up the unanswered text. She wasn't sure if he'd even remembered it. But after days of radio silence, his sudden invitation for dinner had caught her off guard. And yet, she'd said yes. Because even if this was just a casual fling, even if she was a ghost in someone else's story, part of her wanted to trust him.

He parked just a block from the ocean. The restaurant was charming, coastal without being kitschy, the kind of place you find in a travel guide but still feels local. Matt held the door open, smiling like he wanted her to know he noticed everything about her—even the hesitation.

Inside, they were led to a quiet corner table near the window. Soft candlelight flickered against their menus. Penny ordered grilled shrimp with lemon risotto. Matt got blackened fish tacos and an extra side of chips he never touched.

They ate slowly, talked about nothing important—books, bad coffee habits, their shared annoyance with Betsy. Penny forgot, just for a second, that she was someone else.

After dinner, they strolled along the shoreline, shoes in hand, the Pacific lapping quietly at their ankles. The moonlight cast long shadows, and the breeze softened everything.

When they stopped, it was without planning.

Matt turned to her.

"You're kind of hard to read," he said.

Penny smiled. "That's by design."

"Yeah. I figured."

He leaned in. She didn't step back.

Their kiss was quiet, slow, and certain—like both of them needed to stop pretending they didn't want it.

The moon shimmered above them.

And for once, Penny let herself feel something that wasn't work, wasn't worry, wasn't undercover.

Just... her.

They stayed on the beach longer than they meant to, talking about everything and nothing. Matt told stories from his old shifts on the Eastside, the wild characters he'd encountered during graveyard coverage. Penny—

careful, still calculating—offered only half-truths, shaping stories that kept her cover intact while giving just enough vulnerability to let the air between them soften.

"So what's your real escape plan?" Matt asked, tossing a small rock into the waves. "If you weren't working retail, what would you be doing?"

Penny hesitated. "Something that matters. But still lets me sleep at night."

Matt nodded like he understood. "You've got that vibe. Like there's more going on. Not in a bad way. Just... more."

She smiled, heart fluttering at how close he was to the truth.

They ended the night walking barefoot back to the car. His hand brushed hers once. Then again. And finally, they held hands like it was the most natural thing in the world.

At the car, he opened her door.

"Make sure you fasten your seatbelt," he said.

"Only if you promise to answer your phone."

He laughed, leaning down to kiss her one more time. "Deal."

As she watched the lights of the coastline blur behind her in the sideview mirror, Penny let herself feel full.

She knew tomorrow would drag her back into the fray—Tommy, Betsy, the case—but for tonight, she had peace.

Still, as the quiet hum of the car engine filled the silence on the drive home, doubt began to creep in at the edges. Could she really keep compartmentalizing like this? Letting one part of her fall into something soft and warm while the other stayed hard, alert, and braced for betrayal?

She didn't know.

All she knew was that in Matt's presence, she felt the strain of her dual life more intensely. The weight of every half-truth. The ache of wanting more than she was allowed to take.

She rested her head lightly against the window, watching the blur of passing lights, and for a brief second, let the emotions flood her—hope, fear, desire, guilt. All tangled. All real.

When the car finally slowed in front of her building, she sat still for a second longer.

"You okay?" Matt asked gently.

She nodded. "Yeah. Just tired."

But the truth was more complicated.

She wasn't just tired. She was unraveling—thread by delicate thread.

And that was more than she'd had in weeks.

CHAPTER TWENTY-THREE

RISING HEAT

The next morning, the store felt different.

It wasn't just the usual post-weekend inventory scramble or the grumbling of under-caffeinated coworkers—it was something in the air. Like the city itself was breathing heavier.

Penny stepped inside Rock n' Roll Alfie's just after 6:50 a.m., the sun still stretching its way across Sunset Boulevard. She didn't need a memo to know things were escalating. There had been a break-in at a neighboring pharmacy overnight. Rumors were swirling that a crew—young, reckless, territorial—had started claiming corners nearby.

And Alfie's? It sat on the edge of it all, open twenty-four hours, full of cash registers and routine.

She passed Sonia and Annie by the entrance. The officers looked alert. More alert than usual.

"Extra eyes on deck?" Penny asked.

"Just until things cool off," Sonia said, tapping the rim of her coffee cup. "A tagging crew hit two blocks over. Rival stuff."

Annie didn't say much—just nodded in that way that told Penny they both knew the problem was bigger than a few kids with spray paint.

Inside, Nora was already mopping near the bakery, humming to herself but glancing out the front window every few seconds.

"Too much noise outside," she murmured as Penny passed. "Bad noise. I feel it."

Penny did too.

And she wasn't the only one. Matt had returned to morning duty again, walking in through the side entrance with a fresh walkie clipped to his belt and his sleeves pushed up. He scanned the store as if reading invisible threads.

Their eyes met briefly, something unspoken passing between them—an echo of last night's warmth dulled by today's sharp reality.

Business as usual had left the building.

And Penny knew: this shift was going to change something.

It wasn't long before the gossip started to drift in like steam from a fresh brew. Lynn, stacking pastry bags at the counter, whispered to Taurus that a corner store on Fairfax had been held up the night before. No one hurt, but the suspects were young—and bold. Not even masked.

"They're just walking in like it's theirs," Lynn muttered, barely making eye contact. "Like they don't care anymore."

Taurus nodded grimly. "They don't. That's the scary part. They want you to see their faces. That's the message."

In produce, Jorge was unusually terse, snapping at a newbie for misplacing price signs. "Keep your head down and your eyes open," he warned, his voice low but firm. "Ain't the week to get sloppy."

Even the customers seemed different—more distracted, more watchful. A woman with a stroller asked Matt to walk her to her car, citing "too many guys hanging around the lot."

Matt didn't hesitate.

Penny watched him from behind the espresso machine, her hands on autopilot as she steamed milk. He moved like someone ready to react. Not just a shift supervisor—something more. She could tell the walkie on his belt wasn't just for show today.

Trina, meanwhile, had stationed herself in front of the service deli, talking in loud tones about how "certain people" had better not bring drama into her store. Betsy, unsurprisingly, backed her up with enthusiastic nods, casting side glances toward the doors every few minutes.

Something was coming.

The heat wasn't just in the weather.

The neighborhood was shifting. And Penny could feel the whole store bracing for impact.

By mid-morning, a second police cruiser had arrived, parking just outside the side entrance. This time, a pair of plainclothes officers stepped inside, chatting briefly with Annie and Sonia before doing a slow loop through the aisles.

Penny noticed customers pausing more often, glancing over their shoulders, whispering near the refrigerated section. It wasn't panic—but it was close. It was anticipation. The kind that lived in people's throats.

Even Richie was quieter than usual, his typical banter dulled by what he called the "vibe shift." "It's like something's going to break," he said, refilling the pastry display. "But no one knows where the crack's gonna start."

McKenzie, ever observant, came back from her break chewing her bottom lip. "There were three guys parked across the street when I stepped out. No shopping bags. Just staring at the store. Not from around here."

Penny scribbled a note in her pocket notebook, folding it quickly and tucking it away.

She clocked Tommy entering through the main doors, laughing a little too loudly as he tossed a roll of paper towels into his cart. Watching. Always watching.

She couldn't afford to lose focus.

Everything was simmering.

And something—someone—was going to boil over soon.

Just after noon, Penny found it.

The cryptic note was tucked inside the pastry delivery log clipboard—a place only employees usually touched. Folded twice, the edges slightly sticky from powdered sugar.

It wasn't signed.

She opened it under the counter, shielding it from the security camera line of sight.

You're asking the wrong questions. Look where the deliveries go after dark. - A friend

Her pulse kicked up.

The handwriting was sharp, deliberate. Not printed. Someone trying not to be recognized—but not rushed either.

She scanned the floor. Everyone looked busy. But someone had watched her long enough to know where she looked for clues—and how to plant one without getting caught.

She slid the note into her apron pocket and turned back to the espresso machine, steam hissing.

The warning was clear.

And now she had a new thread to pull.

Night deliveries.

Where they went—and what they might be hiding.

Her thoughts spiraled as she tamped espresso for a cappuccino order. Someone inside the store was feeding her information—but how much could she trust it?

Was it truly a warning... or a misdirection? And who was the note from? Richie? Nora? Even Taurus?

Her mind bounced between possibilities. She thought of Trina—always lingering near the bakery, always nosing into things she claimed to hate. Or was it someone quieter? Someone who knew how to move through the back aisles unseen?

She glanced up just in time to catch Matt walking through the rear stockroom doors with a clipboard in one hand, walkie in the other. He looked focused. Alert.

Was he aware of the deliveries? Had he noticed anything off during his overnight shifts?

Penny's gut twisted. She needed to talk to someone, but couldn't afford another misstep. Everyone seemed to be playing some version of the truth—but only a few were playing the same game she was.

She tucked the note deeper into her apron, the paper warming against her skin.

She would follow the trail.

Tonight, she'd find a way to stay late. Watch. Listen. Confirm.

If someone was using Alfie's for something more than groceries... she was going to see it with her own eyes.

But just when her mind should've been focused on the note and the growing danger inside the store, she felt it again—him.

Matt had just walked past her, brushing too close as he reached for the supply cabinet, and the heat between them surged. It was the second time that shift. The air crackled like static. Like they were magnets caught in someone else's storm.

He said nothing. Just gave her a quick glance, one brow raised—like he could read her mind. Like he wanted to.

She tried to concentrate on stacking cups, but her hands betrayed her. She reached too fast, knocked over a lid. He was already there, catching it midair, their hands grazing. They both paused. Looked at each other. Held the moment too long.

Matt leaned in, voice low, rough around the edges. "You're staying late tonight, right?"

Penny nodded.

"Break room. Back hallway. Twenty minutes."

She didn't answer, but he was already gone.

And her heart was racing for reasons that had nothing to do with crime.

Twenty minutes later, she slipped into the break room just as Matt was locking the back door. He slid a chair beneath the knob. No one was walking in.

They didn't speak. They didn't need to.

The room was dim, the overhead light buzzing. Penny was still in her apron. Matt moved with certainty, backing her toward the small table in the corner, pulling her close like she was the only steady thing in the storm.

He kissed her like he meant it. Like he'd been holding back all day.

And she kissed him back like she was tired of pretending she hadn't noticed.

Her hands found his shoulders, his waist, tugging him in as if she could anchor herself there. Matt's hands moved to her hips, steady and confident, pulling her flush against him. Every motion felt electric—like the tension that had been building between them for weeks was finally being lit like a fuse.

They fumbled toward the table, laughing breathlessly between kisses. Matt cleared it with one hand, cups and an unopened box of napkins clattering to the floor. He lifted her onto the edge, her apron bunched at her waist, his belt already unfastened.

"Still want this?" he asked, voice hoarse against her ear.

Penny pulled him closer in answer.

The kiss deepened. Slow and hungry. Their movements grew less careful. Hands explored like they were mapping something sacred. Her back hit the cold edge of the break room mirror as Matt turned them toward the counter, never breaking contact.

She gasped when his hand tangled in her hair, when he kissed along her neck, his stubble scraping her skin in the best way. Every breath came harder now. Everything about this moment was reckless, dangerous, and completely consuming.

And yet—it felt like the safest place she'd been in weeks.

Matt's mouth found hers again, slower this time, deliberate—like he wanted to memorize every breath between them. She could feel the heat of his hands at her waist, grounding her even as the rest of her body buzzed with sensation. He moved her gently to the counter, pressing her back against the cool surface as her fingers curled around the back of his neck.

Her apron strings came loose, and she laughed softly against his mouth, the sound catching in her throat when he slipped his hand beneath the hem of her shirt. Her heart was pounding. So was his.

They moved together like they'd done this before in another life, like they'd been waiting for the right moment—and this one, despite everything, refused to wait.

He whispered her name once—Penny—like it was a promise. And when she looked into his eyes, she saw something raw there. Not just desire, but need. Not just passion, but connection.

Everything around them faded—the buzzing light, the chill of the storage air, even the sounds from the store floor beyond the break room door. All that existed was this moment, this breath, this fire.

When it was over, they didn't rush to move. He leaned his forehead against hers, both of them still catching their breath, hearts thudding in sync.

No words. Just the understanding that something between them had shifted—irrevocably.

And for now, neither of them was ready to let go.

But as they began to straighten their clothes and re-tie apron strings, reality seeped back in. The buzzing fluorescent light no longer hummed like a backdrop to intimacy—it buzzed like a reminder. Of where they were. Who they were.

Penny looked at Matt. "This changes things."

He nodded, brushing a lock of hair behind her ear. "It does. But not in a bad way."

Penny gave him a look, equal parts grateful and guarded. She wanted to believe him. But she also knew things were about to get messier.

As she opened the break room door, the hallway beyond felt brighter, busier. Too loud.

And just as they stepped back into the chaos of the store, Taurus appeared by the back storage racks, mid-conversation with Richie.

"You hear about the guy who showed up during the last delivery?" Taurus was saying. "Didn't sign the manifest. Looked nervous."

Penny froze.

Richie noticed. "You okay, Penny?"

She nodded. "Yeah. Just tired."

But inside, her thoughts were racing.

The note. The warning. The deliveries after dark.

Who was this mystery man?

Matt glanced sideways at her, concern flickering briefly in his expression before they both stepped back into their separate routines.

The heat between them was real. But so was the danger rising just beyond the reach of their stolen moment.

By late afternoon, the store was still tense—quiet in the way a storm cell is just before it breaks. Security lingered at the entrances longer. Sonia had returned for another walk-through. Even Jorge, normally immune to stress, was seen double-checking the back stock doors.

Penny kept herself moving, pretending not to feel the shift—but she did. And when she passed the receiving area near the back loading docks, she noticed a new face—a man in his sixties, wiry, wearing a maintenance vest that didn't quite match the standard Alfie's issue. He stood near the open bay, clipboard in hand, chatting with one of the assistant stockers.

He didn't look like a delivery driver.

And he wasn't the one Penny had seen before.

She quickly noted the time, made a mental mark of his shoes—scuffed leather, not steel-toed—and the way he kept one hand deep in his pocket. He smiled, but not at anyone in particular.

Penny circled back to Taurus when she saw him near the cleaning supply aisle. "That guy from earlier—at the dock—he's not one of ours, is he?"

Taurus shook his head. "I don't know who he is. I just know he's been around twice this week. Doesn't touch a cart. Doesn't lift a box. Always gone before anyone questions it."

Her skin prickled.

The message in the note suddenly felt more urgent.

Night deliveries. And faces no one could place.

She had to move fast—before someone else did.

That night, Penny stayed late under the pretense of helping McKenzie reorganize syrup stations and clean the espresso machine. She kept her apron on, her movements casual, but her eyes tracked every exit, every shadow in the stockroom.

Matt reappeared around 9:45 p.m., this time not flirting, not playful—focused. He pulled her aside briefly, just outside the break room.

"You really think something's happening during the night shift?" he asked, voice low.

"I don't think. I know. Someone's using the store for more than pastries and produce."

Matt crossed his arms. "Then we need to watch it ourselves."

Penny hesitated. "You're in?"

"You trusted me in that break room, didn't you?" he said with a quick smirk. Then serious again. "Let's get answers. Tonight."

They made a plan to slip into the stockroom around midnight. From there, Penny would observe the loading dock. Matt would stay near the service alley in case anyone entered from the outside.

By the time the last of the regular employees clocked out, Penny and Matt were ghosts in the system—still on the clock, but forgotten.

And just before the clock hit midnight, Penny heard it: the low rumble of a truck pulling up out back.

Her pulse steadied.

This was it.

She moved quietly to the back hallway, notebook in hand, crouching behind a stack of unopened bulk flour.

The bay door creaked open.

Voices. Two men. Not familiar.

One handed over a small, unlabeled box.

And that's when she saw him.

Tommy.

Accepting it without a word.

Penny's breath caught in her throat. She pressed herself tighter against the bags of flour, heart pounding, as she watched him tuck the box under one arm and give the man a casual nod.

Matt was somewhere near the alley entrance. She wanted to signal him, but couldn't risk being heard. She focused instead on memorizing every detail—Tommy's stance, the make of the truck, the way one of the men kept glancing over his shoulder.

The exchange lasted less than thirty seconds. Then the truck door slammed shut and the vehicle rolled off without headlights, vanishing into the backstreet shadows.

Tommy disappeared into the walk-in cooler.

Penny stepped back into the light of the hallway, her pulse racing. She needed Matt. Now.

She found him crouched just outside the breakroom with his walkie silent but in hand.

"He took it," she whispered. "Tommy. The box. He just... accepted it. No clipboard. No signature. Nothing."

Matt's jaw clenched. "I saw the truck leave. No plates. You get a look at the driver?"

"One of them. Mid-thirties, white guy, shaved head. But it wasn't about them—it was about him. Tommy's in it. And we need to find out how deep."

Matt nodded. "We've got enough to start documenting. But if we're right... this goes way beyond just stolen goods."

Penny looked back at the hallway.

Something was happening at Alfie's.

And now, she was standing in the middle of it with only one ally and a whole lot of unanswered questions.

CHAPTER
Twenty-Four

NIGHT MOVES

The next morning, Penny barely slept. The image of Tommy taking that unmarked box was burned into her mind, along with every whispered word, every suspicious glance, every unscheduled face that passed through the store in recent days.

She needed answers. Fast.

Before her shift even began, she drove by Alfie's and parked across the street, watching from behind the tinted windows of her car. The neighborhood felt like it was pulsing—nervous energy vibrating beneath the surface of normalcy. Delivery trucks came and went. A few people loitered by the alley. She jotted down plates, descriptions, timing.

Inside the store, Matt was already on shift, playing it cool but keeping his eyes wide open. They hadn't spoken since the night before, but the weight of what they saw—and what they shared—clung to both of them like steam on glass.

Penny stepped inside, greeted McKenzie, nodded to Lynn, kept her routine. But everything felt heavier now. The coffee wasn't just coffee. The customers weren't just customers.

Everything was part of something.

And she was ready to find out exactly what.

By mid-morning, the tension had already thickened.

Nora pulled Penny aside near the juice cooler. "The man with the clipboard? He came again last night. Quiet. No boxes. Just stood and watched."

Penny felt a chill. "Did he talk to anyone?"

"Only Ted. And they didn't smile."

Ted. Of course.

She thanked Nora and made a mental note. That clipboard man was no ghost. He had a name, a role— and maybe, a reason to keep showing up.

Meanwhile, Matt texted her from the other side of the store:

"Front lot, maroon sedan, tinted. Plates match one from last week. Sitting idle."

Penny ducked into the employee restroom and pulled out her notebook. The plates were the same ones she'd spotted during her early stakeout. She matched the timestamp to deliveries and it clicked—every time that car showed, something off-book was happening.

At 11:15, two of the bakery boxes were returned to the back cooler without being scanned. McKenzie noticed it too.

"That's the second time this week," she whispered. "Boxes in, no barcode, no record."

Penny jotted it down.

Then came the twist: Betsy and Joe held a closed-door huddle in the frozen aisle with Ted. Trina lingered nearby pretending to face the freezer shelves.

Too many layers. Too much movement.

When Penny turned the corner near the loading bay, she stopped cold.

Tommy. Talking to the mystery man in the clipboard vest.

Not a word exchanged. Just a box. A nod. And a handshake.

The clipboard man turned, made direct eye contact with Penny.

And smiled.

She swallowed hard.

The game wasn't just on.

It had seen her, too.

She forced herself to look away, heart pounding in her chest. Keep moving. Don't react. She circled back through produce, pretending to inventory the apples, but her eyes stayed trained on the reflection in the glass cooler doors.

The clipboard man was gone.

Matt caught up with her near bulk snacks, his voice low and steady. "I saw him. The guy with Tommy. He's been watching the alley three nights in a row. Sometimes from inside a delivery truck, sometimes on foot. He doesn't work here. And no one's questioned him."

"Except me," Penny muttered.

Matt looked around before leaning closer. "We need to take this up. Officially. You have to call Butler."

Penny hesitated. Calling her handler meant exposure. It meant looping in the department and risking her position if someone leaked. But she also knew the risk of waiting was greater now.

Before she could answer, a crash echoed from the front of the store. Shouts. A scream.

They both ran.

Near the registers, a scuffle had broken out—two teenage boys trying to bolt with unpaid alcohol and a tote bag full of packaged meats. One of them shoved a cart into a senior customer's legs before sprinting for the doors.

Matt was already in motion, intercepting one while Sonia tackled the other outside.

Annie was close behind, clearing a path through the front doors and barking instructions to customers to stay clear. She moved with a calm precision Penny had seen before—rowing champion instincts paired with street-smarts. She knelt by Sonia as they cuffed the boy, checking his pockets and exchanging quick intel.

"They're not local," Annie muttered. "Definitely running a grab pattern. Could be tied to the crew tagging west of La Brea."

Sonia nodded. "One more kid with a burner phone and a pocket full of nothing."

The energy in the store snapped.

Panic. Chaos.

Penny knelt next to the injured customer while security and staff swarmed to help.

And in the corner of her eye—behind the customer service desk—she saw Ted.

Watching.

Not helping.

Just... watching.

And smirking.

After the suspects were secured and the commotion calmed, Annie stepped into the store's back hallway with Penny to follow up. Her voice was firm, but it softened as she looked at Penny's face.

"You good?"

Penny nodded, brushing a strand of hair behind her ear. "I've been better."

"You're holding something," Annie said, narrowing her eyes. "I don't mean emotionally—I mean intel."

Penny hesitated.

Sonia joined them, still adjusting her belt, her hair slightly out of place. "If you know something, you should tell us. The neighborhood's heating up faster than we can track it. We've had three corner stores hit, and the tagging crews are overlapping territories. Something's coming."

"I know," Penny said. "I just… need to be sure before I loop anyone in."

Annie exchanged a glance with Sonia. "We're here. Whether you're ready or not. This thing doesn't just touch you—it touches the whole block. And you're not the only one being watched."

Penny's jaw tightened. She wanted to believe she could handle this alone, but the layers were piling up too fast. Trina and Betsy playing their silent power games. Joe standing just a little too close to every shady exchange. Ted, always watching but never helping—like he already knew the ending of a story no one else had finished reading.

After a moment's pause, she pulled out her burner phone from the bottom of her apron pocket.

"I'm calling Butler," she said.

Annie nodded. "It's time."

Penny stepped outside into the alley, heart hammering as she waited for the line to connect. The phone rang once. Twice. Then: "Butler."

"It's me," Penny said. "We've got movement. Real movement. Boxes being exchanged. No manifests. Possibly tied to the uptick in gang activity around Sunset. I have visual confirmation—Tommy is involved."

A pause. Then: "Understood. Are you safe?"

"For now. But it's getting harder to stay invisible."

"Keep your distance. Keep your logs. I'll set up a meeting. We'll move soon."

The line went dead.

Penny stood in the cool shade of the alley, phone still in her hand. There was no turning back now.

As she stood there, the alley suddenly felt narrower, the world closing in. She tucked the burner into her pocket, eyes scanning the far end near the loading bay. For a second, she thought she saw movement—a flicker of a shadow just past the chain-link fence. But it was gone before she could focus.

Inside, the tension hadn't lifted. Customers moved faster, quieter, as if the earlier scuffle had unsettled something bigger than just nerves. McKenzie met Penny's eyes across the café counter, her brows slightly raised, like she was silently asking: What now?

Taurus approached the café slowly, unusually quiet. "The back door sensor glitched," he said. "It pinged twice around 4 a.m. on the logs. But no one's fessing up to being back there."

Penny's stomach dropped.

That would've been just after the last delivery.

She turned to Matt, who was checking the lobby security cam feed on his phone.

"Is it time?" she asked.

Matt didn't look up. "It's past time."

Whatever was about to break, it wouldn't wait for her to catch her breath.

She would have to move with it—or be buried by it.

A few hours later, Penny slipped out to her car for a break, hands shaking slightly as she sipped her iced coffee. She stared at the edges of the receipt in her pocket—the one she used to jot timestamps and names and plate numbers. Her log was growing fast. Too fast.

When she returned, she found Richie pale-faced by the cleaning closet.

"You didn't hear this from me," he said in a whisper, "but the guy with the clipboard? He was spotted outside the corporate Sunset Star on La Brea yesterday. Ayeda was talking to him. And laughing."

Penny's pulse kicked again. Ayeda—too polished, too smiley, with just enough reach to tie Alfie's to corporate without getting her hands dirty.

"And," Richie added, "I think Betsy knows. She's been acting weird. Checking over receipts twice. Asking who's working what shifts next week."

McKenzie passed them just then, dropping a coffee filter in the bin. "Lynn said Trina's going to be named co-Manager by Friday. No one's even pretending it's about coffee anymore."

Inside the café, the register beeped. Taurus took a step closer to Penny as he wiped down the counter.

"You got people watching out for you?" he asked quietly.

Penny nodded. "I do."

"Good," Taurus said. "Because you're not just in it now. You're under it."

The buzzer on the front door chimed.

Penny looked up.

The clipboard man walked in.

This time, in plainclothes.

And he didn't look away.

He walked in like he owned the floor, his stride relaxed but precise, head on a swivel like he was taking inventory—of the store, of the staff, of her. His eyes found Penny instantly, and they didn't blink.

Matt was a few paces behind the kiosk, watching from the health and wellness section. He clocked the exchange in a heartbeat and subtly reached for the walkie clipped to his belt, his other hand sliding into his jacket.

Penny felt the weight of the man's gaze as he approached the counter. Not fast. Not threatening. Just deliberate.

"Pumpkin spice ooh la latte," he said smoothly. "Extra hot. No lid."

His voice was lower than she remembered. Too calm.

She rang him up, hands steady, voice neutral. "Name?"

He smiled again. "You know it."

The register beeped.

"Order will be at the end," she said.

He stepped aside, leaned against the pickup counter, and watched the floor like a hunter waiting on dusk. Just close enough to intimidate. Just far enough to act innocent.

McKenzie, prepping a cold brew behind her, whispered, "Who is that guy?"

Penny didn't answer. But her spine was stiff, her eyes hard.

Because now she knew—he wasn't just a middleman.

He was the link.

And he had just made this personal.

Penny moved with calculated calm, slipping behind the espresso machine to prepare the clipboard man's drink. Her mind raced. Every movement he made was designed—strategic, calculated. He wasn't here for coffee.

Matt edged closer to the front, positioning himself in direct line of sight, his body language relaxed but ready. Penny could see it in his jaw—he was coiled tight, waiting.

The clipboard man took his drink slowly, wrapping both hands around the cup like he was savoring the heat.

"You all keep this place running tight," he said, more to the room than anyone in particular. "Impressive operation."

Taurus stepped out from the backroom, eyes locking on the man for a brief second before moving behind the bakery case.

Penny forced a polite nod. "We do our best."

He leaned slightly across the counter, lowering his voice. "Keep doing that. And maybe things stay... smooth."

Matt moved then, standing close enough to make his presence known.

"You enjoy your drink, sir?" he asked, tone pleasant but sharp.

The man didn't flinch. "Always do."

He took a long sip, turned slowly, and walked toward the exit.

Everyone watched him go.

Penny's heart was hammering in her chest. This wasn't a threat—it was a warning. A test. A show of power.

The message was clear:

He knew.

He was watching.

And they weren't ready for what came next.

CHAPTER
TWENTY-FIVE

ESPRESSO YOURSELF CAREFULLY

The clipboard man was gone, but the chill he left behind lingered long after the door clicked shut. Everyone resumed their stations, but it was an act—Penny could see the stiffness in McKenzie's posture, the way Taurus kept glancing over his shoulder, how Matt's jaw flexed every time the door chimed.

Something had cracked. And now, no one could pretend it was just caffeine and coupons anymore.

Penny busied herself wiping down the counter, eyes darting toward the alley every few minutes. She checked the clock. Butler hadn't followed up yet, but she knew something was in motion. She could feel it.

Later that afternoon, Penny caught Trina near the walk-in. Alone. Trina was texting, her voice low but annoyed. Penny stepped behind a shelf of plastic cup lids and listened.

"You said it would be fast," Trina whispered. "She's watching everything. And now he just walked in like he owns the place."

Penny's heart skipped.

Who was she talking to?

She backed away quietly, rounded the corner, and nearly collided with Richie.

"You good?" he asked, startled.

"Yeah. Just trying to stay two steps ahead."

"You might need three."

Penny's shift ended without further fireworks, but the silence was louder than chaos.

She knew now—Trina was involved.

And whatever they were moving through Alfie's... was bigger than anyone had guessed.

Later that evening, her nerves frayed and her thoughts tangled, Penny made a decision: she needed a reset. Not a notebook. Not surveillance. Just something—anything—to loosen the grip anxiety had on her spine.

So she found a foot massage place tucked between a laundromat and a nail salon two blocks off Sunset. It smelled like eucalyptus and peppermint oil, the walls painted a soft blue that made her feel like she could breathe again.

As she settled into the chair, her phone off, head tilted back, Penny let the weight of the last week begin to drain from her limbs.

But quiet wasn't meant to last long.

From behind the curtain separating the massage stations, she heard it—voices.

Familiar ones.

Trina.

And Betsy.

"I told you it was meant for Mike," Trina snapped. "Not Donny. But he grabbed the drink. How was I supposed to know he'd be back early?"

Penny froze, heart hammering.

Betsy's voice came next, lower but sharp. "Now we're stuck with a dead guy and a promotion that's moving too slow. If she finds out—"

"She won't. Not unless you screw it up."

Penny's fingers curled into the chair's arms. Her blood ran cold.

They had poisoned Donny.

Accidentally.

And it was meant for Mike.

The pieces shifted, then slammed into place.

This wasn't just smuggling. It was murder.

And now she knew exactly who was behind it.

The weight of it hit her like a cold wave. Penny sat frozen in the dim massage room, heart pounding, her limbs tense again despite the pressure of the massage therapist's hands. She didn't hear the soft chime of music anymore or the gentle hum of the water feature by the door. All she could hear was the echo of Trina's voice—sharp, unapologetic, dangerous.

Her stomach turned.

She had suspected so much. But this? This was murder. And it was personal. The drink was meant for Mike—the Federal Compliance Liaison, another unsuspecting player in this twisted drama. And Donny had just been in the wrong place at the wrong time. A mistake. A casualty.

Penny's fingers gripped the armrest, her breath shallow. She wanted to scream. To storm through the curtain, to confront them both right then and there. But she didn't. She couldn't. Not yet.

Instead, she sat with the rage, the disbelief, the helplessness.

Betsy and Trina were playing puppet masters while the rest of the staff danced. And now, it wasn't just about evidence—it was about justice.

For Donny.

For Mike.

For every person who walked through the doors of Rock n' Roll Alfie's unaware of what was happening behind the scenes.

And for herself—because this mission had just become a war.

She left the massage parlor in a daze, her body tense despite the service, her mind racing with too many voices.

By the time she returned to her car, she had already pulled out the burner phone. Her fingers hovered above the keypad for a moment before she hit dial.

Butler answered on the second ring. "McCool?"

"I just heard them. Trina and Betsy. It wasn't just smuggling. The drink was meant for Mike. Donny took it instead."

A pause. Not surprise, just silence.

"You sure?"

"I'm sure. I heard it myself."

Another pause, then Butler's voice lowered. "We thought it might go that deep. You're close, McCool. Closer than we expected."

Penny leaned against the car door, her breath fogging the window. "What's next? We need to move."

"Not yet," Butler said. "You need to stay in place. Keep collecting. We're pulling surveillance from corporate and coordinating with narcotics. We can't risk tipping them off now."

"But they're talking freely. They think they're in the clear."

"That's why we wait," Butler replied. "They're comfortable. That's when they get sloppy. And that's when we'll strike. Until then—lay low. Stay smart. And don't let them see you flinch."

Penny hung up with a deep exhale, slipping the phone back into her coat.

The war had started.

But she'd fight it in silence—until the takedown came.

The next day at Alfie's, the tension was as thick as the scent of burnt espresso. No one spoke of the clipboard man, or the fight at the register, or the new schedule posted with Ted's name oddly absent.

Penny moved like a shadow, blending in, nodding politely, making drinks and memorizing everything.

She could feel the pressure mounting—like the whole store was holding its breath.

When she passed Nora in the hallway, the custodian paused mid-mop and glanced around.

"The floor's not the only thing slick today," she whispered.

Even Nora knew something was wrong.

Matt avoided eye contact but lingered close, his shoulder brushing hers as he walked by with a shipment receipt she didn't ask for. He was tense too—wound tight like he knew more than he was letting on.

Penny noticed Trina watching everyone, standing near the customer service desk with her arms crossed, eyes sharp.

She knew.

She was trying to figure out who else knew.

And Penny? She just had to keep playing dumb—until she didn't have to anymore.

Around noon, Annie and Sonia returned to the store. They didn't approach Penny, but they made their presence known—slow patrols through the aisles, small nods to the security guards, and long looks at the employee schedule posted by the time clock.

Penny caught Annie's eye as she refilled the condiment station.

Annie gave the smallest of nods.

Confirmation. Support. Maybe even trust.

Across the store, Betsy and Trina were laughing too loudly over the pastry case, but it didn't reach their eyes. It was performance now. A cover.

Behind the veil of smiles and seasonal lattes, something was rotting.

Richie passed by with a mop, whispering as he moved, "Watch the inventory logs. Ted's been changing things in the system. At night."

Penny nodded, fighting the urge to react.

Her list of suspects was growing, and with it, her sense of urgency.

She just needed one more piece—something undeniable.

And then she'd blow the whole thing open.

But even as she plotted her next moves, another weight tugged at her—one she hadn't unpacked.

The break room.

Matt.

That moment had been intense. Needed, even. A release from the constant pressure. But now that her head was clearing, guilt crept in. Not regret—but complexity. She hadn't let anyone close in a long time, and now, of all times, she had. She couldn't afford distractions, but she also couldn't pretend she didn't feel something.

That night, she called Lisa—her best friend since college, now a mom of a teenage daughter and someone who always picked up, even if she only had ten minutes.

Lisa answered on the second ring, voice warm and familiar. "Hey, stranger. You okay?"

"I don't know," Raven said honestly. "It's a mess. The case... the people I'm working with... and then there's this guy."

"Oh no," Lisa said with mock dread. "A guy?"

"It just happened. In the break room. And it was... great. But now I can't stop overthinking it."

Lisa paused. "Do you feel safe with him?"

Raven nodded, then realized Lisa couldn't see. "Yeah. I think I do. But I don't know if he's all in, or if it was just the moment."

Lisa was quiet for a second. "Raven, you don't need to figure it all out right now. But you do need to let yourself feel things. You're not a robot. You're still human. Just don't lose sight of who you are in all of it."

Raven smiled faintly. "You always know what to say."

"Of course I do. I'm your emotionally stable friend. One of us has to be."

They laughed softly. And for the first time all day, Raven let herself breathe a little deeper.

She hung up feeling lighter.

And ready to go deeper into the dark.

That night, Raven sat at her tiny kitchen table, a single lamp glowing overhead, flipping through her notebook. Every scribbled line, timestamp, and detail seemed to pulse on the page like they were leading her somewhere. The air felt thick with purpose.

She turned to a clean page and wrote one sentence:

It's time to set the trap.

Her hands moved methodically as she mapped out the players—Trina, Betsy, Tommy, Ted, the clipboard man, and now Ayeda. She circled the names, drew arrows, timelines. She wrote Donny's name in bold red ink at the center.

He deserved justice.

They all did.

As she worked, she thought about Lisa's words. About what it meant to stay human while undercover. What it meant to protect herself, but not close herself off. She hadn't just called Lisa for advice—she'd called to feel seen. To remind herself she was more than just a role.

Raven closed the notebook and leaned back in her chair, exhaling slowly.

Tomorrow, she would start pulling the threads tighter.

She wouldn't confront them head-on.

Not yet.

But she'd make it clear—someone was watching.

And she was done pretending not to.

Before heading to bed, she left her notebook open on the table—something she never did. Tonight, it was intentional. A symbol. If something happened to her, if the trap didn't spring the way she planned, someone needed to know what she'd uncovered.

She took a long shower, letting the water burn away the panic and pressure that clung to her skin. She stared at herself in the mirror afterward, water still dripping from her hair, and whispered aloud to her reflection: "You're not backing down."

Sleep came slowly, filled with dreams of dim corridors, flickering lights, and footsteps that always stopped just before she turned around. But for once, she didn't wake in a cold sweat.

She woke up ready.

There was no room left for hesitation. Every thread had been pulled taut. She'd gathered intel, she'd made the call, and now her instincts were sharpened like a blade waiting to be drawn.

She brewed a cup of coffee and stood by the window, watching the early light rise over the buildings, bathing the cracked streets in a faint golden haze. Somewhere out there, Trina and Betsy were plotting their next move. And so was she.

She wouldn't go in swinging. She'd go in steady. Unshakable.

The storm was coming.

But this time, Raven wasn't caught in it.

She was it.

CHAPTER
TWENTY-SIX

TURNING POINT

Penny arrived at Alfie's before sunrise.

The air outside still carried that quiet Los Angeles chill that only lasted for a few precious hours before the day's heat took over. She wore her plain black hoodie under the Sunset Star apron, hair pulled back tighter than usual, and her jaw set with purpose.

Today, she wasn't just blending in.

She was bait.

The plan wasn't fully formed, not yet. But she knew the storm was circling. Her presence, her silence, her composure—it all played a part now. Let them think she was just another Barista in the background.

She clocked in, walked the floor, and took her place at the kiosk. McKenzie gave her a tired smile. Taurus was already grinding espresso with a level of focus that bordered on aggressive.

"Quiet morning," he muttered without looking up. "That means it's about to get weird."

Penny nodded. "Isn't it always?"

By 7:15, the rhythm of the morning shift had set in. The usual customers. The regular drink orders. But Penny watched everyone. She studied their faces, their tension, their tells.

She wasn't looking for coffee orders today.

She was looking for mistakes.

And someone—she didn't know who yet—was going to make one.

By 7:40 a.m., the early calm shattered.

Penny first noticed the woman pacing back and forth between the Sunset Star kiosk and the locked entrance to the service deli. She was Black, mid-40s, well-kept—her hair pulled into a tight bun, oversized sunglasses masking her eyes, and dressed in athleisure like she'd just come from a barre class. But it was the duffle bag that caught Penny's eye. It was too big, too full, and the way the woman gripped it like a lifeline, making the hair on Penny's arms stand up.

She wasn't ordering. She wasn't browsing. She was waiting for something.

Or someone.

Penny flagged Jorge near the front registers. "Hey—this lady's pacing with a duffle and keeps checking the deli. You might want to—"

Jorge waved a hand. "It's fine. Probably just waiting for her sandwich or something."

"But the deli's not open yet."

He shrugged. "People get antsy. I'll walk by."

Penny watched him halfheartedly stroll over, offer a tight smile to the woman, and disappear into the stockroom. Typical Jorge.

Two minutes later, chaos erupted.

The woman had entered the kitchen behind the service deli counter. Somehow, she'd slipped through an unlocked prep door. Now she stood in the back, holding a giant stainless-steel chef's knife in one hand and a bubbling pot of boiling water in the other, refusing to leave.

Customers were screaming. Employees frozen. And Penny? She was stuck behind the counter taking drink orders from a customer who wanted an almond milk cappuccino extra hot with two and a half pumps of vanilla.

Her hands trembled as she rang up the drink.

McKenzie whispered under her breath, "Is this real right now?"

Penny wanted to jump the counter and handle it herself.

Where was the armed guard?

Not Matt. He hadn't been on the schedule all week.

Jorge finally called 911.

Twenty minutes later, ten LAPD officers flooded into Alfie's, moving with practiced calm. They set up a perimeter and began talking the woman down. Penny could barely focus as she pretended to steam milk.

It took all twenty minutes, but they got her. No injuries.

They walked her out in handcuffs, her head bowed, still gripping the handles of the duffle like she'd never let go. The line of officers formed a slow parade behind her—right past Sunset Star Coffee.

Customers were whispering. Phones were out.

Penny stood frozen at the register, her face composed.

But inside, she was unraveling.

This wasn't just tension anymore.

This was a powder keg waiting to blow.

When the last officer exited the building, Penny finally stepped away from the counter. She ducked into the employee hallway and braced herself against the wall, breath tight in her chest. The adrenaline was still pumping, but now it left behind something heavier—dread.

This wasn't even connected to the case, and yet it felt like a mirror. Another crack in the surface of something pretending to be normal. Another reminder that chaos could erupt at any moment.

Taurus found her a minute later. "You okay?"

Penny nodded, though she wasn't sure it was true. "Where was security?"

"Don't know," Taurus said. "We're getting the fill-ins now. Matt's shifts keep getting reassigned. Betsy's doing. Rumor is she's trying to get the whole team replaced with people she picks."

Penny's eyes narrowed. Control. That's what this was all about.

She returned to the kiosk just in time to catch Trina whispering to Jorge in the corner. Both of them glanced her way before splitting apart.

It didn't matter what mask they wore—everyone was starting to show their real face.

And Penny knew that the next mistake... might be hers if she wasn't careful.

The store hadn't fully settled when the next explosion happened.

Near checkout lane three, two customers—both regulars—began shouting at each other over who was next in line. One, a wiry man in his fifties wearing a vintage band tee and aviators, accused the other—a younger guy with earbuds in and a cart full of energy drinks—of cutting.

"Hey, I've been waiting ten minutes!" the older man yelled.

The younger guy popped out an earbud. "Bro, I don't care. You weren't in the lane."

"You think you're tough because you've got tattoos?!"

"Why don't you shut it and go back to whatever garage band you crawled out of?"

The shouting drew everyone's attention. Customers stopped mid-swipe at the self-checkouts. Taurus popped his head from the bakery case. McKenzie ducked lower behind the kiosk.

Penny could only shake her head.

A Manager's voice rang over the comms: "Security to the front lanes."

But again, there was no response.

Because there was no security.

Again.

Penny gritted her teeth as the two men nearly came to blows. Jorge finally ran over and stood between them, arms out like a referee.

"Enough!" he barked. "You want to throw down? Do it outside, not next to my cantaloupes!"

That earned a few snickers from bystanders, but the tension didn't fully dissolve. Both men stormed off in opposite directions, grumbling profanities.

Another crack.

Another sign.

Alfie's was losing control.

And Penny was the only one who seemed to notice it all happening in real time.

She slipped away to the back hallway, pulling out her burner phone. Her thumbs flew across the screen as she texted Butler a coded update: "Multiple breakdowns. No security. Internal shifts. Suspects emboldened."

She didn't expect an immediate reply—she never did—but just sending it calmed her breathing.

Then she remembered the receipt log. She hurried to the storage closet where Ted sometimes filed overnight changes. The door was ajar.

Inside, the paper trail was sloppy—boxes half-labeled, timestamps mismatched. She found one note scrawled in Ted's handwriting: "Monday night delivery cleared—do not inventory until after 7 a.m."

That was the night the unmarked box showed up.

She snapped a photo.

Every part of her buzzed with instinct now. Something was happening soon—maybe tonight. She could feel it.

And this time, she wouldn't just watch it unfold.

She'd be ready to move.

As she stepped out of the storage closet, her nerves still crackling with urgency, Penny nearly collided with McKenzie.

"Hey," McKenzie whispered, eyes darting. "You okay?"

Penny gave a small nod. "Just... watching."

"Yeah, well, you're not the only one." McKenzie leaned in. "There's a new delivery on the dock. No barcode. It wasn't scanned in. Jorge said not to worry about it. Said it was special order."

That phrase again—special order. It had come up twice now. First from Tommy. Now Jorge.

Penny's breath shortened. "Where is it now?"

"In the cooler," McKenzie said. "Same shelf where that other box went missing."

Penny made a note in her head. Timing. Location. Language.

The web was tightening. And if she waited just long enough, she might catch them in it.

From the front of the store came the sound of another raised voice—this time, a customer arguing about a double charge. Small, petty. But the tension was thick enough to snap.

And through the store's glass doors, she spotted the clipboard man.

Watching again.

Just for a moment.

Then he turned and disappeared into the crowd.

Penny's pulse ticked up. She wiped her hands on her apron and stepped forward, trying to follow—but he was already gone. Just like that. Like he hadn't even been real.

She turned the corner toward the loading area—just in time to see Jorge coming out from the cooler.

She didn't hesitate.

"That delivery McKenzie mentioned—what was it really?" Penny asked, voice low and sharp.

Jorge blinked, surprised. "Like I said, special order."

"You keep using that phrase like it means something. I want to know what it means."

He shifted uncomfortably. "It's above my pay grade. I don't ask questions."

"Then maybe you should start," Penny snapped. "Because I'm asking."

The hallway was silent for a beat too long. Jorge stared at her, then turned and walked away.

That was it.

A crack in his armor.

Penny turned back toward the front of the store, her gut twisting.

Tonight had to be the night.

The threads were pulling tighter.

And whoever was at the center was starting to feel it.

Then, from across the store, a voice Penny didn't expect to hear rose above the ambient noise.

"You think you can just swap my shifts and not tell me?"

It was Matt.

He was standing near the customer service desk, uniform shirt untucked, clearly not scheduled—but clearly furious. His voice cut through the chatter like a blade.

Betsy stood behind the desk, arms crossed, trying to wave him off. "We had to make adjustments—"

Matt stepped closer. "No. You've been phasing me out. And don't pretend it's scheduling. This is personal."

Penny edged closer, heart pounding.

"Matt, not here," Betsy hissed.

"Yeah, here," he snapped. "You want to treat me like I don't exist? Let's talk about that in front of everyone."

Heads were turning. Employees paused mid-task. Even Trina emerged from the aisle, lips curled into a grin.

Penny saw it then—how easily Trina fed off the chaos. How she liked watching people break.

Betsy's voice lowered, venomous now. "If you don't leave right now, I'll make sure you never get a shift at any Alfie's again."

Matt took a step back, jaw clenched.

He scanned the room. His eyes landed on Penny.

A flicker of guilt. Or maybe warning.

Then he walked out.

No one spoke.

The tension he left behind? It stayed.

And Penny knew—it wasn't just unraveling anymore.

It was coming apart by the seams.

CHAPTER
TWENTY-SEVEN

THE SNARE TIGHTENS

By the next morning, the air inside Rock n' Roll Alfie's felt different—thicker, quieter, like the store itself was holding its breath.

Penny arrived early again, this time not out of habit but necessity. She was expecting something. Anything. Her gut told her the web was shifting, pulling tighter.

And if someone didn't slip soon, she might have to make them.

She moved through her routine, but her eyes never stopped scanning. Trina was unusually chipper. Jorge looked like he hadn't slept. Betsy was in the office with the door closed most of the morning.

At 9:03 a.m., a corporate email hit the kiosk's shared terminal: INVENTORY AUDIT COMING

THIS WEEK. MANAGERS: HAVE PAPERWORK
READY.

Taurus muttered under his breath, "That'll rattle
cages."

Penny smiled, just barely. Good. Rattled was good.

She made an excuse to check the back cooler. The
mystery delivery from the night before was gone.

No record. No trace.

But now she had more eyes. McKenzie was texting
her updates. Richie had taken it upon himself to "clean
near the back office" more often.

Even Nora, sweet Nora, had caught wind of something.

"Trina," she whispered, leaning in while filling the
mop bucket. "She go out back with clipboard man. I see
it. Last night."

That was it.

Confirmation.

Trina wasn't just complicit. She was the key.

Penny's fingers curled around the handle of her cup.

It was time to close in.

That afternoon, just after the lunch rush, a ripple
passed through the store.

A regional Manager from corporate—pressed blazer, clipped walkie, calm but firm—walked straight into
the office.

Ten minutes later, Betsy and Trina were summoned.

"Headquarters needs a word," the Manager said flatly. "It's about the incident involving Donny."

Penny watched from the kiosk as both women froze.

Trina's eyes darted, but she masked it quickly with a shrug. "Now?"

"Yes. Pack your things for the day. You'll be debriefed at Downtown LA. HR will follow up after."

Betsy's lips parted as if to object, but nothing came out.

For once, neither of them had a script.

They disappeared out the front door five minutes later, neither looking back.

And Penny? She didn't move.

She just kept wiping the counter, pulse steady, breath quiet.

The walls were closing in.

And the two women who thought they ran the place?

They were finally out of frame.

But the victory was short-lived.

The next morning, Betsy was back.

She stood in front of the team near the bakery, holding a clipboard and wearing a tight smile. Her voice was upbeat but edged with exhaustion.

"Just to clear the air," she said, patting her midsection, "yes, I'm pregnant. Baby number five. Surprise!"

A few gasps. A couple forced claps. Most employees just exchanged quick glances—so it wasn't just weight gain after all.

The announcement landed like a strange punctuation mark after her abrupt summons to headquarters.

Penny watched from behind the espresso machine, eyebrows raised.

That same afternoon, Joe pulled Trina into the office. By the end of the shift, the news was out: Trina was being officially promoted to co-Manager.

"Temporarily," Jorge clarified. But no one bought that.

The team buzzed with unease. Even the new Baristas sensed something was off.

Penny took it all in quietly, her expression unreadable.

She knew exactly what this was.

A reshuffling of power.

A distraction.

And a sign that the endgame was fast approaching.

But just when Penny thought she'd seen every angle, another twist snapped the tension tighter.

During the late afternoon lull, a new employee from the grocery department—Kenny, barely nineteen, fresh from orientation—walked up to the Sunset Star kiosk with a crumpled note in his hand.

"Hey," he said, voice low. "This was taped inside the break room fridge. It's... weird. Figured it might be yours."

Penny opened the note slowly. Block letters. Marker ink. No signature.

"You're getting too close. Back off. Final warning."

Her blood went cold.

She looked around the store. No one was looking at her. No one was watching. But that was the trick, wasn't it? The ones who knew how to hide never looked suspicious.

She tucked the note deep into her apron and forced a smile. "Thanks, Kenny."

He nodded, oblivious, and wandered off toward frozen foods.

Penny returned to her station. Every cell in her body was alert now.

The game had changed.

Someone wasn't just nervous.

They were threatened.

And it didn't take long before Penny began to suspect why.

Later that evening, as she refilled the pastry display, McKenzie whispered over her shoulder, "Did you hear what Trina said about Kenny?"

Penny turned slightly. "What now?"

"She was telling Richie that Kenny's been acting sketchy. That he said something about Raid and joking about how easy it'd be to poison someone."

Penny's stomach dropped.

That conversation had happened. She remembered hearing Kenny laugh about using Raid to kill the ants in his bathroom. A throwaway comment. One that sounded like a teenager making light of a gross chore.

But now? They were twisting it.

She caught sight of Betsy and Trina in the front corner, talking quietly. Both glanced Kenny's way with faux concern, and Penny knew it wasn't genuine. It was strategic.

They were setting him up.

A distraction. A scapegoat.

Penny clenched her jaw. They were willing to ruin a clueless kid's life to protect their own lies.

And that made them more dangerous than ever.

She needed a strategy—and fast.

First, she quietly warned Kenny. She caught him on his way out by the loading dock, keeping her voice low.

"Listen, if anyone asks about that Raid joke—don't say another word. Don't repeat it, don't explain it, just say you don't remember."

Kenny blinked. "Wait... what's going on?"

"Just trust me," Penny said. "They're trying to make you the fall guy. Keep your head down and let me handle it."

He looked shaken, but nodded.

As a diversion—and maybe something more—another crisis struck that afternoon.

Richie came running from the back cooler, panic in his voice. "All the milk's expired. Every jug, every carton. Even the half and half."

Penny rushed back with him. The refrigerator smelled sour and chemical at once.

The date labels told the story—none had been rotated. Some were over a week past due. Even the specialty creamers were bloated and spoiled.

The dairy Manager had failed to restock properly—or had deliberately ignored the logs.

Taurus, furious, started pouring the spoiled milk down the sink. One container after another. Whole milk, skim, nonfat, oat, almond, heavy cream—all of it.

It felt symbolic. A flood of waste, of mismanagement.

Or worse.

Sabotage.

Because this wasn't just carelessness.

It felt orchestrated.

And Penny had a feeling she was being watched the whole time it happened.

Later that evening, as the floor calmed from the day's chaos, Jorge made an announcement that made everyone look up from their stations.

"Corporate's requesting surprise spot interviews tomorrow," he said, barely hiding his stress. "If they call your name, just cooperate. It's part of the follow-up from the audit."

McKenzie shot Penny a quick glance.

Richie muttered, "They're fishing now."

Penny nodded slowly. The net was tightening, but she wasn't sure if it was theirs or the store's.

Back at the kiosk, Kenny returned to her side, visibly nervous.

"They called me to meet with HR tomorrow," he whispered. "Do you think it's... because of the note? Or that stupid joke?"

"I think it's because you were easy to pick," Penny said gently. "But I've got your back. We'll get through this. Just stay calm. Say only what you need to."

Kenny's eyes searched hers for certainty, then nodded.

Penny watched him go, her mind already spinning. If they were willing to burn a rookie, what else were they hiding?

She'd have to move faster.

And this time, she wouldn't just defend.

She'd strike.

But before she could build her next move, another problem surfaced—and this time, it was close to home.

April, one of the floaters—cashier by day, Barista by rotation—had been seen using Richie's login at the kiosk register. At first, no one thought much of it. A temporary access fix, something April had done before with permission. But during the afternoon drawer count, nearly $300 came up missing.

The investigation moved fast.

Security pulled footage. And there she was—April, alone at the register, sliding bills into her apron pocket during a lull in the rush.

Richie was shaken but cleared. He hadn't even been on shift when the theft occurred.

As the story unraveled further, Penny caught wind of another twist—April's sister, a cashier at the other Alfie's two miles down La Brea, had been caught weeks earlier doing the exact same thing. Corporate hadn't made it public, but HR was already watching both locations closely.

This wasn't just about fraud. It was about the kind of rot that spread in quiet corners.

Penny made a note in her log.

Everyone's scrambling now.

And with every fracture, she got closer to the center of it all.

Then, just before close, another twist landed like a spark to gasoline.

Jorge, red-faced and tight-lipped, stormed out of the Manager's office and slammed the break room door behind him. Word spread fast: someone had called the employee hotline to report "improper store-level bonus allocations"—and Jorge was now under investigation.

Rumor had it, a few top-performing cashiers hadn't seen a dime of the bonus pool, while others with close ties to Trina and Betsy had mysteriously received full payouts.

It was the kind of low-stakes corporate mess that could quietly destroy reputations—and trigger a reshuffling from the top.

Penny didn't even blink. She jotted it down.

The snare wasn't just tightening—it was constricting.

Someone was desperate.

And desperation meant mistakes.

All she had to do now was stay ahead of them long enough to catch them in the act.

And then, just as she thought the day couldn't twist further, a new face arrived at the front entrance—a man in a white long-sleeve button-down shirt with the Alfie's logo embroidered on the chest, khaki pants, and a visitor badge clipped to his belt and a duffel bag in hand. He introduced himself at the kiosk as Brian from Loss Prevention.

He was polite, quiet, but his eyes missed nothing.

He spent the next few hours shadowing Jorge, glancing at receipts, asking questions quietly. No one knew exactly what he was here for—but the timing was too perfect.

By mid-afternoon, Taurus whispered, "That guy gives me internal affairs energy."

And Penny had to agree.

Everyone was watching everyone now.

And the more hands Corporate sent, the more likely it was that someone—anyone—might finally crack.

Penny just needed to be ready when they did.

She noticed Brian glance up at the security camera tucked in the corner above the breakroom hallway— noticing angles, blind spots. He wasn't just auditing receipts. He was reading the whole store.

And he didn't say much, but the questions he asked made everyone nervous.

By the end of his visit, he'd already requested a list of overnight access cards, a breakdown of the dairy logs, and internal reports from the last six weeks.

McKenzie muttered, "Whatever he's looking for, he's close."

And Penny agreed—because she could feel it.

Not fear. Not tension.

Anticipation.

Something big was about to drop.

And the next person to slip... might take everyone down with them.

What Penny didn't expect was who would start to shift under pressure.

Richie.

Normally chatty and upbeat, he began to withdraw. He stopped joking during prep, avoided eye contact, and even flinched when April's name came up.

At first, Penny thought it was just guilt over the stolen register login. But it was something deeper.

Later that night, she found him near the back hallway pretending to clean the cabinet drawers.

"You good?" she asked.

He nodded too quickly. "Yeah. Totally. Just tired."

But Penny waited. Gave him space.

Finally, he sighed and leaned against the wall. "I got an email from HR saying my access was suspended—temporarily. That's when I realized... maybe none of this is accidental."

Penny's stomach sank.

He wasn't just a victim. He was a thread—one more they were pulling on.

She reached for her notebook as soon as he walked away.

The trap was bigger than she thought.

And the players? More vulnerable than they realized.

CHAPTER
TWENTY-EIGHT

FINAL PUSH

By the following morning, Penny felt it: the shift from investigation to execution.

She moved with intention now—quietly gathering, watching, listening—but the pressure was building fast. The store buzzed with strange silences and wary glances. Even customers could feel something off.

The clipboard man hadn't returned, but she felt his presence in every suspicious box that went unlogged and every hallway whisper that died the moment she approached.

Kenny was still walking on eggshells, Richie was barely holding it together, and McKenzie had started texting her from across the kiosk instead of speaking aloud.

Meanwhile, Brian from Loss Prevention had extended his stay. He now showed up two hours earlier, hanging around the receiving bay and casually questioning anyone who passed by. He was building a case.

But Penny knew the window was closing.

If she was going to act—really act—she needed to pull a trigger soon.

She just didn't know which one would fire first.

Then came the slip-up.

Word filtered through Jorge, overheard on a call to another Manager: during her questioning at headquarters, Betsy had inadvertently let something critical slip.

She admitted that the chai syrup had been replaced with a new batch because the old one had expired—and that Trina had fixed the broken pump before the incident with Donny's drink.

It was supposed to be routine maintenance. But in the context of a poisoning? It changed everything.

Betsy casually implied that Trina had been the only one on duty capable of fixing the pump. Her exact words were: "I didn't even touch the new chai—Trina handled all that."

That statement flipped the script.

It threw Trina off completely.

Penny learned the rest from Richie, who'd overheard Trina cursing in the break room, furious and shaking.

"That wasn't the plan!" she'd shouted, slamming a locker door. "We were setting up Kenny! What is she doing?!"

Apparently, Betsy had chalked up the confusion to her pregnancy—"too many hormones, too much nausea"—but Trina didn't buy it. For the first time, there was a visible crack in their alliance.

And Penny knew: the pressure was splintering them from the inside.

By midday, the fallout deepened.

Trina couldn't keep it in. She cornered Ted near the dry goods aisle, pacing, frantic.

"I need to tell you something," she hissed. "She's throwing me under the bus. Betsy. She told them I was the only one who touched the chai pump. That's not what we agreed on."

Ted, who usually played it cool and unreadable, actually blinked in surprise. "Why are you telling me this?"

"Because you said you had my back," she snapped. "You said you'd help if things went sideways. Well, they're sideways now."

Penny, stacking syrups nearby with her back turned, caught every word.

Ted didn't respond right away. Then he muttered, "You should've kept it clean."

Trina's face fell. "Are you serious?"

"You let it get messy," he said, turning his back to her. "You let her see too much."

And just like that, Trina realized she was more alone than ever.

But Trina wasn't one to fold easily. Anger had always sharpened her instincts, and now it kicked into high gear.

She followed Ted into the small elevator equipment room behind the Sunset Star kiosk—one of the few quiet corners in the store no one ever checked unless something broke.

Ted raised an eyebrow. "This better be good."

Trina crossed her arms, her tone low but loaded. "You and I both know I've been useful. But if you're thinking of ghosting me now, you'd better remember how much I know. About the deliveries. About the side deals. About you."

Ted's face remained stoic, but a flicker of tension passed through his eyes.

"I'm not the one who brought heat to this place," he said.

"No," Trina replied. "But you are the one who's still standing to gain—if I stay quiet. So make your choice."

There was a long pause.

Then Ted nodded, slow and silent.

It wasn't trust. It was strategy.

And that made them even more dangerous.

But Ted's mind was already elsewhere.

The dream he'd been clinging to—becoming Store Director—felt like it was slipping through his fingers. Betsy had used up all her favor, and with Trina cracking under pressure, Ted knew he was running out of places to hide.

For the rest of the afternoon, he kept his head down and busied himself in the cleaning products aisle, facing detergent bottles like they were the only thing he could still control. It was quieter there, just the soft hum of the overhead lights and the occasional squeak of a rolling cart.

But his thoughts were loud.

He ran through every decision, every shortcut, every loyalty he'd sold. Was it all still worth it? Would someone like Brian from Loss Prevention sniff out his involvement next?

He straightened a bottle of bleach that didn't need straightening.

The shelves didn't talk.

But they also didn't lie.

And that made them more trustworthy than anyone else in the store right now.

What haunted Ted more than anything was what he'd have to tell his wife—if it all came out. She was counting on this promotion. Had already started planning around it, whispering about moving closer to the Valley, picking out a new car. She had no idea he'd been cheating—no idea he was tangled up in side deals and backroom threats.

The idea of disappointing her churned deeper than his fear of getting caught.

But still, he couldn't undo what he'd done.

Now, all he could do was keep stacking bottles and pretend he still had time to fix it.

Even as that time evaporated with every whisper down aisle seven.

Back near the kiosk, Penny had begun assembling her own plan—not just to protect Kenny, but to lock in every thread she'd followed from day one. She spent the rest of her shift casually asking clarifying questions about inventory procedures, checking timestamps against her notes, and confirming which Managers signed off on what during Donny's final week.

By closing, she slipped into the break room under the guise of retrieving a misplaced apron. Instead, she opened the utility closet and pulled out the second burner phone she had stashed weeks ago—just in case.

She texted Butler a single line:

"Need a sit-down. In person. Tonight if possible."

No one else knew what she was planning—not McKenzie, not Richie, not even Matt. But she had reached the point where silence would only protect the wrong people.

She was done watching.

Now it was time to speak—and strike.

But the universe had other plans.

Just after Penny sent the text to Butler, her burner phone buzzed with a strange number—then immediately shut off. She tried powering it back on, but it stayed dark. Dead battery? Maybe. Or maybe not. She checked the charger she'd left hidden in the backroom cabinet. Gone.

Then came a second blow: McKenzie rushed into the break room, pale-faced. "You didn't hear this from me, but Jorge is requesting a full lock on all employee lockers overnight. He says corporate requested it, but... something's off."

Penny's stomach twisted.

Someone was getting nervous. And someone else was getting sloppy.

She couldn't risk waiting for Butler's reply. Not if her message hadn't gone through. Not if her evidence could be tampered with.

She slipped out of the break room and back onto the floor, her eyes scanning for Brian from Loss Prevention.

But he wasn't there.

Not in receiving.

Not near the office.

Gone.

Vanished.

And that's when she knew—something was moving beneath the surface.

Faster than she thought.

Aisle ten was dark when she walked past—the overhead light flickering erratically like a warning signal. She ducked into the backroom hallway again, only to find the utility closet now locked with a temporary sign: "Under Maintenance—Do Not Enter." The lock was new.

That was her signal. Someone knew about the burner.

At the kiosk, Taurus leaned in and whispered, "They moved the camera angle over the mop sink. It's pointed at the lockers now."

Everything was being watched. But not by who she'd expected.

Jorge walked by her without making eye contact. He looked pale. Sweaty. Like a man who knew the ship he was on was about to sink.

Penny turned to McKenzie. "We're out of time. Meet me at the alley door in twenty. Bring your phone."

If she couldn't wait for backup, she'd make her own.

The takedown wouldn't be clean.

But it would be real.

And tonight, it would begin.

She returned to the kiosk just long enough to make it look like she was closing up. Her hands moved automatically, wiping counters and emptying the tip jar, but her ears were trained on the store's rhythm—the sounds of carts rolling, scanners beeping, murmured conversations. The calm before whatever came next.

Aisle thirteen went silent.

Then: a crash.

Penny jerked her head up. McKenzie came running from the back, breathless.

"Someone knocked over the mop bucket. But get this—it wasn't cleaning solution in it. It was milk."

"Milk?"

McKenzie nodded, whispering fast. "Smelled spoiled. Thick. Like someone pulled it from the trash. Why dump it in the middle of the floor?"

Penny's mind snapped to the recent milk spoilage—entire cases discarded. Could this be a message? A warning? Or maybe an attempt to cover something else?

She narrowed her eyes and glanced toward the rear aisle. The spill hadn't just caused a mess. It had redirected the night crew—pulled Taurus, Richie, and even Kenny off their usual routines.

And just like that, the floor was open.

A gap.

A perfect window.

Penny grabbed her notes, stuffed them under her apron, and made for the alley door.

Whatever was coming—they were moving first.

But so was she.

She pushed the alley door open slowly, scanning the lot. A light drizzle misted the concrete, and the only sound was the soft clink of an empty cart nudging the side of the loading dock.

McKenzie slipped out behind her, phone in hand. "Are we really doing this?"

"We don't have a choice anymore," Penny said.

Just then, a shadow moved at the edge of the lot.

Brian.

He stepped out from behind a delivery truck, face unreadable. "You're not the only one getting followed.

Someone's been trailing me too. I had to step out before they shut me down."

Penny stepped closer, voice low. "How bad is it?"

Brian's jaw tightened. "We're not dealing with petty theft anymore. There's something deeper—financial laundering, organized misreporting. Names are showing up in different stores. Not just this one."

McKenzie let out a shaky breath. "This is bigger than Alfie's."

Penny nodded. "Then let's make it count."

Brian handed her a flash drive. "Everything I've got. It's not enough to finish them, but it'll start the fire. You better move fast. They're planning something tonight."

The crash hadn't been a distraction.

It had been a signal.

And the next move was coming fast.

Too fast to stop.

But just slow enough to catch—if Penny was ready.

CHAPTER
TWENTY-NINE

COUNTDOWN TO CLOSE

The flash drive burned in Penny's pocket.

She and McKenzie slipped back inside through the alley door, ducking into the service hallway just as the overhead lights dimmed for closing procedures. The store was thinning out, but tension still clung to the walls like a storm cloud refusing to break.

Penny didn't wait. She headed straight to the kiosk, motioned for Taurus to close up early, and gave Kenny a nod that said: stay low.

She passed Brian's drive to Richie in a folded napkin. "Get this to your friend in IT. Quietly. Tell him it's an audit request."

Richie blinked, then nodded and pocketed it with practiced ease. "He owes me one."

"Make it count," Penny said.

McKenzie covered the register while Penny slipped toward the employee hallway, where Jorge was already talking to someone on the phone, pacing tight circles. She caught only a few words: "…didn't sign off on that… I told you we needed more time…"

He hung up when he saw her.

"You're not scheduled back here," Jorge said flatly.

"I'm not following schedules anymore," Penny replied.

He opened his mouth to respond—but never got the chance.

The front doors buzzed open. Four uniformed officers entered the store, followed by a woman in plainclothes with a badge around her neck.

Sergeant Butler.

Her presence shifted the entire store.

And this time, Penny didn't stay in the shadows.

She stepped forward.

"It's time."

But the takedown would have to wait.

The next morning, before the adrenaline had fully left Penny's system, Nora shuffled into the back hallway carrying a small white box with a wax paper lining. Her hands were dusted with flour, and her smile was bigger than usual.

"Para ti," she said, handing the box to Penny.

Inside was a soft, round cookie sandwiched with caramel filling and dusted with powdered sugar. An alfajor.

"I haven't had one of these since I was in Argentina," Penny said, touched.

"You need inspiration," Nora said, nodding proudly. "For your drink. The contest. Remember?"

Penny had almost forgotten.

Nora leaned in, whispering like it was classified. "You call it 'The Alfaretto.' Dulce de leche, espresso, whipped cream—like the cookie. I can see it already."

Penny couldn't help but smile.

She scribbled the idea on a napkin: 2 ristretto shots, 3 pumps dulce de leche, steamed almond milk for hot / cold almond milk for iced. Topped with whipped cream, caramel drizzle, and coconut flakes.

Nora clapped her hands. "You practice now. Win for us."

In the middle of espionage and betrayal, a cookie from a friend was the most grounding thing Penny had felt in weeks.

She tucked the napkin into her pocket beside the flash drive.

One was for justice.

The other—for joy.

And both, she now realized, were worth fighting for.

Later that day, Nora brought Penny into the break room kitchen during her break and insisted she test the first version of the Alfaretto on her.

"I trust your hands," Nora said, sipping with dramatic flair, eyes closed like she was judging a talent show. "Mmm. Sweet like heartbreak. Bold like revolution."

Penny burst out laughing. "That might be the best review I've ever gotten."

They stood together at the prep sink, sharing bites of another alfajor and sipping from a single trial cup. It was a quiet, rare moment—a stolen breath between chaos.

"You know," Nora said, "everyone thinks I don't pay attention. But I see how much pressure you carry. How much you pretend not to care."

Penny's smile faltered, just slightly.

Nora placed a warm hand on her arm. "Don't let them take your joy. That drink? That's you. You're more than whatever this place tries to pin on you."

Penny blinked fast, caught off guard by how deeply it hit.

"Gracias, Nora," she whispered. "Really."

Nora winked. "Now go. Practice. And win. I want to tell my grandkids I trained the best Barista in Los Angeles."

From then on, Nora became Penny's biggest cheerleader. Every shift, she checked in on her progress, dropping encouraging notes scribbled on napkins or sliding her fresh ingredients she'd "accidentally" over-ordered. A small jar of dulce de leche here, a hidden stash of almond milk there. Penny played along, smiling more than she had in weeks.

Sometimes, they'd steal five minutes to sit near the back sink, sipping quietly and talking about life beyond Alfie's—about Nora's grandkids and her late husband, about Penny's dreams of one day opening a place of her own.

"You got the heart for it," Nora told her. "You just need the right door to open."

Penny knew she was right. And maybe, just maybe, this contest wasn't about a trip or a title—it was about proving to herself that she could still dream, even while working undercover in a storm of lies.

One afternoon, while Penny was fine-tuning the iced version of the Alfaretto, Nora pulled up a metal chair, plopped down with a sigh, and said, "You know, I used to be scared of people like Betsy. Loud ones. The kind who think a title makes them holy."

Penny raised an eyebrow. "Used to be?"

Nora smirked. "Now I just outlast them."

Penny laughed, wiping caramel from the edge of a to-go cup. "That sounds like a motto."

"It is," Nora said. "Life teaches you how to endure. But the magic? That's in the moments you dare to dream again. You're doing that now."

Penny paused, hands stilled over the espresso machine. The weight of Nora's words settled in her chest like something sacred.

She wasn't just making a drink. She was reclaiming something.

Hope. Identity. Herself.

Just as she added a final dusting of coconut flakes to the iced version, the break room door creaked open and in walked Lupe—the floor Manager, clipboard in hand and reading glasses perched on her head.

She paused at the doorway, eyeing the setup.

"What's this?" she asked, squinting.

"Just practicing for the Barista contest," Penny said, trying not to sound startled.

Lupe raised an eyebrow and walked closer. "Looks... impressive."

She took a sip from the sample cup Nora nudged toward her.

"Oh wow. That's good." Then, almost as an afterthought, "You made this?"

Penny nodded.

Lupe looked surprised—genuinely, but not without a trace of something else—an edge in her voice, the faint curl of a competitive smirk. "Didn't know you had a creative side."

Neither did I, Penny thought.

After Lupe left, Nora nudged her. "Watch your back with that one. She's got jealousy hiding behind her compliments. But forget her. You're better than you think."

And for the first time, Penny believed it too.

But Lupe wasn't done.

Over the next few days, she hovered around the kiosk more often than usual—asking subtle questions, rechecking Penny's schedule, and making offhand remarks about how the contest was just "corporate fluff" and didn't reflect true store performance.

"She's threatened," Nora whispered one morning, watching Lupe pretend to reorganize stir sticks. "She's got power, but no spark. That drink you made? It scares her."

Penny tried to shrug it off, but she could feel the shift—how Lupe would linger too long, how her tone was always just a degree too sharp, her praise always carrying a hint of sarcasm.

One evening, Penny found her practice ingredients moved to the wrong shelf, and her prep notes mysteriously missing from the break room corkboard.

Not sabotage, exactly.

But not far from it either.

Nora found her fuming in the corner, restocking everything.

"Let her squirm," Nora said. "The brighter you shine, the more shadows show up. Let her see you fly."

What Nora didn't say aloud—but Penny could feel—was that Lupe's bitterness ran deeper than competition. It wasn't just about the drink, or even the contest.

Lupe didn't like how close Penny had become to her.

Seeing Nora, an older Latina from a generation above hers, pour her energy and warmth into Penny—a younger, white outsider—made Lupe quietly seethe. That kind of loyalty Lupe couldn't control, and it stung.

She'd spent years commanding respect through position, and now Nora's warmth and wisdom were being poured into someone else. Someone younger. Someone who reminded Nora of who she used to be.

And that, more than the drink, made Penny a threat.

Lupe's bitterness wasn't born overnight. Her parents had come to the U.S. from El Salvador, working two jobs each so she could be the first in their family born on American soil. She learned early how to navigate both cultures—when to soften her tone, when to stand her ground. In the Alfie's ecosystem, she'd built her own niche: tough, sharp, no-nonsense. But the truth? She often felt alone.

She struggled with the expectations—both cultural and corporate. There was always pressure to stay polished, to lead without cracking. She used her toughness like armor. And sometimes, her femininity too, though it never sat comfortably. Seeing someone like Penny—a woman confident in herself without playing the same exhausting game—grated on her.

Because deep down, Lupe wasn't sure if her way had ever really worked. Or if she was just too far in to turn back.

Alone with many insecurities she never dared speak aloud, Lupe had always been a survivor. Survival taught her to be strategic, to stay two steps ahead. But it also made her guarded, suspicious of kindness that came too easily. She watched Nora and Penny laugh over caramel drizzles and coconut flakes, and something inside her ached—not just jealousy, but the sting of being left behind by the kind of warmth she'd forgotten how to receive.

———

That night, Penny checked her messages.

Nothing from Brian.

She stared at her burner phone, scrolling through old texts. The last one from him had been short: "Get it to someone you trust. Then lay low." Nothing since. No calls. No check-ins.

She called Richie.

"Did your friend pull anything from the drive yet?"

Richie sounded winded. "He's trying. But he says there's encryption. Like someone tried to bury it behind layers of decoy files. He's working through it. But it's gonna take time."

Time was the one thing Penny didn't feel like she had.

She hung up, heart thudding. If Brian had disappeared, if the files were buried too deep, if someone was onto them—this whole thing could collapse before it even started.

Penny sat alone in her apartment that night, staring out the window, her fingers still dusted with coconut from her latest batch of test drinks.

She needed Brian to resurface.

She needed something to break.

Because the silence was starting to feel like a threat.

And Penny wasn't the only one feeling it.

Brian had sensed something off about her from the beginning. Not in a suspicious way—more like curiosity. She didn't act like the others. She asked smarter questions, kept better notes. She tracked patterns in staffing and supply without ever writing them down where they could be seen.

Most Baristas didn't conduct reconnaissance during milk deliveries.

She wasn't just observant. She was strategic.

He didn't know who she really was, but he'd bet money she wasn't just here to win a coffee contest. No one carried that much focus without a mission.

And if he was right, that meant she was walking a tighter line than anyone realized.

And she was doing it alone.

That's what pushed Brian to go further.

Before going dark, he had started pulling footage—not just from Alfie's, but from two other locations linked by a pattern of irregular vendor shipments and falsified returns. He'd flagged the same names cropping up in late-night logins and supply runs: Trina. Ted. And a third—Biola.

Then he'd found a discrepancy.

A deleted report. Timestamped the day before Donny died. Edited under a generic Manager login. Covered over with a clean replacement.

He took a screenshot. Emailed it to himself.

Then... silence.

The kind that left Penny checking over her shoulder the next morning as she walked into work. The kind that told her whatever was coming next—it wouldn't wait for anyone to be ready.

CHAPTER
THIRTY

THE FINAL FROTH

Penny arrived at work early the next morning, but this time, she didn't linger at the kiosk. She went straight to the back hallway, where the store's energy always pulsed quieter and closer to the truth.

McKenzie met her near the lockers, eyes wide and tired. "Still nothing from Brian?"

Penny shook her head. "Not a word."

"Richie's guy says it's layered deeper than expected. Hidden metadata. Altered file trees. Corporate-level security encryption."

Penny muttered under her breath. "Someone was serious about hiding this."

She scanned the hallway. Jorge was in the office with the door half-closed. Trina hadn't clocked in yet. Ted was stacking produce like his promotion depended on symmetry. Lupe walked past without saying a word.

Everything looked normal.

But everything felt off.

At the kiosk, Taurus was already setting up. Penny slipped behind the bar and pulled a new milk crate forward, her hands moving automatically.

"You see how quiet it is?" he asked.

"Too quiet," she murmured. Then, louder, "Anything weird on your shift last night?"

Taurus paused. "They're moving people again. A night loader just got transferred. No warning. And the overnight guy who usually stocks the dairy—he didn't show."

Penny looked up sharply. "Was that scheduled?"

Taurus shook his head. "Nope. Just... didn't come back."

Her stomach clenched. Names were dropping. Staff was shifting. Surveillance tightening. The silence wasn't just unsettling—it was strategic.

Whoever was behind it all wasn't waiting for someone to catch them.

They were cleaning house before the storm broke.

And Penny was still inside.

Earlier that week, HR had quietly summoned Betsy and Trina for a meeting in the back conference room. Word spread fast, but few knew the details.

Penny later heard snippets from Taurus: "Anonymous report about racist behavior at the kiosk. Everyone's getting mandatory training now. Apparently, Alfie's is cracking down hard—they're not brushing anything under the rug anymore."

Lupe, lips tight, didn't say much afterward, but her eyes narrowed every time someone mentioned it. Rumor had it Ted filed the report, hoping to cover his own tracks and distance himself from the fallout—but others believed Lynn had submitted it before she quit. Quiet and observant, Lynn had endured more than people realized.

No one had seen her since the schedule changed unexpectedly three weeks ago. She hadn't said goodbye. She just... stopped showing up. Her locker was cleaned out within a day. And when HR was asked, they only responded with, "Lynn resigned."

HR made it clear: Alfie's had no tolerance for racism or microaggressions, regardless of position or tenure. Betsy and Trina were given a formal warning and required to complete training immediately. Afterward, they were told to address the team directly.

The apology wasn't scripted, but it was stiff. Betsy muttered something about "not realizing how certain jokes might land" and Trina offered a quick, forced nod, saying she "never meant to hurt anyone."

No one clapped.

Taurus crossed his arms. McKenzie barely looked up from restocking pastries. Penny held her gaze steady, watching both women squirm under the weight of their words.

The training might have been mandated—but the damage was already done.

And it wouldn't take much to ignite.

By midday, Butler texted her to meet in the alley behind the store.

The wind was dry, the sun harsh. Penny pulled her hoodie up and waited next to the dumpsters, heart thudding.

Butler pulled up in an unmarked sedan, sunglasses on, her expression carved in granite.

"Get in."

Penny slid into the passenger seat.

"Gus is out," Butler said without ceremony. "Internal Affairs pulled him. He was caught drinking on the job—Negronis in a thermos. Classy."

Penny blinked. "You're serious?"

"Deadly."

Penny slumped back into the seat. Gus had been her initial handler. A mess, but reliable. Mostly.

"Who's taking over?"

Butler sighed. "No one yet. So, I'm here. You're mine now."

Penny gave a dry laugh. "Great. That's not terrifying at all."

Butler looked at her. "You're deeper in than I thought. And now you're the only one still embedded. We need that drive decrypted. We need something actionable."

Penny handed her a slip of paper. "Richie's friend. Working through it. But someone's pulling strings inside. Staff disappearing. Roles shifting. They're scrubbing things."

Butler folded the paper and tucked it into her pocket. "Then scrub back harder. You've got 72 hours before I have to escalate this. I'll do what I can from the outside, but in there? You're the eyes."

Penny nodded slowly. "Got it."

As Butler pulled away, Penny stayed seated on the back steps, watching her reflection in the tinted glass.

No more handler. No more fallback.

Just her, the lies, and the unraveling storm.

She took a long breath, letting the alley's stale, sun-baked air settle into her lungs before standing. Inside the store, everything was shifting—alliances, schedules, even personalities. The tension had a rhythm now. People spoke in clipped tones, avoided eye contact, lingered too long near the break room doors.

Back at the kiosk, Penny caught Trina watching her—closely. Not the usual smug glances or power-posturing. This was different. Measured. Suspicious.

Richie handed her a receipt but slipped her a note beneath it: Camera over the dairy fridge moved again. Facing inward now. Someone's watching us.

Penny read it once, nodded, and pocketed it.

Then she did what she knew how to do—she blended in.

Took a customer order. Smiled politely. Called out, "One Cappuccino for Ava!"

All the while, she counted seconds between glances, clocked where every department lead was standing, and timed how long the break room door remained open when Jorge slipped inside.

She wasn't just undercover anymore.

She was hunted.

And the trap was tightening.

Joe was back from vacation, strolling the store with a fake tan and a tighter jawline. His presence, while meant to reestablish control, only deepened the sense of unease. He lingered too long near the front registers, didn't greet the regulars like he used to, and seemed to watch Penny with a little too much curiosity.

Mike popped in again, appearing at the counter like a ghost Penny hadn't summoned. He ordered the same drink as before but asked about Donny—casually, like he was just reminiscing. Penny kept her answers vague, sensing he was fishing.

Meanwhile, Betsy waddled down the hallway, clearly further along in her pregnancy than she'd been just a week ago. She barked instructions at Lupe and Jorge between heavy breaths, her usual sharpness blunted by discomfort—but not completely dulled. She still knew how to tighten the screws when no one was looking.

The store was a stage.

And today, everyone was stepping back into character—too aware, too rehearsed.

Something was coming.

And it didn't take long to arrive.

The explosion began near the break room—verbal, not literal, but just as incendiary.

Trina's voice could be heard halfway through the stockroom, sharp and unmistakable. "You think you can pin this on me now?! After everything?!"

Penny froze mid-pour at the kiosk. Heads turned throughout the store. Even customers glanced toward the back with raised brows.

Betsy's voice followed, strained but cutting. "Watch your tone. We discussed this—"

"No, you talked. I listened. You let me take the fall for Donny's drink, and now you're waddling around like Queen of Rock n' Roll Alfie's while I mop up your lies!"

A crash. Something metallic hit the floor.

Then, silence.

Trina stormed out of the hallway still in her apron and ball cap, her ponytail swinging behind her like a fuse ready to light. She ripped off her name tag and hurled it into the customer service desk like a final grenade.

She didn't stop to clock out. Didn't even acknowledge the gawking onlookers.

To Penny, it looked like a scene out of The Joker—except the hospital was Alfie's, and Trina was walking away with the match in her hand.

"If this place is going down," she shouted as the sliding doors opened dramatically for her exit, "I'm not going with it!"

And just like that, Trina was gone.

But even after the doors shut behind her, the store didn't quite return to normal.

Everyone was watching—craning their necks to see where she was going. Trina's car was parked in the upstairs parking lot, but she didn't head in that direction.

Instead, she stomped past the front entrance, toward the sidewalk. For a moment, it looked like she might be heading to the bus stop across the street. A few people whispered, others exchanged looks.

"She forgot her car's upstairs," Taurus muttered under his breath.

"Maybe she's going to Domino's," Richie quipped. "One last pizza before the apocalypse."

Her behavior was strange, erratic. But no one dared chase her.

And with every step she took, it became more obvious—Trina hadn't just walked out of a job.

She'd walked out of a war zone.

But later that evening, Penny overheard Jorge muttering to Lupe behind the dairy cooler.

"Turns out she did clock out," he said, annoyed. "Used the backroom register on her way out."

Lupe scoffed. "She's planning on coming back. Mark my words."

And she was.

In Trina's mind, the contest wasn't over. She still had a drink idea tucked in her apron pocket and dreams of taking her husband to the Bahamas. This wasn't a resignation—it was an intermission.

The only question now was what she'd walk back into.

Trina may have walked out with dramatic flair, but in her mind, she was still in the running—still the star of her own show. The Alfie's Barista Contest was her ticket, her fresh start, her excuse to cash in on years of loyalty and long shifts. She had already told her husband to keep his calendar open for the Bahamas trip, speaking like it was already hers.

And she wasn't wrong to think she had a shot. Trina had a flair for flavor, a knack for dramatic presentation, and just enough charm to sell her creation to the judges.

But Penny knew better than to underestimate her. Trina's exit may have been messy, but it was never final.

It was a move. A calculated one.

And Penny had to be ready when she returned—because if Trina was coming back, she wouldn't just be fighting for a vacation.

She'd be fighting for redemption.

Meanwhile, Biola—Betsy's mother—had become conspicuously absent from her usual perch near the bakery. She hadn't been around much lately, but when she did appear, it was with pursed lips and tight nods. Word around the store was she wasn't thrilled about Betsy's latest pregnancy.

"She already has four kids and a full-time job," Taurus murmured to Penny. "And now another on the way? Biola's probably praying for early retirement just to get some peace."

Biola had always been fiercely proud of her daughter, but she also had strong opinions about responsibility and image. The gossip swirling through Alfie's wasn't just about Betsy's condition—it was about whether she could still lead effectively. And Biola? She wasn't defending her this time.

Whatever support she had once offered seemed to be fraying, right along with Betsy's grip on the store.

But in the midst of Biola's disillusionment, something unexpected happened—she and Taurus began to connect. It started over small talk near the bakery racks, then grew into longer conversations while cleaning up after close. They shared a love of classic music, strong coffee, and a no-nonsense attitude about life and work. Where Betsy saw competition, Taurus saw humanity—and Biola, tired from years of silently standing in the background, appreciated being seen.

Meanwhile, the Doppio Twins—Dustin and Dylan—turned in their aprons without warning. The chaos had worn them down. They'd relocated from North Carolina with dreams of acting, and the constant tension at Rock n' Roll Alfie's was killing their spark. They wanted back in the creative world, the one that brought them to Hollywood in the first place.

"We didn't come all this way to fight over espresso shots and freezer logs," Dustin had said.

"And besides," Dylan added, "we look better on camera than in aprons."

Their departure was quiet but symbolic. Even the dreamers were walking away.

Technically, Dustin had worked in the cheese department and Dylan at Sunset Star Coffee, but their twin energy had made them a fixture of the store's personality. Without them, the vibe felt different—quieter, like a record had stopped spinning.

Around that same time, a new Barista named Pam had started picking up shifts. She was quiet but sharp, often blending into the background until she spoke. Most of the team didn't know she was referred by her brother Ricky, the sushi master behind the sushi bar. But Joe knew—and he noticed her.

Too much.

Joe, married with kids and an inflated sense of authority, had already started hovering near the kiosk more often, asking Pam if she needed help with restocks or offering to walk her to the backroom cooler. Everyone saw it.

"She's his next promotion from within," McKenzie whispered sarcastically to Penny one morning.

Penny didn't laugh. She just kept an eye on it.

Joe's interest was inappropriate. And if things continued in this direction, it wouldn't just be awkward.

It would be dangerous.

CHAPTER
THIRTY-ONE

TENSION UNLEASHED

Pam had always been the rebel in the family. Her brother Ricky, the sushi master at Alfie's, had always tried to keep her on the straight and narrow, but Pam never followed anyone's rules—except her own.

She wasn't here to impress anyone, least of all the people at Sunset Star Coffee. In fact, when Ricky had referred her for the Barista position, he'd told management, "She'll earn it on her own, not because of me."

But now that Pam was here, her skills were undeniable. She had a knack for blending flavors, creating combinations that no one else had thought of. The problem? She didn't want to be seen as "just Ricky's sister."

So when Penny noticed the tension growing around her, she wasn't surprised. Pam had been quiet at first, working her shifts without fanfare, but recently, her presence was becoming impossible to ignore. Everyone in the store was starting to talk—especially Joe, who had become unusually interested in Pam's movements.

Pam didn't seem to care, though. She was cool, collected, and focused on her work. Her eyes occasionally darted toward Joe, but she never let him get under her skin. Ricky had always told her to be careful of guys like Joe, but Pam wasn't worried. She could take care of herself.

Still, Penny couldn't shake the feeling that something was building. And now, as the Barista contest approached, it seemed like Pam was starting to get pulled into the drama, whether she wanted to or not.

The next day, as Penny worked through the lunchtime rush, the tension reached a boiling point. Ayeda—corporate's overbearing Manager from Sunset Star Coffee—waltzed into the kiosk like she owned the place. Her icy demeanor immediately chilled the air as she looked over the Baristas working.

"Gather 'round, everyone," Ayeda said in a sharp tone, her eyes flicking from Barista to Barista. "I just wanted to remind you all of something very important. That contest you're all so eager about?" She paused, letting the words hang in the air. "You will not enter it. Under any circumstances."

The moment her words landed, the room felt smaller. Penny could see the reactions around her—Trina stiffened, McKenzie shot a quick glance at Penny, and even Richie seemed uneasy. Ayeda wasn't just giving a suggestion; she was laying down a command.

"I'm sure you all think it's cute, some little coffee contest to bring in customers," Ayeda continued. "But I've got my orders. And if anyone dares to enter, there will be hell to pay. Consider this your final warning."

Her voice was cold, calculated, and Penny could feel the pressure mounting. Ayeda wasn't making idle threats—she was asserting control, and her eyes lingered on Penny as if daring her to protest.

With one last cold smile, Ayeda turned on her heel and left, leaving the atmosphere in the kiosk thick with the aftermath of her visit.

The confrontation with Ayeda was a sharp reminder that Penny wasn't just working in a coffee shop—she was embedded in a much bigger, more dangerous game. The contest, once a personal challenge, was now wrapped in layers of resistance. Penny couldn't help but wonder—was winning the contest even enough? Was it a diversion from something bigger, or was this her moment to break free from the chains they'd all been locked into?

But Penny wasn't about to back down. Ayeda had no idea what Penny was capable of when she had something to prove. Her competitive fire had been sparked, and there was no turning back now.

As the evening shift wound down, Penny's phone buzzed, pulling her from her thoughts. It was a text message from Taurus: "You really think you're gonna beat

Trina? She's going all-in on this. She's already practiced with a blowtorch." LOL

Penny smiled, knowing that Trina's intensity was exactly what she needed. It was time to go all-in too.

The following evening, Penny's phone buzzed again as she was closing up for the night. She reached for it, half-expecting it to be Richie with some new intel on the drive, or maybe McKenzie asking about the contest rules.

Instead, it was her Uncle Sidney.

"Raven, it's Uncle Sid," came his voice, warm and steady on the other end. "How's everything going with the... work?"

She smiled despite herself. Her uncle always danced around the topic, never directly asking about her undercover assignments, but always hinting at his curiosity. A retired history teacher, Sidney had a knack for being fascinated by all things law enforcement and criminal justice—though he had never pursued it himself.

"Busy as usual, Uncle Sid," Raven replied, trying to keep her voice casual. "Same old, same old."

"Same old, huh?" Sidney chuckled. "You know, I've been reading a lot of books about the FBI lately. You wouldn't believe the stuff they get into! It's all so thrilling, just like something out of those crime shows you used to watch. Makes me think you've got quite the exciting life, don't you think?"

Raven could hear the gleam in his voice even over the phone. Her uncle always saw her job as a thrilling adventure, something right out of a spy movie.

"Yeah, it's... exciting, alright." Raven laughed softly, but there was a touch of unease behind it.

"I'm sure it is," he replied, his tone shifting just a little more serious. "But be careful, Raven. I know you're smart, but this kind of work—it's dangerous. I don't care how many gadgets you have or how many people you've got backing you up. Stay safe, kid."

Raven smiled, warmth flooding her chest. "I will, Uncle Sid. Don't worry."

"I'll try not to. Just remember, your old Uncle Sid is always rooting for you."

"Thanks," she said softly, her thoughts momentarily drifting to her family back home. The people who cared about her, the ones she couldn't risk letting down.

"Alright, take care of yourself, Raven. And don't be afraid to take a break from all that excitement once in a while. You deserve it."

"I'll keep that in mind," Raven replied with a quiet laugh.

As she hung up, Raven sat in the break room for a moment, the weight of her uncle's words settling over her.

Exciting. Dangerous.

Her life was a balancing act now, one that wasn't just about doing the right thing, but staying in one piece long enough to finish what she started.

CHAPTER
THIRTY-TWO

DOUBLE LIVES, HALF TRUTHS

Julissa breezed in like she always did at 7:12 a.m. sharp, the sliding glass doors catching the tail of her ponytail like a trailing ribbon. Her cloud-patterned scrubs matched the sunrise behind her. She looked like she hadn't slept in days—and didn't care. She carried herself with the energy of someone who had long since accepted that the world didn't pause for rest.

"Extra large vanilla latte," she said, placing her phone on the counter, already unlocked to a photo of a baby wrapped in a knitted yellow blanket. "Heavy on the vanilla—light on the existential dread."

Penny chuckled automatically, already reaching for a clean cup. "That bad?"

Julissa nodded, then shook her head. "That's real. Night shift on the infant floor. One baby coded at 3:10

a.m. Another had to be rushed for a shunt procedure. But," she added, straightening a little, "Baby girl born at 25 weeks finally went home last night. You should've seen the parents. They brought cupcakes. Frosted smiles, real tears. The whole room needed tissues."

"Cupcakes make everything a little better," Penny murmured, focusing on tamping espresso.

"Not when they're your fifth meal replacement of the week," Julissa laughed. "You ever think about kids?"

Penny froze.

The hiss of the milk steamer filled the pause. She didn't look up.

"I did," she said quietly. "Still do. Sometimes. Life's... complicated."

Julissa leaned forward, eyes soft. "Complicated doesn't mean impossible."

Penny managed a faint smile and slid the cup toward her. "Extra vanilla. And I sprinkled some hope on top."

Julissa lifted it like a toast. "See you tomorrow. Same time, same hope."

When the doors jingled shut behind her, Penny stood still, gripping the edge of the counter.

The scent of vanilla lingered, mixed with steam and the distant whirr of the fridge. Outside, the sky was turning orange, the city waking up one honk and siren at a time.

But all Penny could hear was the echo of that question:

You ever think about kids?

She had. With Josh. She used to picture weekends in the park, tiny shoes by the front door, maybe a dog that the kid would name something ridiculous like Captain Toast. But that life had slipped away—casually, silently, like sand through fingers. Josh couldn't wait forever. And the job had no finish line.

Now she was twenty-nine, hiding behind an apron, an alias, and a burner phone. Still undercover. Still lying. Still running out of time.

She pulled that burner phone out now, almost instinctively. Nothing.

Still no word from Butler.

Four days.

She tapped the screen again, like maybe it hadn't loaded. Still no messages. No check-ins. No codes. Not even a sarcastic meme, which was her usual way of easing tension.

That silence meant something. And in this world, silence was never benign.

To distract herself, Penny turned toward the corkboard above the prep station, where a pink flyer with hand-lettered flair mocked her.

Sunset Star Signature Sips Showdown! Submit your original drink by Friday at 6 p.m. The lucky winner will enjoy a dream vacation—win a trip for two to the Bahamas! Their drink will also be featured on Sunset Star Coffee's menu.

Two days left. Her submission slip was still blank.

Everyone else had entered. Trina had thrown in her "Peach Ginger Frozen Delight" like she was applying for a Michelin star. Even Charles had entered his "Spiced Apple Diesel," which tasted like cinnamon gasoline. Penny had written one phrase in her notebook and crossed it out twice: Lavender smoke?

She closed the notebook. There was no inspiration. Only static.

And then came the moment that snapped everything.

Late afternoon. The café lights were dimmed just slightly for the lull. The air inside felt warm and heavy from steamed milk and overused vents.

Penny stepped outside, needing air, needing clarity, needing something. She walked across the street to the local Lebanese Restaurant to order food to go for later.

And there he was.

Matt. Sitting inside the restaurant. His back to her. Relaxed.

Across from him was a tall, striking blonde with loose waves and a laugh that echoed over traffic. She reached across the table and touched his wrist gently.

It looked like he was smiling. And then there was the laughter.

Not nervously. Not hesitantly.
Comfortably.

Penny's body went still. Her hand still held her cold brew, the condensation dripping onto her wrist.

She watched for longer than she should have. Until the laughter from that table started to sound like something personal.

She proceeded to order.

"Chicken breast plate, tabouleh, baba ganoush, green salad. Extra turnips. To go."

The cashier nodded. "You got it. Want utensils?"

She didn't respond. Just stood there with her arms crossed, jaw tight, blinking hard.

The bag was warm in her hands. But nothing about her felt steady.

Back inside the store, she stashed the food in the fridge and leaned against the metal door. The chill seeped through her shirt, but she didn't care.

Then came Trina.

"Long lunch break?" she asked sweetly.

Penny didn't turn around.

"I saw Matt too," Trina added. "He and the blonde looked... cozy."

Penny's voice was ice. "I don't need commentary."

Trina smirked. "I just hope it's not distracting you. Only two days left. You're still entering, right?"

"I am," Penny said.

"Oh good." Trina leaned in close. "Just don't let heartbreak ruin your flavor profile."

She walked off with a flick of her hair.

Penny clenched her jaw. She could still feel the warm takeout bag against her palms. The smell of garlic and lemon and turnips now nauseated her.

At the end of her shift, she finally pulled out her personal phone and messaged Nora.

Can I ask you something?

It's about Matt.

Nora responded instantly.

Call me.

Penny stepped out into the alley behind the store and dialed. The line connected almost instantly.

"Hey," Nora said gently.

"Is he married?" Penny asked.

A beat. Then another.

"Yes," Nora said quietly. "Technically. They've been separated for over a year, but it's not finalized. He doesn't talk about it. He didn't want people at work to know. Especially not you."

Penny's voice cracked despite herself. "Why not me?"

"I think he didn't want to lose what was starting," Nora said. "Or maybe he knew it was doomed and didn't want to watch it die in real time."

Penny leaned against the wall. "You could've told me."

"I didn't want to hurt you."

"You didn't. He did."

A long silence passed between them.

"I'm sorry, Pen," Nora said. "You deserve someone who's not hiding."

Penny hung up before her voice could tremble again.

The alley felt colder now. The air stung. She stared up at the sky—blue fading into gray.

She didn't cry.

But something inside her hardened.

She was tired of being lied to. Tired of being a temporary place for men to rest while they figured themselves out. First Josh. Now Matt. Always second. Always after.

She reached for her burner phone and saw it buzz.

A single line.

We need to talk. Tonight. Come alone.

No name. No location.

But Penny didn't need either.

Butler.

And the fact that she didn't say where? That said it all.

Only one place she could mean.

The fallback.

The rooftop.

She moved like someone waking from a dream.

Out of the alley. Across the back lot. Past the dumpsters and rusted gate. Up the side of the laundromat next door, where the old fire escape waited like an invitation.

Each step groaned under her boots. The wind picked up as she ascended, tugging her hair back, slicing cold against her skin.

She reached the top and paused.

The rooftop was empty.

Quiet.

The city buzzed far below, a grid of flickering lights and endless traffic. But up here, everything slowed.

Penny walked to the edge and looked out. Her body was still tense. Her chest tight.

But something inside her clicked.

The tears never came.

Not because she wasn't hurt—but because she was done being hurt.

Matt had her secrets. Butler had her silence.

But she had clarity.

No more distractions. No more waiting.

This case, whatever it was now, needed her full focus.

She wouldn't let anyone take it from her.

Not Trina. Not Matt. Not even her own doubt.

The wind rustled her sleeves. Her pulse calmed. Her hands steadied.

Somewhere below, a siren wailed into the night.

And Penny waited.

Ready.

CHAPTER
THIRTY-THREE

THE ROOFTOP DIRECTIVE

The rooftop wind had teeth.

Penny pulled her sleeves over her fingers and paced slowly along the gravel perimeter. The city stretched out below her in blinking yellows and silvers, its chaos muted at this height. Somewhere down on Sunset, someone was blasting synth-pop from their car stereo. The contrast only made the silence up here feel deeper.

She checked the time on her burner.

9:58 p.m.

Butler was never late. Which meant she was already here—or something was wrong.

Just as Penny began to scan the shadows, the stairwell door creaked open.

There she was.

Butler stepped out quietly, a slim figure in a dark jacket, scarf wrapped tight, her sharp features caught in rooftop light. She moved with the stillness of someone who expected to be followed.

"You came," Butler said.

"I thought you were dead," Penny replied.

"I nearly was."

"What happened?"

"Someone made me," Butler said. "I don't know how. I kept my routine, stuck to fallback protocol. But someone inside Alfie's knew I was watching. Knew I was your handler."

Penny's stomach tightened. "So it wasn't external?"

"No. It was inside. That's why I vanished. Had to burn the apartment, switch gear. I've been in the wind. Monitoring. Carefully."

Penny couldn't hide her alarm. "Burned the apartment?"

Butler nodded. "There was a warning. Unmistakable. A burner phone I'd already decommissioned. Planted in my bed. Open. Recording. Whoever it was wanted me to know they'd been close."

She pulled a flash drive from her coat pocket and handed it to Penny. "This has everything I could salvage. GPS logs, payment trails, off-the-books shipments. All linked to an offshore shell company with Betsy's name on it."

Penny's mouth went dry. "And the poisoning?"

"The Chai syrup was spiked with Raid. Intentionally. This was an execution, not an accident."

"Do you think Trina was in on it?"

"She's sloppy and self-absorbed," Butler replied. "Which makes her the perfect scapegoat. But she's not smart enough to be the architect."

Penny turned the drive over in her palm. "So what now?"

"You stay the course. Keep eyes on Betsy. Keep smiling. Play the role. But don't trust anyone—not even the ones who act like they're just pouring coffee."

"And you?"

"I'll disappear again," Butler said. "No contact unless absolutely necessary. Dead drops only. And if they suspect you—vanish."

She stepped toward the stairwell door, but then paused. Her voice dropped.

"Be careful, Raven."

The sound of her real name in the night air caught Penny off guard. She hadn't heard it spoken aloud in weeks.

She nodded once.

And then Butler was gone.

Sleep never came.

Back at her apartment, Penny sat curled on the couch with a mug of lukewarm tea and the flash drive on the table in front of her like a ticking bomb. Her hair was still windblown from the rooftop. Her hands itched from adrenaline.

She stared at the wall and thought about Matt. His silence. The woman. The way he'd vanished like a magician folding into smoke. She wasn't sure what was worse—not knowing why, or realizing she didn't need to anymore.

A knock jolted her from the silence.

She froze.

"Raven?" a voice called gently. "It's Anselmo."

She exhaled and opened the door. The curious maintenance man stood with his tool kit and a tired smile.

"Disposal check, right?" he asked.

She stepped aside. "Right. Forgot I even submitted that."

He knelt under the sink and got to work, his movements steady. "You've been keeping to yourself a lot more lately. You okay?"

She leaned against the counter. "Define okay.'"

He glanced up. "Still using Penny?"

Her mouth parted slightly. "You knew?"

"I knew by your third day here," he said. "I used to be military police. Saw a lot of folks pretending to be who they weren't."

She didn't deny it.

"You don't have to explain," he said. "Just don't lose your own name in the process. That's all I'll say."

He tightened one final bolt and stood.

"Disposal's good," he added. Then he paused. "Whoever made you forget how to trust people? They don't deserve to take your softness, too."

She nodded, trying not to show how much that cracked her open.

After he left, she plugged in the flash drive and began scanning encrypted files. GPS logs, offshore payments, flagged documents—one file labeled Sunset Payroll – Level 7 Access blinked behind a password wall.

She made a note to decode it.

But first—there was a drink contest to survive.

The café was buzzing.

A hand-lettered sign hung by the espresso bar: SUNSET STAR SIGNATURE SIPS SHOW-DOWN! Taste, Vote, Win!

Ballots were stacked beside tiny pencils. Kevin, Sunset Star Coffees Regional VP worked crowd control like a carnival barker. "Try the drinks! Vote anonymously! Get a caffeine buzz and a say!"

Penny stood behind the bar with quiet confidence, pouring samples of her Alfaretto—a balanced almond-amaretto flavored espresso drink with a creamy caramelized sugar, and velvety coconut finish that worked hot, iced, or blended. Adaptable. Practical. Hers.

Across the café, Trina was surrounded by a flock of customers snapping selfies with her Peach Ginger Frozen Delight—tall, frosty, neon-colored and crowned with candied peach slices and a paper umbrella.

"This drink is a moment," Trina purred. "Bright, refreshing, and sweet with a little kick. Just like me."

Penny rolled her eyes. But she had to admit—the presentation was stunning.

As the crowd thickened, Penny's focus sharpened—not on the drinks, but on something else.

The man in the hoodie.

He was back. This time upstairs—pacing outside the glass elevator that connected the store to the upper-level parking lot. He kept checking over his shoulder, gripping his refilled cup like it owed him something.

Penny saw it.

The RV.

Same as before, wedged up top between two rusting cars. But this time, she looked closer.

A girl—fifteen? Sixteen?—peeked out from the RV door, then quickly disappeared back inside.

Tommy passed by her, heading toward the trash station.

"Hey," Penny said. "That guy—he's been up there a lot, right?"

Tommy paused. "Yeah. Yeah, he has."

"You said there were teenagers?"

Tommy hesitated. "I... I think so. A few. In and out. Hard to say."

Penny's gut twisted.

She slipped into the break room and fired off a text to Butler:

RV parked upstairs. Man pacing outside elevator. Teens seen going in/out. Looks like trafficking. Need coverage.

The reply came quick.

Annie & Sonia en route. The elevators must be blocked without disrupting flow. Watch Tommy.

Penny's eyes narrowed.

She walked back out just in time to see Annie and Sonia enter the café—blending in perfectly, one with a shopping basket, the other sipping a drink. They moved separately but in sync, communicating with glances.

Sonia veered toward the elevator vestibule.

A group of customers waited to go up. Sonia smiled politely and stood nearby, casually reading her phone—but when the elevator doors opened again, she stepped in just enough to stop the suspect from entering. A subtle maneuver. No one noticed the block.

Annie circled toward the produce section, taking a back route toward the store's side stairs.

Then it happened.

The suspect saw her. Or sensed something.

He turned. Ran.

Straight for the elevator.

Sonia was faster.

She shifted the rolling cart beside her into position. The man tripped. Annie pounced from behind.

It was clean. Efficient.

The cuffs snapped before customers could even process what had happened.

A woman dropped her cold brew.

Kevin shouted, "What the—?"

"Security matter," Annie said calmly, flashing her badge. "No danger. Please remain calm."

But Penny was already moving—eyes scanning.

Something was missing.

Tommy.

Gone.

His apron was draped neatly over a stool. But he'd vanished during the takedown.

She stepped outside to the rear alley. A flash of motion disappeared behind a dumpster. She caught only a glimpse—brown hoodie, low cap, fast feet.

She texted Butler immediately.

Suspect apprehended. But Tommy slipped out. Might be connected.

Copy that. We're tracking. Good instincts.

Back inside, Kevin tried to bring the mood back up. "Okay, folks! Drama's over. Drinks still flowing!"

Trina turned to Penny, eyes narrowed. "You always in the middle of the chaos?"

Penny smiled. "Sometimes I'm the eye of it."

When the voting closed, Kevin sealed the box with dramatic flair.

"Votes are locked! Results at the Friday staff meeting!"

Trina clapped politely, but her eyes stayed on Penny.

"Whatever happens," she said, "you made it interesting."

Penny tilted her head. "And you made it peachy."

Trina blinked.

Penny smiled.

Let the votes speak for themselves.

But for now—she had bigger things brewing.

And she was ready.

CHAPTER
THIRTY-FOUR

PASSWORDS AND SHADOWS

The café was quiet, long after closing.

The grinders were silent. The last syrup pumps had been rinsed. Outside, the streetlights cast long slants of amber across the tiled floor. Penny sat in the corner booth near the emergency exit, her laptop open, fingers hovering over the keyboard.

The flash drive Butler gave her gleamed faintly in the port like a secret waiting to be weaponized.

Her coffee had gone cold. She hadn't noticed.

Most of the files had taken hours to comb through—shipping logs, falsified receipts, strange account routing—but one folder had held its password like a deadbolt: Sunset Payroll – Level 7 Access.

Six digits. Five failed attempts before it locked her out.

She had one try left.

She glanced down at her notebook, where she'd scribbled anything that might mean something: initials, vendor names, drink orders, aliases.

Then she saw it—Zara Belcourt. The name had appeared twice.

Once as a vendor of honey-almond extract. And again—quietly—as a Barista who'd supposedly worked two shifts and earned over $5,000 in bonuses.

And Zara had once ordered a drink with "three pumps almond, two honey, six ice cubes."

She typed: ZBelcourt326

The screen blinked.

Access granted.

Penny inhaled sharply.

The folder bloomed open with dizzying precision. Dozens of entries.

Names, IDs, pay bonuses, fake timecards. The operation wasn't sloppy—it was sophisticated. Entire identities had been fabricated to push funds into three known accounts.

Each account tied to a shell company.

Palm Echo Ventures. Indigo Root Holdings. And one she hadn't seen before: Basham Group LTD.

All offshore. All scrubbed clean.

And one of the names receiving those bonuses?

Kenny Ramirez.

Her eyes widened.

Kenny had been on the inside. Whether by force or design, he'd been playing a role. And now he was gone.

Penny sat back, heart pounding. Without him, Trina and Betsy no longer had a buffer.

The collapse was beginning.

The next morning, the espresso machine sputtered reluctantly to life. Kevin was already behind the bar when Penny arrived, sleeves rolled up, mood unreadable.

She set her bag down. "Long night?"

He didn't look up. "Kenny quit."

Penny blinked. "When?"

"Last night. Dropped his apron on the counter, said he was 'done being the fall guy,' and walked out. No notice. No explanation."

"Did he tell anyone why?"

Kevin finally looked at her. "No. But Ted's been pacing all morning. Betsy's locked in her office. Trina's pretending it's business as usual, but she smells like she's been stress-sweating since dawn."

Penny's brow furrowed. "Something's unraveling."

"Yeah," Kevin muttered. "And I don't like being in the blast radius."

Just then, Ted walked in from the back. The Assistant Store Manager's usual swagger was off—shoulders tense, eyes flicking around. His shirt was half-tucked. His face glistened with a sheen of nervous energy.

He motioned for Kevin to join him near the mop closet.

They spoke in low tones. Penny pretended to re-stock the straw dispensers while listening as closely as she could.

Kevin's voice rose slightly. "You're joking."

Ted said something Penny couldn't catch.

Then Kevin stepped back—clearly offended.

Ted slipped a small envelope into his hand.

Kevin looked down, then up again, his mouth pressed into a line. He said nothing, turned, and walked away—straight into Betsy's office.

Ten minutes later, corporate was on the line.

Fifteen minutes after that, an Alfie's VP of Protocol was present via video call.

By noon, Ted had been asked to gather his things.

He tried to protest—loudly.

"It was just a little encouragement! For morale! She's our best Barista!"

"No one cares," Kevin said flatly. "And Sunset Star does not tolerate contest tampering."

Betsy stood in the corner, arms crossed, jaw twitching, watching Ted's career dissolve.

Trina? She pretended not to notice. But her face was pale.

And worse—she stank.

Penny caught the scent first during a mid-morning rush. A sharp, unpleasant wave that hovered near the register. A customer visibly flinched. Another pulled her sweater over her nose.

Kevin gave Penny a helpless look. "I can't tell her."

"No one can," Penny said. "She's a ticking time bomb."

Trina's eyes darted toward them once—almost like she knew. Like she'd heard everything.

Later that afternoon, Penny stepped into the storage hallway to restock bottled water when she nearly collided with Phil.

The former sheriff's deputy turned security guard was solid as ever, arms folded across his chest.

"Hey, Penny," he said. "Can I ask you something?"

She nodded.

"You seen Matt?"

Her stomach flipped. "Not since last week."

Phil frowned. "That's what I figured. He missed two shifts. Didn't call. Not answering texts. His brother said he's gone dark. That's not like him."

Penny's voice was quiet. "No. It's not."

"I know you two were close."

"We were... starting to be," she admitted.

Phil looked down the hallway. "He talked about you. Said you were smart. Said you saw things other people missed."

Her throat tightened. "Thanks for telling me."

"If I hear anything, I'll let you know."

He walked off without another word.

Penny stood still for a long moment.

Matt was missing.

And her instincts told her he didn't leave voluntarily.

That night, long after the café closed, Penny returned to the files.

She plugged the flash drive into her laptop, pulled up the security folder again, and rewound to the previous afternoon.

There—on the break room feed.

Trina. Alone.

She looked around. Reached into her apron. Pulled out a USB drive.

Penny watched as Trina plugged it into the shared café laptop, typed something rapidly, and then wiped her fingerprints off the surface.

It wasn't subtle.

And it wasn't innocent.

She texted Butler:

Trina planted something on the shared computer. USB. Saw it on footage. 3:18 PM yesterday.

Butler replied instantly:

Secure the device if you can. And Raven? Watch your back.

Penny pulled up her hoodie and headed back to Alfie's, breaking protocol just this once. She entered quietly, using her staff key to unlock the back door. The store was dark except for the glow of the emergency exit signs.

In the break room, she opened the shared laptop.

The USB was still inserted.

She carefully pulled it free and slipped it into an anti-static pouch she kept in her coat pocket.

When she turned, she noticed something else.

On the whiteboard beside the fridge, someone had written:

DO NOT TRUST HER

No name. Just the message.

She erased it. Quietly. Without a word.

Back home, she stared at her reflection in the darkened window.

Matt was gone. Kenny had quit. Ted was fired. Trina was spiraling. Betsy was running out of shadows to hide in.

The game had changed.

And she wasn't just watching it anymore.

She was in the middle of it.

And whoever had written that message on the whiteboard?

They weren't wrong.

Trust would only get her killed.

CHAPTER
THIRTY-FIVE

THE TASTE OF CONSEQUENCE

The sky over Hollywood that morning was the color of old linen—cloudy, stretched, waiting for something to snap.

Inside Alfie's, the tension was already boiling beneath the surface. Even the espresso machine hissed like it knew something was coming.

The drink contest results were set to be announced at the end-of-day staff meeting, and despite the week's chaos—missing coworkers, bribery scandals, silent departures—the store marched on, grinding beans and blending smoothies as if nothing had changed.

Penny arrived early with a second cup of coffee already in hand, her shoulders squared and jaw tight. She didn't expect celebration. Not in the traditional sense.

But she had a feeling—deep in her bones—that today would shift something.

And not just for her.

Kevin was already behind the kiosk, double-checking inventory.

"She's not in yet," he said without looking up.

"Trina?" Penny asked.

Kevin nodded. "Or Betsy. No one's seen them since yesterday. And Ted... well, he's radioactive now."

Rumors were swirling. Ted had allegedly been calling corporate, trying to salvage his job, while Trina had left Kevin a voicemail that sounded more like a voice memo from a breakdown.

"Good riddance," Kevin added under his breath.

Penny didn't argue. She was watching everything—and everyone.

Including Joe.

The Store Director had been oddly visible all day—walking the aisles, straightening product displays, even making small talk with customers like he was auditioning for a role. His usual polish seemed duller, his smiles tight at the edges.

Penny could see it in his eyes.

He was sweating something.

He'd pulled Trina and Betsy into his office twice already that morning—closed door, muffled arguing. And afterward, both women had come out looking brittle and tight-lipped.

The pressure was mounting.

And Penny was no longer beneath it.

She was right in the middle.

<hr>

By midday, the air inside Alfie's felt too still, like the entire store was holding its breath.

Penny stood behind the counter wiping down surfaces that didn't need it, her nerves itching beneath her skin. She'd barely slept. Her thoughts kept circling the USB Trina had inserted into the breakroom laptop. Butler had responded only with: "Hold steady. We're watching. Watch them."

Them.

Who was "them" now?

Betsy hadn't left the office. Trina had arrived an hour late, her hair still damp, her eyes glassy, and the faint but unmistakable odor of alcohol clinging to her like bad perfume. No one mentioned it, but everyone noticed.

Phil, the security guard, stepped in around 12:30 and made his usual lap. He paused briefly at the counter where Penny was refilling napkin dispensers.

"You good?" he asked.

"As good as this place lets you be," she replied.

He grunted, eyes flicking toward the back. "Saw Joe talking with Betsy in the alley behind the loading bay this morning. You think he's involved?"

"I think he's in too deep to back out," Penny said.

Phil nodded like he already knew. "Matt would've sniffed this out. That guy had instincts."

Penny swallowed. "Still nothing?"

Phil shook his head. "Not a word. And now Ted's off the grid too. You starting to feel like the last clean one in the building?"

Penny gave a dry smile. "That assumes I ever was."

He didn't push her on it.

<hr>

BY 3:45 PM, THE ENTIRE TEAM HAD GATHERED IN the breakroom for the staff meeting. The air smelled like leftover donuts and nervous sweat.

Kevin stood at the whiteboard, a sealed ballot box in front of him. He was composed, but Penny could see a vein pulsing at his temple.

Trina was slouched in a folding chair near the mini fridge, arms crossed, her knee bouncing uncontrollably. She wore a too-tight floral top and thick makeup that was starting to smear under the fluorescent lights.

Betsy stood in the back, silent, phone in hand, tapping her nails against the case.

Joe leaned against the wall near the windows, arms folded, lips pursed like he was chewing the inside of his cheek. He looked oddly satisfied, as if he already knew what was coming.

Kevin cleared his throat. "Alright. Today's the day. Thanks to everyone who entered the Sunset Star Signature Sips Showdown. Every drink was unique, and we had a solid turnout for the vote."

He broke the seal, unfolded the slips one by one, counting aloud.

Trina exhaled, like she'd been holding her breath for a week.

Kevin paused, lips parting slightly.

"Second place—Trina Kingsley, Peach Ginger Frozen Delight."

A few claps. One from Phil. Another from Sandra, the bakery lead.

Trina clapped once, then stopped.

Kevin pulled out the final slip. "First place—Penny Padlock, for the Alfaretto."

Applause broke out louder this time. Penny's heart pounded, but her face stayed calm. She stood as Kevin handed her a small white envelope and a laminated sign with her drink's name printed in bold script.

Joe stepped forward. "On behalf of the regional team, I want to congratulate Penny. We'll be piloting the Alfaretto in two test stores starting next month. Great job."

There it was.

Everything Penny had held back—every slight, every moment of invisibility—collapsed under the weight of quiet recognition.

She smiled. Not out of pride. But relief.

She had earned this.

Trina, meanwhile, stood without a word and walked out of the room.

Kevin cleared his throat again. "That concludes our meeting."

But it didn't.

Not really.

By 4:30 PM, most of the staff had returned to their stations, but something was wrong. The store felt off-kilter. Customers were whispering. The lights flickered once, then again.

Penny was refilling the grab-and-go fridge when she caught movement in her periphery—Trina, pacing near the breakroom, eyes wide, fists clenched. She looked like she was having a conversation with someone who wasn't there.

Penny moved closer.

"—always the favorite, huh? Bet you planned this," Trina was muttering, tugging at her necklace until the chain snapped. She didn't even flinch.

Joe emerged from the hallway suddenly, grabbing Trina by the arm and pulling her aside. He didn't yell, but his voice was sharp enough to cut drywall.

"You need to pull it together," he hissed.

"I'm not your problem anymore," Trina spat.

"You're everyone's problem right now."

Penny ducked behind a merchandise rack, watching their silhouettes break apart.

She headed for the back to get paper towels and saw the mop closet door hanging open.

She glanced inside.

The gas can was gone. A trail of oily footprints—small ones, like Trina's size—led toward the electrical room.

Penny's pulse shot up.

She turned to run—

BOOM.

The shockwave tore through the store with a concussive pop. Lights exploded overhead. Shelves toppled. Smoke poured down from the ceiling as customers screamed.

Sprinklers activated.

Penny hit the floor, heart pounding, hands over her head.

The air filled with the acrid sting of burning wires and scorched plastic.

She crawled toward the front, coughing, eyes watering.

Phil was already on his radio, calling in the emergency. Kevin was trying to get customers to the exit. Alarms blared.

Penny stumbled past the breakroom.

Trina was curled against the wall, covered in debris.

Betsy was trying to pull herself out from under a table. She was yelling "my baby, my baby!"

Joe was gone.

Just... gone.

Gone before the smoke had cleared.

Gone before anyone could ask him what he'd been hiding.

And Penny, chest heaving, stared at the carnage and knew—

This was only the beginning.

The emergency lights flickered overhead, casting everything in jerky flashes of red and white. The sprinklers had stopped, but water still pooled in places, mixing with shattered glass and burned paper.

Penny crouched next to Trina, who was coughing violently, her makeup streaked and her blouse torn at the shoulder.

"You okay?" Penny shouted, barely able to hear herself over the alarm.

Trina blinked up at her, dazed. "Did I... did I do this?"

"I don't know," Penny said, even though she was fairly certain Trina hadn't set the explosion—but she might've enabled it.

Phil moved past them, helping Betsy limp toward the breakroom door. Her pantyhose were singed at the knees, and there was a cut on her forehead.

"Where's Joe?" Kevin asked from the hallway.

No one answered.

"Wasn't he in the back?" Sandra asked, hugging a soaked jacket to her chest.

"I checked the office. He's not there," Kevin said. "We need to get people out now."

Penny stood, helping Trina to her feet. She felt the adrenaline in her joints like acid. Her fingers were shaking.

Outside, sirens wailed—fire, paramedics, maybe even police. Through the blown-out front window, she saw flashing red and blue begin to smear across the sidewalk.

"Evacuate now!" Phil barked. "Everyone out!"

Penny followed Kevin toward the front. The air was thick and tasted metallic. Children were crying. A teenager was live-streaming the scene on her phone, narrating like it was a blockbuster.

Only once they were out on the curb did Penny realize how close the explosion had come.

The blast had taken out part of the back storage hallway. Electrical wires now dangled like jungle vines. The mop closet door was gone.

Smoke billowed from the vents.

She looked around.

Phil. Kevin. Trina. Betsy.

Still no Joe.

It didn't make sense.

Unless... he knew it was coming.

Unless he made it happen.

And then vanished.

By the time the fire department arrived, smoke had started to leak into the neighboring stores. Alfie's was cleared, the sidewalk lined with dazed employees and jittery customers wrapped in emergency blankets.

Flashing lights bathed the storefront in chaos. Firefighters pushed inside with hoses. EMTs worked methodically through the crowd, checking for concussions and burns. Police officers cordoned off the scene with yellow tape, already taking statements.

Penny sat on the curb, her hands wrapped around a bottle of water someone had handed her but she hadn't opened. Her apron was soaked and streaked with ash.

Phil stood a few feet away talking to a fire captain. Kevin gave his statement to a pair of uniformed officers, arms crossed over his chest. Trina had stopped shaking, but she stared at nothing, her pupils still wide.

Betsy, bandaged and furious, refused help from paramedics. "I don't need to go to a hospital. My baby is fine! Just get me a phone. I need to call corporate. I need to call Joe."

No one answered her.

Penny pulled out her burner and texted Butler:

Explosion. Back hallway. No fatalities. Joe is missing. Trina and Betsy rattled. No one knows who triggered it.

She waited.

The reply came sixty seconds later:

He knew. We've been tracking funds. He was the last unconfirmed variable. Get out of there. I'll send Annie and Sonia.

Penny read the message twice.

Joe knew.

She stood up slowly, scanning the street again. No sign of him. No text. No apology. No explanation.

He was gone.

Disappeared into the smoke like he was never there.

And maybe he never truly had been.

Across the street, the Lebanese restaurant still had its lights on.

A normal dinner crowd.

A couple laughing at a table by the window.

Life moved on.

But Penny didn't move.

Not yet.

CHAPTER
THIRTY-SIX

FULL EXTRACTION

The smoke curled low in the ceiling vents, as if reluctant to leave.

Outside, the fire trucks had pulled back, but the scent of scorched wires and plastic clung to every surface. The front of Alfie's was boarded up in makeshift plywood. The windows had been cracked, one blown out completely. Yellow police tape fluttered like a warning.

Penny stood across the street behind the bus stop, her arms folded across her chest.

She could still hear it.

That boom. That instant where everything went white.

The screech of metal. The silence afterward. The screams.

She still hadn't told anyone how close she'd been to the blast. How she'd seen the oily footprints leading to the electrical room. How she'd almost stopped it.

Almost.

But not quite.

By morning, the media had descended.

Local news anchors interviewed shaken customers and quoted fire marshals. "An isolated incident," they called it. "Under investigation."

Penny didn't speak to anyone.

She waited for Annie and Sonia.

They arrived at 9:04 a.m. in an unmarked grey van with tinted windows and a silent engine. Both wore jeans and jackets, unassuming but sharp-eyed.

"Raven," Annie said as they approached.

Sonia nodded once. "Butler sent us. We're moving now."

"Is Joe dead?" Penny asked.

They didn't answer right away.

"We don't know yet," Annie said. "But we think he ran. There was a car waiting behind the loading dock. Surveillance from two weeks ago shows him moving cash into the trunk after hours."

"And Matt?" Penny asked. "Have you found him?"

Sonia's expression softened—just slightly.

"We did," she said. "He's alive."

Penny blinked.

"He was drugged. Left in a safehouse in Riverside. Joe needed him out of the way. Thought he'd seen too much."

Penny's heart dropped into her stomach. "Can I see him?"

"You will," Annie promised. "But first, we finish this."

THE TEMPORARY CONFERENCE ROOM WASN'T much—folding chairs, a flickering light overhead, and a stale pot of coffee that no one touched—but it was enough. Enough to confront what had been buried. Enough to rip the mask off what had nearly gotten Penny—and Matt—killed.

Betsy sat with her arms crossed, a corporate-branded fleece draped over her shoulders like a shroud. Her eyes were red but dry. She wasn't someone who cried. Not in front of anyone.

Trina lingered outside the door, pacing like she was in a holding cell. Her eyeliner had run, and her hands trembled every time she paused.

Penny walked in slowly, her steps deliberate. Annie and Sonia followed silently behind her, their energy sharp and professional.

"Ms. Padlock," Betsy said, voice clipped. "What a surprise."

Penny ignored the sarcasm. "You've had every opportunity to walk away from this. You didn't."

"You don't know what I've dealt with," Betsy said. "What Joe promised. What we were *building.* You see a ledger. I see ten years of loyalty."

"Ten years of laundering," Penny corrected. "Of manipulation. Of setting people up to fall while you stayed clean."

"I ran a tight ship."

"You blew it up."

Trina stumbled into the doorway. "Is this what this is now? You're going to pin it all on *us*? After everything?"

Betsy stood. "You said you took care of it!"

"You told me it was just a program!" Trina cried. "That it was nothing. That I just had to plug it in and walk away."

"You were too easy to use," Penny said, her voice lower now. "That's why they picked you. You wanted to win so badly, you didn't care what you compromised to do it."

Trina turned to her, her expression crumbling. "You don't get it. You had *people* looking out for you. Matt. Kevin. Even that weird maintenance guy. Me? I was on my own. I just wanted one thing—just one stupid thing—that would make someone finally see me."

For a moment, Penny saw it. The scared, desperate girl inside the armor of performance. But she didn't flinch.

"You got seen," Penny said. "And now you have to deal with it."

Annie dropped a folder on the table—thick, tabbed, and damning. "We have it all. The siphoned payroll funds. The shell companies. The timed surveillance footage. And the flash drive Trina plugged in? It uploaded a keystroke tracker—one designed to search for system-level passwords and auto-forward to an off-site IP. That's espionage, Betsy. You don't just lose your job over that."

Betsy laughed—short and brittle. "You people think this ends with me? That Joe's just going to vanish? You're not even in the deep end yet."

"Then throw us in," Sonia said, stepping forward. "We swim."

Annie pulled out the cuffs. "Betsy Gomez, you are under arrest for conspiracy, wire fraud, data manipulation, and accessory to attempted arson."

"I want a lawyer," Betsy said, standing with an odd sense of pride.

"You'll get one," Annie replied. "At the precinct."

They walked her out first, silent but not resisting.

Trina lingered. Frozen. Staring at Penny.

"You know I didn't light anything," she whispered.

"I know," Penny said. "But you struck the match."

Trina sank into the nearest chair, head in her hands.

THEY HADN'T BEEN PART OF THE TAKEDOWN, BUT they'd been part of everything that led up to it—the quiet support that had kept her grounded when everything else threatened to spin out.

No one said anything. They didn't have to.

Penny walked up to Amira and handed her a hot, steaming MED BOMB.

Amira took it, held it up high like a silent toast, and nodded.

Charles wandered out from the back room, blinking like he hadn't seen daylight in weeks. He gave her a crooked smile, the kind that said *you did good* without needing the words.

Dante leaned against the checkout lane, arms crossed, a rare look of calm on his face. He'd been keeping watch longer than most people realized, making sure things didn't spiral while Penny was buried in her role.

As the dust settled and the sirens faded into the background, the store slowly began to breathe again.

And Penny?

She exhaled.

For the first time in months, she breathed without bracing.

***

Two days later, the air was warmer. Lighter.

Penny stood outside a recovery center in Riverside, clutching a paper bag with a thermos and a chicken quesadilla. She hadn't said she was coming. Butler had arranged it.

The door opened.

Matt stepped out.

He looked thinner. Eyes shadowed. But alive.

They didn't say anything for a full five seconds.

Then he smiled.

"You still make that almond drink?"

Penny laughed, even as her eyes welled. "Only every day."

He stepped forward and hugged her—tight, real.

She let herself be held.

But only for a moment.

That night, Butler met her on the rooftop of Penny's building, wind tugging at her scarf.

"It's done," Butler said. "Trina's cooperating. Betsy's not. Joe is still off-grid. But we'll find him."

Penny nodded.

"You did more than survive there," Butler added. "You dismantled a system."

"I just didn't want anyone else to get hurt."

Butler tilted her head. "So what now?"

Penny looked out at the city, blinking lights stretching into the night. She took a long breath.

"I think I want to open a place. My own café. No secrets. Just good coffee."

Butler smiled. "Then you better start sourcing coffee beans."

THE END

The Alfaretto

A rich, smooth espresso with sweet almond amaretto notes, creamy caramelized sugar, and a velvety coconut finish.

Get your Alpha Rewards Points!

CHAPTER
THIRTY-SEVEN

Penny Padlock is back—and this time, the secrets are thirty thousand feet in the air.

In the pulse-pounding sequel to *Revealations*, Penny goes undercover as a flight attendant for Alpha Airways, a once-glamorous airline now steeped in scandal. A string of brutal murders has rocked the company, and whispers of conspiracy echo through every gate and cabin aisle. When Penny boards her first flight, she doesn't just carry a service manual—she carries a mission.

What begins as routine safety checks and beverage service soon spirals into a labyrinth of lies, cryptic conversations, and deadly coverups. As flight attendants vanish and suspects circle closer, Penny forges unlikely alliances with fellow crew members—each with secrets of their own.

From late-night layovers in shadowy hotels to high-stakes standoffs in the cockpit, *Revealations: Airways* hurtles toward a truth that's been hidden behind polished uniforms and closed doors. Penny must navigate betrayal, corporate corruption, and her own growing fears before the final descent.

Fasten your seatbelt. The next Revealation is airborne—and it's not going to be a smooth ride.

EPILOGUE

One year had passed since the case closed at Rock n' Roll Alfie's, but the scent of espresso and the echo of footsteps in those tiled aisles hadn't left me. I stood just outside the sliding doors, eyeing the place like an old crime scene that had been scrubbed clean but never truly forgotten.

They'd repainted the front entrance—brighter colors, friendlier signs. A cosmetic facelift to mask the memory of what had gone down in the upstairs parking lot. I wasn't in uniform anymore, no apron, no alias. Just me. Raven McCool. Back in jeans, boots, and the kind of jacket that said I didn't come for groceries. I came for closure.

Inside, Alfie's looked deceptively normal. Sunset Star Coffee still stood near the florist, espresso machines hissing their usual steam symphony. Trina was long gone. Betsy had served her time, or at least part of it, but no one really talked about her anymore. The new baristas smiled, oblivious to the drama that had unfolded just a year earlier.

I approached the counter, half-expecting a ghost to rise up from behind the pastry case. Instead, a teenager with a pierced eyebrow asked for my order. 'Med Bomb,' I said. He didn't flinch. It was still on the secret menu. That meant something hadn't changed.

I took my tea and moved to the same corner table where I used to sketch suspects in my notepad. The table still wobbled. Classic. I sipped and scanned the room like old times. Joe was still here—of course. Alfie's didn't let go of people like him. Corporate had a way of sweeping things under the rug if the numbers stayed high.

Then I saw him. Matt. Hot Stuff. Still leaning near the doors, scanning the room with that same effortless awareness. Our eyes met. No fist bump this time. Just a small nod. The kind that says, 'Yeah, I remember too.'

I wasn't here for a new case. I wasn't even here for answers. I just needed to know the place survived. That the people who'd stayed behind still breathed easy. That Alfie's, for all its chaos, had found its rhythm again.

But as I took another sip, I noticed a man near the back exit. Early forties. Business casual. Watching the registers a little too closely. A nervous twitch in his foot. A hand that hovered near his pocket like he was debating something.

I'd come here to remember. Not to work. But instinct doesn't retire. And something about him didn't sit right.

I grabbed a napkin, pulled out a pen, and started a new page. Just in case.

Because maybe Alfie's wasn't done with me after all.

AUTHOR'S NOTE

Thank you for reading *Revealations*. This book has been a labor of love—born from a fascination with mystery, humor, and the hidden dramas that unfold in everyday places.

Rock n' Roll Alfie's is a fictional grocery store, but it's inspired by the strange, chaotic beauty of real-life jobs, where personalities clash, secrets linger, and community forms in the most unexpected corners. While the characters, events, and Sunset Star Coffee are imagined, the energy of late-night shifts, impossible customers, and workplace politics are very real.

Writing Raven McCool's journey as Penny Padlock gave me a chance to explore duality—the way we all wear masks, sometimes out of necessity, sometimes to survive. She's flawed, fearless, and often funny even when she's in danger. I hope she made you root for her the way I did while writing each chapter.

To everyone who's ever worked retail, food service, or undercover (in any form): this one's for you. Your resilience is the real story.

With gratitude and coffee-fueled creativity,

— Ruth Drabkin

ACKNOWLEDGMENTS

To my incredible parents, Harry and Mary — thank you for believing in my imagination from the very beginning. Your love and encouragement have meant everything to me. You gave me the roots to grow and the wings to chase stories.

To my brothers, Andrew and Roger — Andrew, thank you for the laughs, support, and for always having my back. Roger, though you left this world before I arrived, I carry your name with pride and purpose. You are a part of my story, and this book carries a piece of you too.

Much love and appreciation to my friends and extended family who have cheered me on, lifted me up, and celebrated every small victory along the way. Whether it was a kind word, a brainstorm session, or a much-needed reminder to take a break — I couldn't have made it through this journey without you. Your voices echo in my mind even when I'm at the keyboard alone: 'Go Ruth!' and 'C'mon Ruth!' — those cheers have meant more to me than words can say.

To the unforgettable characters who spoke to me, challenged me, and demanded to be written — thank you. You made *Revealations* come alive.

This book was born from a combination of persistence, support, and love. To everyone who's been part of my life's story: thank you for helping me tell this one.

ABOUT THE AUTHOR

RUTH DRABKIN IS AN AUTHOR BASED IN LOS ANGELES, California. Known for her heartfelt children's books and now branching into adult fiction, her writing blends sharp wit, emotional depth, and an eye for mystery in everyday life.

Her debut adult novel, *Revealations*, showcases her ability to weave humor, suspense, and unexpected moments of beauty into stories that reflect the hidden layers of human experience. Ruth's storytelling is inspired by real jobs, real people, and the wild heart of Los Angeles.

When Ruth's not writing, she loves to travel, indulge in great entertainment, bake up something sweet, and spend time with her precious dog Maximus. She thrives on moments shared with friends and family, whether it's a heartfelt chat, a shared meal, or a spontaneous adventure.

Stay classy — and keep turning pages.

You can find more of her work at
www.ruthdrabkin.com.

9 7 9 8 9 9 9 4 0 3 1 0 0